Unmasked

BRANDON BOOTH

ISBN: 0692066632
ISBN-13: 978-0692066638

BRANDON BOOTH

Dedication

To my one and only, the found to my lost, the half that makes me whole. This book was written for you and exists because of your grace and patience.

There has never been another like you, and there never will be again.

Part One

"The winds of change blow ever fierce,
a violent tempest's roar,
some are blown out to sea,
but others to the shore."

Chapter One

The water was as blue as he'd ever seen it, even as it rocked the dingy sailboat back and forth on the growing waves. Usually the waters off the coast of Cannes were calm this time of year, but this storm threatened to grow into something fearsome. Even so, Jason couldn't help but be mesmerized by the deep blue color of the water, its intensity was unlike anything he'd ever seen in his short sixteen years. Was it a warning of something to come, or reassurance amidst the mounting storm? He wasn't sure, and before he could ponder the question further, his father yelled something over the wind.

"Pull the boom windward, let's get to dock before…," the rest was unintelligible over the wind, but Jason understood the point. *Let's get the hell into dock before the storm tips us over.* Working quickly, Jason pulled the horizontal boom pole towards the wind, which was now pushing the boat directly towards shore. The boat itself was unremarkable, a simple sailboat with more than its fair share of scars. Nonetheless, it served its purpose and had yet to fail them.

His father had purchased it two years ago when they'd moved to the small Ile Sainte Marguerite in France. The boat was necessary for their occasional voyages to the nearby Cannes for provisions and other essentials that could not be grown, or made, on the island itself.

Located just off the Golfe de la Napoule, the island was the home of the Fort Royal prison, a formidable and foreboding presence amidst an otherwise beautiful island. His father had moved them here at great expense for reasons that Jason had never been privy to. His mother had anguished at the move. He had heard her crying and pacing the floor on many long nights before the move from America. There had been shouting, too, and the closer their departure had been, the more frequent the arguments. Jason was an intensely curious young man, convinced that knowing was always preferable to not. His father, Dean, had tired quickly of his questions. On one particularly confrontational evening, Dean had made it clear that he would no longer tolerate being questioned by his only son.

"You'll know when the time is right and not a damn minute before, do you hear me, boy?"

"Dad," Jason started to reply, "I just want…," his voice fell silent as he saw the look of anger in his father's eyes.

"When you're ready to hear it, when we're ready to say it, you'll be told. This will be the last time you mention this to me.

And if I hear you troubling your mother about it, there will be hell to pay. Don't test me, boy."

Jason hadn't. His father was generally a patient man, but he was determined to enforce his rules when he believed them to be for the best. The faded leather belt that he wore was functional in more ways than one as Jason had learned on more than one occasion. Once, when he was a boy of no more than eight, he'd taken one of his mother's canning jars outside to catch fireflies. The way they lit up the trees in the evenings had always fascinated him; he'd wanted to keep some of that magic in his bedroom at night. Armed with a net his father used to scoop fish out of the lake when fishing, he'd run back and forth across the property to the rear of their home. He caught dozens of the flashing bugs, bottled lightning and wonder to a boy of eight, and had capped the jar with a piece of fabric stolen from his mother's sewing drawer.

A few days later, he overheard his parents talking about the missing jar. Panicked, he'd quickly tossed out the dead bugs and hidden the jar behind the horse cart near the barn, fully intending to return it to the cellar as soon as there was a free moment. Instead, his father had found the jar when he had gone to seat the horses.

"Did you take this jar? Did you put it here?" his father had asked.

"Noo... no, it really must have been Matthew. He was over yesterday and we were playing outside. He must have found it on the window sill and been playing with it and forgotten." The story was laughable, believable only to eight-year-old boys who were sure that their parents hadn't been born with the wits given to the barn cats.

"This is your last chance, son. Tell me the truth. Did you take this jar?"

The young boy didn't like lying to his father, but liked the thought of extra chores and a tanned hide even less. The decision wasn't so much out of fear as it was practical avoidance of more work. His chores already seemed overwhelming, and the last thing he wanted was a morning spent milking the cows or trenching his mother's garden.

"No, sir, it wasn't me, I swear it."

The lie that he had thought so clever had been undone in an instant. His father's belt, however, took an eternity, at least to Jason. *One! Two! Three!* The belt had cracked across his reddening buttocks eight times, one for every year he'd been alive, as was his father's custom for punishment. However, just when he'd thought the torture complete, *whack!*, the belt cracked again, and then once more. Ten times instead of eight.

"Those extra two are for lying to me, and swearing before God. The good book says, 'let your yes be yes, and your no be no.' The next time you lie to me, son, you'll be sorry you did."

Dean was not a particularly religious man. He didn't often quote scripture, and he viewed Sunday meetings as 'women's clubs'. But he went, and so did Jason's mother, Kathleen. Apparently, this particular bit of scripture had struck a chord in Dean, and that fact was not lost on Jason. His rear end had burned for hours and had been sore for nearly a week afterwards. Lying to his father was not something that was going to be tolerated, and the lesson of the ten lashes was not quickly forgotten.

The city of Cannes, located in the southeastern part of France, was far busier than the small island where they lived. After docking their boat in the port of le Vieux, Jason and his father headed towards the center of town. It boasted vendors and rooms for rent, among other amenities and pleasantries associated with a hub of commerce. Walking along the rambling, cobblestone streets, Jason took in the fragrance of the place. The smell of freshly cut flowers from a shop on a corner, of exotic spices from a nearby cart, and of fresh fruit from street side merchants. Considering the growing storm, vendors and patrons rushed to complete their business before the rain inevitably began. His father's already brisk pace quickened with the first crack of thunder. Though miles away, the storm was moving fast, and Dean wanted to reach their destination with as much haste as possible. As vendors began to close their stands and pack away their carts, Dean frowned and looked back.

"Keep up, son, we're nearly there. Come."

"Yes, sir," Jason replied, his thoughts elsewhere. In spite of the hustle and bustle of the marketplace, his thoughts still drifted back to the blueness of the ocean. There was an importance there that he could not quite identify, and his mind stubbornly refused to move beyond it.

Jason wore a simple outfit of cotton trousers, an old shirt that could probably stand to be replaced rather than patched, again, and a vest meant to make him more presentable. His father was similarly attired, although his shirt was much too big for him and his shoes were ill fitting as well. His father had lost a considerable amount of weight over the last year, whether from the increased work, or stress, Jason did not know. Not that his father cared about his weight or his clothing. His primary concerns were the health and well-being of his family, and if that meant wearing clothes past their actual lifespan, so be it.

By the time they reached their destination, the rain had started. The old building was a ramshackle place wedged between a dilapidated bar and a small eatery, seemingly kept upright by the very force that saw it squeezed there. The windows were dirty to the point of being purposeless; no one could possibly see through them. The sign overhead simply said, 'Apprendre', and nothing more. *Learn? What was that supposed to mean? What was this place?* Jason wondered silently.

When Jason was just barely fourteen and the decision to upend their family had been made, Jason's mother had set about teaching both Jason and Dean French. His mother was fluent, albeit quite rusty, and was diligent in her teaching. Competent teacher though she was, Jason did not have an ear for language, and his grasp of the spoken word was minimal, at best. His father was far better than he was, although Jason suspected that his mother invested much of their private times forcing him to speak in the foreign tongue. Jason had grown quite proficient at reading French, although that skill was not particularly helpful to him at this moment. *Learn? Is this some sort of library? Bibliotheque?*

His thoughts were cut short by the rapid opening of the heavy door at the front of the building. While it seemed like the door should be immovable, caked in grime and showing rust at every hinge, the brute of a man standing in the doorway had opened it almost silently and clearly without significant effort. His broad shoulders filled the frame, crammed there almost like the building itself had been so many years ago. His face wore a strange expression. It certainly wasn't happy, but it wasn't angry or severe, either. It was a wearied hopefulness, perhaps. The look of a man who had waited a long time for something but who had been disappointed before. Looking at him, Jason was more taken by his sheer volume. Like his shoulders, his pot belly was nearly as wide as the doorframe, making it seem like he had consumed too much beer, keg and all. As if to distract from his belly, he had grown a mane of hair that extended past his shoulders. Dark brown and unkempt, it was in desperate need of more care than he was giving it.

As the rain started to fall with more vigor, Jason and his father jogged towards the open door. Upon approach, the man moved aside and, to his great surprise, greeted his father in English, albeit fragmented.

"Hello, you've made it. I have been keeping time for your arrival," the man said, while giving Dean a pat on the back.

"Yes, we have. I apologize for the delay, it has taken me longer than I expected to procure the information you requested. It was not avoidable."

"So you've found it then? The proof?"

"Yes. It took me a while to find, but it is there. Just where the letter said it would be," Dean replied, letting each word fall from his lips as if it weighed a ton.

The man's eyes grew wide, if only for a moment. His previous look of weariness transformed into profound relief.

"Merci, merci, merci," the large man replied, slipping back into his native tongue, "now that we have this final piece of proof, we can reveal everything. We can tell the truth."

"That's why we've come," his father replied, "why we've been here all along."

Stepping inside, Jason coughed at the dust that covered most of the visible surfaces. Rickety tables were filled with books, charts, and scraps of parchment. They consumed nearly every available inch of the room. Most of them looked as though they had not been touched in years, the dust thick and uninviting. Others, however, looked well worn, their pages dog-eared and showing signs of use. Even inside, Jason had no idea what to make of this strange place.

Watching the man move around the cramped interior was oddly captivating. His bulk should have made the process difficult, but he moved around the tight quarters with practiced grace. Though the books and parchments covered the room, and though many of them were balanced precariously, the man caused nary more than a faint rustle as he moved. These were the movements of a man who had walked these floors for years, for decades. The wooden floors clearly showed the preferred pathways of this portly scholar. *Or was he a scholar?* Jason wondered. He wasn't exactly sure who this man was or why they'd traveled to Cannes to speak with him. It was obvious that his father and the man were well acquainted, but his father had made no effort to introduce the two or explain their reasons for being there. *You'll know when the time is right*, his father had said to him seemingly so many years ago.

Was now that time? Would he finally understand why they had moved halfway across the world?

As if sensing the boy's musings, the large man began to speak. Slowly, the words came out, pronunciation exaggerated and elongated beyond need.

"I am Thomas Dauger, son of Jacques Dauger, and I am what you might call a collector. Not a collector of trinkets or other parcels, but a collector of information. Your parents and I have corresponded for many years now concerning an interest we share. A piece of information that I have searched most of my adult life for and, I suspect, a piece of information that your father has sacrificed much for as well."

Jason wanted to interrupt; he was wet, tired, and hungry, but most of all he was ready to know. He was ready to be told the answer to the great mystery of why his life had been turned upside down. He wanted to tell the man to skip the hors d'oeuvres and proceed onward to the main plate. However, in France, that was not the way of things. Conversations, much like meals, were served in a strict order. First hors d'oeuvres, then entremets, then plates, and so forth. To rush the man through his words would be an insult coming from anyone, but especially from someone as young as he was. His patience would have to see him through.

"You see, there are many types of information. Information is neither good or bad, but some information is better than others. Some of it can be trusted, and some cannot. Discerning between the two is, how do you say it?, the trick." Half of those words were butchered almost beyond recognition, but Jason had adapted well enough to French accents to understand. "Once you have information, you must then decide what kind is it that you have."

Thomas looked away from Jason and turned back to Dean. "Now that you have confirmed it, I have much to prepare and will need a few days to do so," Thomas intoned, still struggling with passable English pronunciation. "When can you return?"

"Next week. Monday, perhaps. Wednesday at the latest. I want to make sure that everything is in place before we...," his eyes turned to Jason, "before we go," he finished.

"Yes, alright," Thomas said, glancing around. "I will work here. I will put together the documents that I have, and we will hope that it will be enough to convince the right people of the truth. Next week we will begin," he finished with a growing smile.

"We will go now, before the rain washes us away. Please have everything ready when I return," his father said, and the man nodded, gesturing towards the door.

"I will. Please make sure you do not speak of this. We are nearing the end, but we could still face... problems if word were to get out. I fear that some of my own inquiries have already raised too many suspicions," Thomas said quietly, handing Dean a lantern.

"I have spoken of this to no one, and won't start now," his father replied, and Jason could certainly testify to the truth of that statement.

As they rushed out of the building, it took everything in his power not to riddle his father with questions about what had just happened. *This strange man knows more about what is going on than I do,* Jason thought sullenly. A thousand questions flew through his head, but none of the important ones passed through his lips.

"Will we return to the island tonight?" Jason asked instead, hoping to eke out any information that he could, even if it required a roundabout approach.

"Tonight? In the storm?" his father asked with surprise. By now, the storm was in full swing. The raindrops were like pebbles being thrown from the sky above. The thunder was coming every half minute now; each boom louder than the previous. Lightning made the clouds into something magical, almost ethereal. As they walked, the rain soaked them through, along with everything else.

The streets were streams, each one meeting the next until they connected with one of the troughs that lined the cobblestone streets. A deluge this intense was rare for Cannes, and those troughs were littered with bits of refuse, rotten fruit, and other left behind items that had been collecting in nooks and corners. It was like the storm was trying to clean the city of all its sins. For some reason he couldn't explain, Jason suddenly felt calm, even in the midst of the downpour. In that moment, he remembered the blue water that had so transfixed him earlier. He felt as though that same water was falling on him now, temporarily distracting him from the questions and doubts that ran through his mind. His moment of reprieve was interrupted by his father's reply.

"No, not tonight. I have arranged for us to stay at Madame Moreau's boarding house. She is expecting us, although I fear that she may not hear us knocking over this tempest! It is not far. Let's run!" his father finished.

With that, they ran. They ran over the uneven stones, slick with rain. They ran by the streets that just an hour before had been busy with the commerce of life, that had smelled of curry and lavender and pears. They ran past buildings both ancient and new, all the while sopping wet. It had been a long time since Jason had seen his father run. Since he had seen his father look happy. In spite of his previous anger, he found himself grinning in a way he couldn't remember doing since they had moved to the unknown island on the other side of the world.

Soon enough, they reached the white building where Madame Moreau was to be waiting for them. The rain had slowed and Jason studied the exterior of the narrow, two story building where they were to sleep. The outside was white, although it was clear that it had not been painted in many years. The shutters were a dark blue or green, it was difficult to be sure in the darkness. His father had the lantern given to him by Thomas, but it had petered out before they'd arrived. Due to the storm, all the shutters were closed and only the faintest of light escaped, leaving them in near perfect darkness. Jason thought that there was actually a full moon behind all the clouds, but couldn't be sure.

Bang, bang, bang! Dean knocked loudly at the door. Moments passed without any sound to be heard over the rain. Just as Dean was about to knock again, the door peeked open. Slowly at first, then thrown wide as Madame Moreau ushered them inside.

"Entrer! Vous êtes trempé! Déshabillez-vous immédiatement!" She handed them towels and pointed to a small room off the main entryway where shoes and coats were neatly organized. Pointing to the east end of the room, she indicated for them to put their wet clothes in a wicker basket in the corner. After removing their sodden garments, and modestly wrapped in the towels she had provided, Jason peeked out of the room to see Madame Moreau heading towards them with two robes. Handing them both to Jason, he awkwardly fumbled to hold them while keeping one hand on his towel. He probably looked like a fool, and the Madame's smirk confirmed that likelihood. Ducking back inside the room, both Dean and Jason put on the robes and returned to the entryway. The robes were ill fitting for both of them, but they were a dramatic improvement over their previous garb, and Jason was glad for them.

"Merci beaucoup," Jason attempted in halting French.

"Oui, c'est rien, pas de problem," she replied, speaking the most beautiful French that Jason had ever heard. It was a far cry from his own.

"Combien de temps allez-vous rester?" she turned and asked his father. Jason wasn't sure, but he thought that she was asking when they would be leaving.

"Nous partirons demain, pas plus tard que midi," his father replied, and he understood those words. Tomorrow by noon would be soon enough. He was looking forward to a good night's rest and, hopefully, some breakfast in the morning.

"Votre chambre est sur le premier étage, au bout du couloir. Il y a deux lits. Je suis désolé s'ils ne sont pas confortable. Nous n'avons pas d'invités souvent," Madame Moreau instructed, gesturing upstairs.

"Ce n'est pas un problem, j'apprécie votre volonté de nous emmener. Ma femme envoie des cordiales salutations." His father's French was not excellent, but it was slower and much easier to understand, even if not nearly as beautiful. Hearing his father mention his mother made Jason wonder how this woman knew her; she rarely left the island, and when she did she was almost always accompanied by the entire family. They had certainly never visited this establishment before. Leaving him to ponder that question for another time, Dean nodded and ushered Jason upstairs. The last door on the left was theirs, a modestly appointed room with two small beds, a dresser, a bedside table, and a single rocking chair. It wasn't much, but it was dry and quite warm. The fireplace downstairs was doing an excellent job of warming the entire home and Jason truly appreciated it. Although it was only 9PM, Jason was tired. He felt the weight of the day settle down upon him, and before he recognized quite how exhausted he was, he fell fast asleep.

Tomorrow would bring changes that would alter the course of his entire life. Tonight, however, he slept.

Chapter Two

Heather Burdett was ready. The trip had been long, the voyage miserable, and she was eager for it to come to an end. She studied the coast as their vessel made its way south. The waves crashing against the rocks, the stony outcroppings littering the shallows, the birds swooping and diving for their next meals. She had worried that the storm last night would prevent them from reaching Cannes today as they had planned. They had studied the storm from many miles off, watching the clouds fill with lightning and then hearing the thunder let out its rage on the hostile sea. Just the storm's edges had reached them, sending only moderate wind and a smattering of rain across their bow. The captain, a surly man named Pierre, had instructed the crew to hold the sailboat there, fearing the worsening storm's potential to wreak havoc.

"We haven't sailed this far for a storm to beat us on the rocks, we'll wait for morning. We will bring up the sails and make sure we're ready at first light," Heather's father, Edward, said. He apparently noticed the look of apprehension on her face, and sought to sooth Heather's nerves.

Her father was not actually one of the crew, but he worked alongside them to prepare the ship to hold overnight. Wrenching in the sails, adjusting the lines, all completed with familiar ease. Although he was not a sailor by trade, he was a practiced hand. Edward's father had owned a number of sailboats, and he had spent his youthful summers on the water, growing dark with tan. His sandy blonde hair, which lightened in the sun, was now turning gray as he aged. Edward's calloused hands, however proficient, weren't as strong as they once were. Time had taken its toll on her father, and Heather wondered whether he would ever be ready to stay in one place and enjoy the spoils that he had toiled so many years for.

Edward was a merchant, selling a great variety of goods in many different locations. Truth be told, he would sell pretty much anything, to anyone, if the price was right and the opportunity was interesting. He was an honest man, although that had not always been the case. His wanderlust was perfectly suited to his profession, giving him the excuse he needed to travel across the country, and now even the larger world, and explore. He'd pick up goods in one merchant town or another and set out to places unknown to sell them. If they were taking off from home and staying to the coast, they would sail. Otherwise, they would travel over land if the cargo called for a specific destination beyond the reach of their sailboat.

The previous year, a prominent woman named Claire, and her only daughter, Elise, had passed away after their carriage had run off the road and fallen into a small ravine. The family had originally immigrated from France, but had become extremely active within the community, including founding charitable organizations that helped the poor and downtrodden. In the years since they had arrived, they had become a fixture of the city's upper class. Their passing had been a great tragedy for their entire community.

When their estate had been sold, Edward had been able to purchase a large assortment of bustle dresses, formal evening dresses made of fine silk, and even imported cotton garments, along with some other pieces of furniture and some books. Although it had required a bank loan, the purchase had been well worth it. Even though he likely could have sold the merchandise for nearly the same sum in San Francisco, only a hundred or so miles from their home, he chose to travel to New York to offload the finery.

While there, he had purchased yet more merchandise and had made the decision to sail to Cannes, booking passage on a ship called the Neustria. The large, 328ft passenger ship could carry more than 1100 people from New York all the way to Marseille, France, and from there they had boarded this vessel rather than travel overland.

Heather was glad that her father had done so. She, too, loved to travel, and France would be the greatest adventure of her life so far. For years, Heather had fantasized about visiting Paris and walking its historic streets and alleyways, not to mention shopping at the finest stores in all the world. Cannes was not Paris, to be sure, but it was closer than she had ever thought she'd get. *And who knew, perhaps the winds of adventure that had brought them here would sweep them there next?* Heather thought, staring out over the water.

They docked early the next morning, hardly waiting for morning light. At the first opportunity, Heather left the boat, choosing to walk along the beach. She came to a crag of rock and sat, dipping her toes down into the shockingly cold water and touching the sand beneath.

Her mother was nearby, waiting patiently as her father and the crew unloaded boxes and crates full of chattel. A few kegs of beer were also being unloaded, although her father would have little to do with those. He wouldn't even allow himself to carry it, much less partake of any himself.

Years ago, her father had been an abusive drunkard, seemingly dedicated to only two things, his love of drink and his love of travel. Her mother, Lynn, had always taken the brunt of the abuse, and she'd done her best to hide it from the children. With Heather she'd been mostly successful, shielding her from nearly all of the violence. Micah, however, had not been quite so well protected. As the eldest and the only other male in the house, he'd taken a significant share of the abuse, even if not as much as Lynn. Heather preferred not to think about those times. They felt like another lifetime, and she was determined never to return to it.

Nearly five years ago, they'd taken a trip to Texas to sell whatever items her father had thought Texans were interested in. At the time, she'd been only about ten, although she'd have proudly informed anyone who asked that she was 'almost eleven, which was almost twelve.' While traveling, they had stopped in a bustling town to make repairs to their carriage and to visit a mercantile for supplies. Edward had insisted on stopping at the local saloon for a drink, so Lynn took the children next door to wait for him.

When they returned, her father was already well into his cups. Lynn had been eager to get him out of there before he drank anymore. At the suggestion he leave, he'd shown his displeasure with the back of his hand. Heather had watched from outside as it happened.

Sitting at the end of the bar had been another man. He was enormous, with shoulders wider than any Heather had ever seen. He was dressed in a faded overcoat and worn boots, and his shiny bald head gleamed even from outside the saloon.

After Edward had hit her mother, Heather saw the bald man stand up, righteous anger in his eyes. She was not able to see what happened next, but as her mother rushed outside and pulled her away, she heard yelling and the tipping of chairs.

Her father had not returned that night, nor by noon the next day. Her mother had been as nervous as Heather had ever seen her.

"He's gone and done it this time. He's picked a fight with the wrong man or he's drunk himself to death. He should have been back by now, before nightfall yesterday, even. It's…,"

At that very moment, a rustling outside caught both of their attention, and they turned to see Edward standing there, flowers in one hand and a book in the other. His newly clean-shaven face looked naked without his customary beard. Heather was not sure that she had ever seen her father without it. She liked it very much. He stood up straighter than she was used to as well. A hush fell over the space, everyone unsure of who would speak first.

"Edward… are you…," her mother trailed off, unsure of what to say in light of his appearance.

"I'm fine. More than fine. I'm… I'm sorry, for what I did. For what I've done," Edward said. He continued, "Things are going to change. I am going to change."

Heather knew that her mother had heard similar words before. Change was always coming but never arrived. It was a tired and worn path, packed hard by many footsteps. However, never before had he brought flowers, and he had certainly never come home without his beard. *What had happened?* she wondered.

"Yesterday was the last time I will ever drink. Yesterday was the last time that I will ever lay hands on you. Yesterday was the last day of my past, and today is the first day of my future. That I swear to you, Lynn."

He broke down at that point, tears falling from his eyes as he moved to embrace his wife. Heather now had another first. She'd never seen his bare face before, and she'd never seen him cry. Perhaps things really were going to change. Perhaps.

It was only then she noticed the gold lettering on the spine of the book her father carried. *Holy Bible*, it said.

There had been change. Her father kept his word; never again did he hit her mother and never again did she see him drink alcohol. The shelves that had previously been filled with liquor bottles had been taken down. Often she would see him reading from that same Bible, holding it gingerly in calloused hands. It was his most prized possession and rarely was it far from him. His anger still flared up on occasion, but it was quickly restrained, and over the years that, too, faded away. She watched her father transform from one person to another, from someone she feared to someone she trusted. The change had been visible in her mother as well. She had always been a strong woman, firm, but now she had the opportunity to be relaxed. She could let her guard down. This new comfort suited her, and Heather often saw her attending to the household chores with a smile or humming a melody.

Her father's promise had changed their lives, and she thought back on that moment often.

Her father's love of travel did not abate, however. If anything, it grew stronger. Previously, her father's travels had been restrained by his dependency on drink. He spent too much time and money on booze, and it limited his ability to go where he wanted to, or when. Deadlines are fickle things when they reside in the hands of an alcoholic, after all. Now, her father's passion for travel was not held back by any such need, and he was free to put his entire mind toward the effort. Their trips escalated from brief journeys of less than a fortnight to full blown adventures, months in the planning and making. They'd been to New York, to Chicago, and all across the country. Now they had even travelled across the ocean, finally landing here, in France.

"Are you ready to go, darling?" her mother asked softly.

"Oh, yes, let me put my shoes on," Heather responded. She shook off as much of the cold water and wet sand as possible before slipping into her shoes that had been previously discarded on the beach.

"Your father has arranged for us to board here in town. Once the boat is unloaded and prepared, he'll join us. Until then, I thought we'd go and walk the markets, what do you think?"

"Yes, mother, that sounds wonderful."

They walked from the dock towards the city of Cannes. It was still early, hardly past 9AM, but already Heather could hear the sounds of the city. Heather's brother stayed behind to help unload the boat along with the crew. At nearly twenty, Micah was every bit as large as her father. His long hair, well past his shoulders, was his only feminine characteristic. Micah was his father's son, in more ways than one, and so many of Edward's tendencies anchored Micah down. Although Edward attempted to stop him, he'd almost certainly partaken of an ample portion of the kegged beer on board the craft before they'd ever docked. Heather was glad that he was staying with the boat.

As they walked along the winding roads, Heather was struck by the beauty of the place. Cannes was unlike any city that she had ever visited, and she drank in the sights at every turn. The architecture was so different than anything in the States, and the old buildings had indescribable charm. The roads dipped and rose, never seeming to maintain an even direction. As they got closer to the center of the city, the smell of baking bread and buttered savories met their nostrils. Heather's stomach murmured with hunger.

The streets were full, street vendors filling every available nook and cranny to peddle their wares. There were stands of linens and silks in a rainbow of colors, alongside carts where women did their daily shopping, choosing fresh pears and grapes for their evening meals. One merchant sold fresh fish, probably caught that very morning. Heather took it all in, stopping only to run her hands along the soft fabrics or smell the flowers available at one stand or another. Everything was alive and vibrant with color and beauty.

They walked up and down the crowded streets, covering nearly every avenue and alleyway until the marketplace had all but faded away behind them. After browsing for several hours, they stopped at a shop at the edge of the market that was selling bread, and they bought two small loaves. Sitting nearby, they ate quietly, taking in the sight of the water below.

As they sat and took in the beautiful surroundings, they did not go unnoticed by the other patrons in the marketplace. Heather's fiery red hair stood out proudly against the browns and blacks much more common in this part of the world. Her hair made her distinct, it always had. Red hair has a way of separating people, of distinguishing them from others, and that separation carves out a personality, one that is resilient and bold.

Eyes may have been drawn in by her hair, but the rest of her was no less stunning. Although she was short, like her mother, she was lovely in appearance. Her hips were wide and her breasts full, but her face was her greatest physical blessing. Dotted with freckles, she was breathtakingly beautiful, and her smile was infectious. Most striking of all, perhaps, were her eyes. Azure portals ringed in sapphire blue, they were eyes that men wrote poems and sonnets about. Eyes that, if you didn't watch your step, you could find yourself falling into. At nearly fifteen, Heather was already a standout beauty.

"Has daddy told you how long we will stay?" Heather asked.

"No, he doesn't know how long it will take to sell the goods, and I think that he wants to be patient for the best price."

"That's okay, I like it here. I like the way it smells, I like the feeling the air gives me," Heather responded, a smile on her face. The air was crisp, carrying the smell of salt and fish and flowers. An intoxicating mix of the unknown and the mysterious.

"Let us go, shall we? The place we will be staying is nearby, I think. Right down that road, perhaps?"

Heather looked, but didn't see where her mother was indicating.

"Okay, that's fine, my feet are starting to hurt anyway," Heather said, getting up and starting to walk.

They wandered down the streets, searching for a white, two story building with green shutters. Before long, they were completely lost.

"Your father said that the sign would say M.Moreau and that if we walked north of the market we'd be certain to find it."

"North? Which way is that?" Heather asked. She had never been good with cardinal directions.

"It's the way we've been walking, I'm quite sure of it. I'm one hundred percent certain," her mother replied.

Looking around, Heather analyzed the area. They were standing at the bend of a road, set slightly above the marketplace, and overlooking the sea. The wind coming off the water was chilly, and Heather suddenly wished that she'd brought a shawl. Shivering, she saw another roadway on the far side of the market, leading to a cluster of white buildings. She strained to see, but couldn't tell whether there were any signs or what color the shutters might be.

"There, look there," Heather pointed, "those white buildings. Is that is?"

"Oh, it could be, I cannot tell from here. Let's go look," her mother replied.

They headed west, back towards the market. Now, taking a right when they'd previously proceeded straight, they saw a row of buildings set into the top of the hill. The shutters were faded and in need of paint, but they were green. In front of the building was a faded sign, just as her father had said there would be. Knocking on the door, an elderly woman of nearly seventy opened the door. Her hair was pulled back into a tight bun and the house smelled of fresh bread and cinnamon. She ushered them in, speaking in beautiful French.

"Bonjour! Vous êtes Mme Bennett, n'est-ce pas? Entrer, entrer!"

Her mother spoke very little of the language, only what she could learn in the last few weeks of travel.

"Je ne parle pas français bien, est-ce que nous pouvons attendre ici?" her mother said, doing her best with the strange tongue.

"Ah oui, bien sur!" the woman said, smiling enthusiastically and returning to the stove top.

Sitting down on a upholstered couch near the window, Heather took in the room. In one corner was an open doorway that looked like it led to a coat room, as there were several coats hanging on pegs just inside. There were also shoes on the floor, so Heather surmised that there must be other guests. At the opposite end of the room was a staircase leading to the second floor, and beside that a rocking chair that looked like it may be as old as the house. To the south were two large windows, now open and letting in the fresh air. Between the staircase and the windows was a huge fireplace, with plenty of dried wood in a box beside it. *What a wonderful place to spend a cold evening*, she thought.

"My English is not very good, I apologize," the woman said in English, and with a smile. "Tea?" she asked, holding up a kettle. Heather thought that her English was surprisingly good and that she had no reason to apologize. Lynn began to speak, but Heather cut her off.

"Oh yes, please," Heather said, "that would be wonderful."

The tea was excellent, tasting of oranges and spice, and Heather drank it eagerly. It was exceedingly hot, just the way Heather liked it, and it warmed her from the inside out.

Chapter Three

It was nearly noon, and Jason was eager to return home. His father had left early in the morning, before Jason had awoken, without a word about his whereabouts. Jason figured that he'd gone back to see Thomas, the large man from yesterday, so that they could speak in private. He got the feeling that whatever was so important to his father had convinced him to go back, even though he had told the man that he wouldn't return until next week.

Until his father reappeared, he had nothing to do but wait. He ambled around the small room, tracing fingers over the desk and dresser, the only furniture in the room other than the two beds. The beds had been surprisingly comfortable, either that or he had just been so tired that he didn't notice that they weren't. Either way, he felt well rested and ready to go. His mother would be waiting for them, and he knew that he would still be expected to help with the chores.

Looking out the window on the southern side of the room, it seemed like it was going to be a spectacular day. Warm enough to be pleasant with just a hint of chill in the air, exactly his type of weather. Jason grew hot easily and was always glad for a small breeze to cool his skin.

Why were they here? Why had they come to this place? Jason wondered as he looked out the window, staring past the buildings and towards the sea. *What were they doing?* It wasn't the first time that he'd gotten lost while thinking about those questions. His family was not wealthy, and his father had no business here. Ostensibly, they were still farmers, raising sheep and goats and a few crops to sell to the prison. The farmhouse they had lived in for the past year had been decrepit when they'd first arrived, hardly more than four walls with a shabby roof holding them together. How his father had heard of this place, or acquired the farmhouse and land, was beyond him.

His father was a practical man. A man who made decisions based on more than hunches and dreams. This adventure was entirely out of character, and Jason was ready to get to the bottom of it.

Nonetheless, they had spent two years making the ramshackle house into a livable home. His father had gone immediately to work on the roof, rebuilding both structure and façade in order to prevent the rain from dripping in from a dozen different holes. Next, he'd insisted that they address the windows, most of which were broken or frozen in place from years of neglect. Last, he had insisted that they dig around the foundation stones of the home, adding additional bracings and packing mortar into every crack and crevice. Jason had not seen much reason for that particular labor, but his father attended to it constantly nonetheless. Even after they had nearly excavated the entire house, his father continued until every stone had been reinforced and secured. It all had taken time, his father's work on the stones only being completely finished weeks ago, but the results were something that a man could be proud of. Even after the work had been done, no one would call the home anything except modest, but Jason felt proud of the work that he'd contributed.

They had purchased some pieces of used furniture from the mainland, and his father had crafted many others. Their beds, dining table, and most of their chairs had all been lovingly created in his father's workshop, which was housed in the far back of the barn behind the house.

The barn's upkeep had not been given the same priority that the rest of the home had. It, too, had four walls and a roof, but on days with heavy wind, those walls creaked and groaned, threatening to abandon their posts.

"One of these days, we need to get serious about our work in here," his father had once told him while they were tending to the animals.

"I suppose so."

"I'd like to get the roof patched up before winter comes around. Before the rain settles in," his father had said aloud, although primarily to himself.

It was now early August, the last full month of summer before the chillier seasons ahead. *Will we still be here in spring?* he wondered. *Was whatever was happening today going to change this? Were they finally leaving?* He certainly hoped so. Jason was ready to back home in Iowa, back in his real home.

Jason was ready to be home for many reasons, but most of all he missed his friends. Here, in the middle of nowhere, he had none. The population of the island was small to begin with, and the population of teenagers was limited to himself alone. Those few people that were there spoke only French, leaving no realistic options for meaningful friendship with someone of any age.

Back in Iowa, Jason didn't have many friends either, but the ones that he did have were important to him. His oldest friend was Heather Brownell. Their friendship went back to the very first day of school, Jason having pestered her until the teacher had reprimanded them both. Heather, being a teacher's favorite from the first roll call, had not been happy about the scolding. However, in spite of Jason's infraction, the two had become close friends.

While several other kids spent time in their circle, Heather had been the only one to remain consistently at Jason's side. Throughout the years, others came and went, but Heather remained his only real friend. That is, until Calvin arrived just after Jason's tenth birthday.

Calvin was, in many ways, Jason's opposite, both in stature and personality. Whereas Jason was often brash and straightforward, Calvin was more cautious and more reserved. He was willing to speak his mind, but he had a more polite way of doing so than Jason ever managed. Physically, the two also shared little in common. As they grew older, both would end up being tall, but Calvin was slighter of build and far fairer of feature. His blonde hair was quite the contrast to Jason's dull orange mop. They may have been opposites, but those differences worked. They balanced each other out.

Calvin instantly turned their twosome into a threesome, becoming an integral part of both of their lives. Jason spent countless summer hours walking the woods or swimming in one farm pond or another with both of them. Their favorite was an out of the way pond on Jason's farm where they'd constructed a crude dock and a small structure in which to house a few old towels and fishing poles.

In the winter, the three of them would most often end up at Calvin's house, spending hours playing cards or just talking about their lives.

The three of them created a bond that was not lightly broken or abandoned. Over the course of the next five years, they grew together as friends and individuals, leaning upon one another in hard times and celebrating in good times.

Jason's connection to Calvin was as that of a brother. Although they had not met each other until after Jason had turned ten, they now shared everything, and there was nothing that was off limits. Their conversations spanned far and wide, ranging from the mundane to the intensely private. Before Jason had left for France, many of those conversations had started to revolve around the third member of their group, Heather.

The topic of Heather had come up late one evening as they sat outside Calvin's house, his wraparound porch being the setting for many of their deep conversations. The night had been still, the cool September air scarcely moving. Stars had begun to peek out as the sun's final rays disappeared beyond the horizon.

"Do you know what you're going to get her for her birthday yet?" Jason asked, gazing upward.

"I don't know. I was thinking it should be something nice, you know? Maybe some jewelry."

"Jewelry? I didn't know you could afford jewelry. I didn't know that you'd get her something like that," Jason said, raising his eyebrows in surprise.

"I can't, you're right. I'm just not sure what she'd like," Calvin said as he glanced across the yard, watching lightning bugs as they searched for mates. Soon the air would cool and the bugs would be gone for another year. He glanced at Jason as a thought occurred to him. "What about a book? Didn't she say that she wanted to read... what was it she said...," Calvin trailed off, trying to remember.

"It was Jules Verne. *Journey to the Center of the Earth*," Jason said with a sad smile, although in the darkness it went unnoticed.

"That's it! Maybe I'll get her that. What do you think?"

"I think that it's unlikely she'd need two copies," Jason said, the small sadness he felt creeping into his tone. As he said it, he felt sure that Heather would be much happier with it if Calvin had gotten it for her.

"Did she already get it? I didn't kn... oh, you got it for her already?"

"It arrived in the post two weeks ago. Sent away for it when she first mentioned it in July. It cost two dollars."

Calvin let out a whistle. "Two dollars?" His look of surprise was distinguishable even in the minimal light. "Helluva birthday gift."

"I've been saving for a while. Didn't really have anything to spend it on any way, ya know? Besides, it'll be worth it if she likes it."

"Well she'd better. Anyway, now I really don't know what to do. Whatever I buy her is going to seem like junk by comparison."

But it hadn't. When they'd given their gifts to Heather on her birthday at the end of September, she beamed at both. She'd thanked them profusely and seemed ecstatic. The book found a home in her growing library, and the sapphire blue scarf that Calvin had given her was instantly wrapped around her neck, a smile adorning her face.

"You two are the best! I don't know what I would do without you!" she'd said, giving each of them a hug in turn.

Jason and Calvin had given each other knowing looks and exchanged a thumbs up, both seeming to have succeeded at finding an acceptable gift for Heather's fourteenth birthday.

That had been about six months before they had left for this accursed rock in the middle of nowhere. As Jason thought back to it now, he smiled ruefully, wishing that he could be transported back to that moment and away from this place. Away from isolation and loneliness, away from France, away from the feeling that he'd never see his friends again.

Chapter Four

As Heather Burdett sat and sipped her tea, she thought absentmindedly about how far they'd come. From the port of San Francisco to the shores of France. An entire world of land and ocean between the two. They'd traveled to New York to sell the clothing and other items her father had purchased at auction, intending to head directly home afterwards. Her mother constantly harped about the perils of travel and the treacherous weather. In truth, Heather thought that she just wanted to be home. Heather wanted to be home, too, but she also loved everything about this place. The streets, the smells, the people, everything about it made her smile.

Coming here had not been a part of their plan. They'd taken the railroad to New York, first boarding a train from Sacramento to San Francisco and then boarding another train from there. It was the Pacific Railroad, brand new and still a source of national pride. The line stretched from San Francisco to New York, exactly what they needed, and her father said it would change the country forever. Her mother said that the tickets cost too much, but was secretly glad for the level of comfort and speed the train provided. Five days in a sleeper car was far more appealing than many months in a wagon.

However, at nearly one hundred and thirty dollars per ticket, it had not been cheap. Her father had made a significant wager on the success of their trip, and had it not been profitable they would have struggled to even make it back. Whether by fortune, providence, or otherwise, she did not know, but their luck was found in New York City. Amidst the swarming masses, her father had not only sold their goods at nearly twice his hoped for price, he had discovered something that compelled him to travel here, to France.

Whatever that was, he had not spoken of it to Heather. She only knew of its existence by bits and pieces of overheard conversations between her parents. Even though it must have been of great consequence, they didn't feel the need to inform Heather about it. Not that she minded, she was just glad to be here, with the sun shining through the open window and the cool ocean breeze rustling gently outside.

"Honey, I'm going to go down to the market, just down here," her mother said, pointing in the direction they'd just come from.

"Why? We just got here," she said, a confused look crossing her face.

"I want to have some food available when your father and Mike get here. I should have grabbed some on the way," her mother answered, referring to her brother by his nickname rather than his given name of Micah.

"I'd like to stay here, alright?" Heather asked, certain her mother would insist she come along.

"I don't see why not, I'll be back in just a few minutes."

Surprised, Heather smiled and picked up her teacup, holding it under her nose and inhaling the pleasant aroma. Closing her eyes, she sat there in content silence until her mother arrived back a few minutes later, her small basket now full of apples, pears, and grapes, all of which looked delicious.

"Shall we go up to the room and wait?" her mother asked, still standing.

"Sure, is the room ready?" Heather responded.

"I'm not sure, let me ask." Turning to Madam Moreau, who was standing just a few steps away, she tried her best to ask about their room. "L'espace est prêt? Nous pouvons aller?"

The woman looked puzzled momentarily, her mother's French apparently not getting the message across perfectly. Realization dawned on her, and she smiled before simplifying the matter by speaking in English. "Yes, of course. Let me show you."

Heather wasn't quite finished with her tea, but she stood, albeit with some reluctance. She supposed there would be time for more tea later.

They walked up the creaking steps with Madame Moreau leading the way. Heather took note of how narrow the walls were. She thought it was quaint, and it made her love the place even more than she already did. It was old and charming and simply wonderful, she was certain that she could stay here forever.

The room at the top of the stairs was theirs. Madame Moreau opened the door for them and handed her mother a small key before leaving the room. The room held less charm than the common area downstairs. The walls were mostly bare, only one painting hanging in the far corner above a flimsy table with two chairs. There was a bed in the main room and a powder room off to one side. On the other side she saw an open door. Walking towards it, she saw that there were actually two bedrooms, the other housing two smaller beds with a table and a lamp between them.

Both rooms had surprisingly exquisite rugs, crafted from vivid blue fibers with patterns of a light cream. They were stunning in every regard and stood in stark contrast to the rest of the simple adornments of the rooms. They seemed so out of place that Heather had the urge to reach down and touch them, as if feeling the fibers could explain their presence. Resisting the urge, she sat down on the bed in the main room. It, too, was surprising. She wasn't sure whether its comfort was genuine or simply a result of their long voyage, but she quickly stretched out fully on the bed.

She was asleep before she even realized how tired she truly was. Sleep had always come easy to Heather; this instance was no aberration. Whether day or night, Heather had always been able to fall asleep with ease.

She awoke to the sounds of loud noises at the door. Startled, she shot upright, certain that someone was attempting to break in. It took a few moments for her to realize that the voices behind the door belonged to her father and her brother. Smoothing her skirt, she got up and opened the door for them, their hands full of cases.

"Let me guess, you decided to take a nap? Left us to all the hard work, as usual," her brother mocked.

"I... I was tired," came her weak reply. Her brother ribbed her at any and every opportunity.

"Enough with all that," her father cut them off, "help us with these. Let's get clothes unpacked. Madame Moreau said that there

34

was a dresser in the far room." Heather hadn't actually gone into the far room previously, but now that she did, she immediately noticed the large dresser along the south side of the room, nearest the hallway. It was made of an extremely dark wood and looked completely immovable. It was intricate in its detail, with decorated inlays and perfectly crafted dovetails. It seemed even more out of place than the rugs. *What was this place?* Heather wondered, perplexed by the out of place details. *How could a small inn afford to have items like this?*

Although it had felt like longer, Heather had only slept for a little over an hour. Groggily, she helped her mother remove their various garments from the suitcases and transfer them into the dresser in the adjacent room. They had brought less than they needed, never having returned home from New York to properly prepare for a voyage across an ocean. Heather's wardrobe was even more limited than her mother's, who had a penchant for fine dresses.

Although her wardrobe was minimal, what Heather had brought along all looked stunning on her, from the fanciest dress to the simple skirt and blouse that she was wearing today.

Her brother was forced to run back to the boat for their last suitcase, and by the time he returned and everything had been unpacked, it was nearly 4PM. Heather was hungry again, her stomach not satisfied with the loaf of bread she'd eaten earlier. Glancing around, she found the basket of fruit, although it appeared that much of it had already been consumed. Her brother, no doubt, was to blame. Of the single apple and pear that remained, she selected the apple and took a large bite, crunching into it with satisfaction.

"I've spoken to Madame Moreau, dinner will be served downstairs at 8PM. I'm going to the market to investigate what sellers may be interested in our wares before they close for the day," her father declared, not so much initiating a conversation as simply providing information.

Nodding to Micah to come along, they walked out and down the steps. Looking over to her mother, Heather saw that she was likely to fall asleep in the chair sitting in the corner of the larger room. Smiling, she told her mother she was going downstairs for tea. Her mother murmured her approval and closed her eyes. Heather glanced at the beautiful rugs one more time as she left, still curious as to how they fit in.

Back in the main room, she sat in the same chair she had previously, with her back to the stairs and a teacup in her hands. Madame Moreau had been kind enough to pour her another cup, and she sat there content with it once more.

The inn was modest, only about four guest rooms so far as she could tell. There were the two rooms upstairs, two down the hallway to her left, and possibly another one beyond the kitchen. She knew that Madame Moreau's living quarters were in that direction as well, so it may only have been the four she could see. For such a limited space, it felt surprisingly roomy and as guests came and went, she never felt like she was in the way. So far, she'd been able to ascertain that a woman and her husband were staying in one of the rooms down the hall, and the other room downstairs was currently occupied by a large man that Madame Moreau had called Albert. Albert smelled of body odor and unwashed hair, a combination that made Heather glad that he did not stay long and quickly retired to his room. She had no idea who might be staying in the room beside her own, or if it was currently unoccupied.

Blowing softly on her tea, she drifted off into thought. *Perhaps the inn keep was secretly wealthy, running this inn only to fill her days*, Heather thought, her mind wandering back to the rugs and dresser. *Or maybe she stole them!* she thought, now letting her imagination run wild. *No, she's much too old to be sneaking around stealing rugs. Not to mention that it would take at least three strong men to move that dresser.* Holding back a grin at her own foolishness, she looked up just as a boy about her age walked down the stairs. Her back was mostly to him, but she caught just a glimpse out of the corner of her eye. Something about him attracted her gaze and she knew immediately what it was.

Just like her, he had a head full of red hair.

Chapter Five

He made his way downstairs for the second time, his first trip having been earlier to investigate the delicious smell of baking bread that had initially awoken him. His nose had not disappointed. Madame Moreau had prepared a simple breakfast of bread and fruit and, although it wasn't the breakfast of bacon, sausage, and toast that he was used to, Jason savored every bite. His appetite had been extraordinary, but he had not asked for seconds. Being polite was something that had been instilled in him since birth. There would be more food later, he was sure.

Now, downstairs again, he took a seat at the northwest corner of the room. Tucked away, the small table and few chairs were almost hidden from view of the doorway. He imagined that this area was where guests might spend their evenings, sipping wine or enjoying a pinch of whiskey. He didn't even turn around to survey the rest of the room or who might be in it. He was preoccupied with thoughts of his father. *Why hadn't he returned yet? He should have been back hours ago*, he thought, worried and confused.

His father had told the innkeeper that they would leave no later than noon, and yet it was nearly 4PM. His father was not a man who tolerated lateness, so a four-hour delay was more than slightly concerning. Jason sat there, deep in thought, until Madame Moreau walked by and offered him tea, which he accepted as much out of courtesy as anything else.

Taking a sip, he recoiled, the hot liquid burning his tongue. Annoyed, he pushed the cup away from him and towards the middle of the table. His irritation at his father was spilling over, making the too hot tea seem like something more than it actually was.

"Son, good, you're here," his father said suddenly, seeming to appear out of nowhere.

"Where have you been? You said we were going to leave hours ago, and you disappeared this morning without saying a word!" Jason responded, his anger apparent.

"I know, it couldn't be helped. Something... I had something I had to do. It could not wait," his father said, not bothering to offer a meaningful explanation.

"What couldn't wait, what was so urgent that you couldn't even tell me?" Jason said, challenging his father to give him a more appropriate response.

"That's not something I can get into. Not... not here. Not now," his father said quietly, looking around at who may be listening.

Jason was even more annoyed now than he had been before. Yet again, his father refused to tell him anything. At sixteen, he was trusted enough to do anything the family required, but not enough to be told even the smallest detail about a trip that had taken away his home. Taken away his life. Taken away his friends. The fury rose up in him little by little until he could hardly contain it. Rather than screaming at his father, he turned and walked away. He walked out of the suffocating room and into the cooler air outside. Down the streets and alleyways, down through the market, down and down and down until he reached the ocean.

He paced the beach, his anger boiling and raging within him, threatening to burn through his good sense. *He could run,* he thought. *Just leave and never return. But to where? Where could he possibly go? He was trapped. Trapped in the middle of a foreign country with no hope of escape.*

"Ahhhhhhhh!" he shouted, grabbing a stone and throwing it into the ocean, its splash barely discernable in the midst of the tides coming in. Reaching down he grabbed another and threw it even harder than the previous. After that another, and another, throwing stone after stone until his shoulder ached and he was out of breath.

Sitting down in the sand, he buried his head in his hands. The wet sand from the rocks had found its way into his sweating palms and now freckled his red hair with coarse grains. Still angry, Jason made no effort to avoid the tide as it ebbed and flowed on the beach. The waves barely reached his boots now, but shortly they would soak him from head to toe. He didn't care. Why did a little saltwater make a difference anyway? Soaked or dry, he was still a prisoner here, trapped in a cell of someone else's choosing for reasons that no one would tell him.

The walk back took far longer than the walk there had. His steps were shorter and slower than they had been before. His anger and rage exhausted on the rocks and the ocean. He was spent, and his slow pace reflected the change. As he walked back up the sloped roads, he noticed how beautiful the city truly was. Rows of pristine white homes lined the streets, washed clean by all the recent rain.

He was not looking forward to returning to the boarding house, or to the cramped room where his father surely remained. He knew that there would be hell to pay for his outburst. It was also clear that they would not be leaving tonight. It was too late, and there was no reason to risk sailing in the dark. That meant that he would have to spend the entire night trapped with his father.

It wasn't dark yet, however, and the sky was remarkable. Reds and oranges covered the horizon, illuminating the clouds in a brilliant display of God's artwork. The storm had washed the buildings and streets, and now it provided this sunset as a parting gift.

By the time he reached the building where they were staying, the sunset's color had peaked. It was as beautiful as it was going to get. He took a few moments to soak the sight in before proceeding inside.

He kept his head low as he entered, hoping that his father was waiting in their room and not sitting at one of the tables in the main part of the inn. His anger had subsided, but not completely abated, and he wanted to take a little more time to cool off before he was forced to confront him.

He took a seat at the same table he'd been sitting at when his father had returned earlier in the day. Unlike then, the room was busy with activity, and people occupied most of the available seats. Madame Moreau was busy in the kitchen, hovering over a large stew pot, clearly preparing dinner for her tenants. The smell filled the room, mixing wonderfully with the smell of burning wood emanating from the fireplace. Madame Moreau noticed his arrival, and made her way over to his table and smiling warmly.

"You are returned! Your father was worried," she said, attempting her best English. "Do not worry, I told him that you would be back. He is in the room if you'd like to go see him." she finished.

"No, I'd like to sit here for a while if that's okay," Jason said, hoping that she would not press the issue or alert his father.

She didn't respond, just nodded and returned to her cooking, this time tossing some green vegetables into an iron sauce pan. Whatever she was making, Jason certainly hoped that there would be enough for him. He hadn't eaten since lunch and he was famished.

He looked over to a clock that sat on a countertop, its hands indicating that it was nearly 6PM. He hadn't been gone nearly as long as he'd thought. He decided that he'd go upstairs at 6:30PM, whether he was ready to or not.

Less than ten minutes had passed when he looked up to see a redheaded girl standing next to his table. His breath caught in his throat.

"Hello," she said, a smile revealing a mouthful of beautiful teeth, straight and pearly white.

"Hello," he replied simply, unable to formulate something more substantial.

"I usually wouldn't be so forward, but you look like you could use some company. Plus, there's no one else our age here. Can… can I sit here?"

Jason didn't know how to respond. He wasn't used to girls showing any interest whatsoever in him, much less being the one to make the first move. He breathed deeply at the exquisite smell of her perfume. Instead of responding, he simply nodded, pushing the chair beside him out with his foot.

"Thank you, my name is Heather," she said.

He laughed out loud, unable to stop himself.

"Of course it is," he replied, staring into the most captivating blue eyes that he had ever seen, eyes that reminded him of the sea.

Chapter Six

Heather was too taken aback to sit. A simple introduction had taken a sudden turn towards awkward. *Of course it is?* she thought. *What is that supposed to mean?* Even so, she was intrigued. Anyone so bold as to laugh at an introduction must have a story to tell.

"Of course it is? And why is that?" she asked, not skipping a beat.

"I'm sorry, I didn't mean…, my name is Jason. It's a pleasure to meet you," he said, obviously trying to recover from his disastrous beginning. "I have a…," he paused.

A girlfriend. Of course, she thought, a trifle annoyed. *Why did guys always mistake common courtesy for some sort of come on?*

Why could she not even introduce herself without being thought of as one of 'those girls'?

"...friend," he finished. "I have a friend named Heather. A best friend actually. It seems she follows me even to France."

"Oh. Well, I just thought perhaps you could use some company, like I said. I heard you speaking English to your... father?" she said, a question in her voice.

"Yes, we were having a discussion. Sort of."

"Anyway, I heard you speaking English, and I couldn't help but come over and introduce myself. There aren't many teenagers around, and fewer still who understand our language."

"That's true, we are pretty isolated. You're the first pretty face I have seen in months," he said, suddenly blushing with recognition of what he'd said. She blushed too, her freckled face simultaneously reddening and lighting up.

"Have you tried the tea?" Jason asked, smiling at her.

"Oh yes, it's wonderful. I think that I've singlehandedly quartered Madame Moreau's supply," Heather said with a giggle.

"It is very good. She is a very attentive host."

Looking around for Madame Moreau, Heather wasn't sure where she had gone. Just moments ago, she had been busy with meal preparation, but now she was nowhere in sight. She'd been too occupied with the conversation to notice her departure.

"Are you staying long?" Heather asked, bringing her eyes back to his.

"No, well, I don't think so. We were supposed to depart for home earlier today but my father disappeared."

"Disappeared?" Heather asked, with genuine concern in her voice.

"Not disappeared exactly, more like left. He left this morning before I awoke but did not tell me where he was going. It's why we were fighting earlier. He won't tell me anything."

Heather glanced around, feeling a connection to his story. Her own father was often secretive, never giving a full telling of the story they were a part of. Even this trip was mysterious. Why travel to France to sell rugs and furniture? Her mother had been insistent that it was a sort of vacation, a reward for an abundant sale in New York. Heather had her doubts. Her father was closer to skinflint than celebrant. He loved his travel, yes, but he was also too pragmatic to make such a daunting and expensive trip without hope of significant reward.

"Yes, I'm sorry. Parents can be frustrating," she replied, opting for simple agreement.

As if he was just noticing that she was still standing, Jason said, "I'm sorry, sit down."

Heather sat, opting to take the seat across from him rather than the one beside him. There was a proper way to sit, after all. Heather may not be a stickler for etiquette, but she shuddered to think of her father's reaction if he came back to find her sitting next to a strange boy. Even sitting here across from him risked a rebuke, although that rebuke was likely to be delivered with a smirk.

"So where is home?" Heather asked after sitting and straightening her skirt.

"Ile Sainte Marguerite. It's an island close by. We have a farm there, mostly providing rations for the prison."

"Prison?" Heather asked, surprised.

"Yes, there is an old military prison there. It's not heavily occupied anymore, but they still need food for both prisoners and guards. We've been here for almost two years. I'm not really sure why. We moved here from Iowa. I like it well enough I suppose, but there's not too much to do, and I miss my friends."

"Your 'friend' Heather?" she asked, grinning.

Now it was his turn to turn red. "Yeah, she's one of them. She really is just a friend. But I miss them all. Well, both of them, to be precise."

"What about you? Where do you call home? Are you staying here in Cannes for a while? What brings you here?" One question turned into four, pouring out of him one after the other. Heather was caught off guard by the sudden bombardment.

"Well, I'm from California. We live in Sacramento. My father is a merchant, and we travel a lot to sell goods, although we've never travelled overseas before. My mother calls it a vacation, but my father is already trying to sell in the market, and we haven't even been here a day yet."

"You missed a question."

"I did? And what was that?"

"Will you be staying long?" he repeated, and Heather wondered whether perhaps he was feeling the same way that she was. Her palms were damp, and she felt her heart beating faster than was necessary.

"Oh, I'm not sure. My father never really makes plans about how long our trips will last. A few weeks, I imagine. At least long enough to see the sights, wander the streets. Long enough for him to sell his trinkets."

"Perhaps we should start that process right away? Go see the sights. Walk around the city?" he asked, and Heather thought she detected a tone of hope in his voice.

"I... I don't think I can. It's getting dark and my parents would not want me to leave after the sun goes down. Maybe tomorrow? If you're still here?"

"Sure, of course. Maybe tomorrow."

"But you don't have to leave now, do you? My father hasn't yet returned, I'm sure I can stay at least until then."

She watched as Jason glanced back at the clock. She saw him move his head back and forth slightly, as if debating his options.

"Sure, I can stay. I don't have anywhere else to be," Jason replied, and Heather felt herself smiling once more.

They sat there and talked for nearly another hour.

Heather was equally enthralled. She knew right away that Jason was smart, his words precise and bordering on eloquent, even though he hitched and paused as they spoke. There was something about him that both intrigued and excited her.

It was almost 7:30PM when her brother and father returned, looking accomplished. Her father caught her eye, noticing her companion, and wandered over to their table.

"And who is this, Heather?" her father asked, his voice firm.

"Uh, Daddy, this is Jason. He's an American, too. We've just been chatting."

"Is that so? And where is your mother?"

"She is upstairs. Probably still sleeping."

"I see. Well, come up darling, we should get ready for dinner. I'm sure you'll see... uh, Jason, again before we leave."

"Alright Daddy, I'll be right up," she said, giving a look to her father that hinted that he should make his exit. With a gentle nod, they left Jason and Heather alone once again.

"Will I? See you again?" Heather asked.

"I hope so. I need to go anyway. I need to talk with my father. Get everything sorted out."

"How about tonight?" she dared, a bold question easily misunderstood.

"Tonight?" he asked, surprised, "What do you mean?"

"Tonight at 10PM. Meet me here again? Just to talk."

"Ok, yes. I'll be here," Jason said, his voice full of enthusiasm.

"I'll see you then," she said, rising up from her chair. She headed towards the stairs at the corner of the room. As she left she glanced over her shoulder, just once, and quickly hid a furtive smile before ascending the stairs. She couldn't help herself, she was already contemplating their upcoming rendezvous.

Jason sat at the table for a few more minutes, not bothering whatsoever to hide his own.

Chapter Seven

Heather entered their room, knowing full well that she was walking into an interrogation at best and a lecture at worst. Even if her father didn't give her a thorough talking to, her brother was sure to mock her mercilessly. Her mother would be her only port in the storm, always seeming to understand what her daughter was going through.

She opened the door quietly, hoping to sneak in and delay any confrontation until after dinner. Stepping through the doorway, she knew immediately that was not to be. Her mother sat in a rocking chair in the front corner of the room while her father sat on the bed. Her mother's hands were busy knitting, a pastime she'd developed over the course of the last few years. Her father's hands were also busy, although not with knitting needles. Instead, he was occupied with the process of lighting his briar wood pipe. The smoke from it rose into the air and scented the room with its sweet aromas.

"Did you say goodbye to Jason for me?" her father teased playfully. *Good*, she thought, *at least he's not going to make a big deal about it.* Her mother looked up quizzically, apparently unaware of the interaction Heather had been having downstairs. She was surprised that her father had not mentioned it.

"Oh?" Lynn intoned, "and who is Jason?"

"He's no one. I mean, he's just a boy I met," Heather said, feeling her cheeks redden and unable to do anything about it. "He's an American staying here as well. We just bumped into each other and started talking. That's all," Heather finished, intentionally failing to mention that she'd been the first to initiate conversation with the unknown stranger.

"It looked like you were deep in conversation indeed," her father said, now grinning more widely. *He was in a good mood*, Heather thought, *perhaps he'd already arranged a promising sale.* As that thought hit her, she felt a pang of sadness in her stomach. She was in no rush to leave, and a quick sale likely meant a shorter trip than she'd anticipated.

"We were just talking!" she said, just a little too forcefully.

"Flirting is more like it, based on what I saw," her brother Micah called out from the adjoining room.

"Shut up, Mike! We were just…," Heather trailed off, searching for a word other than talking but far away from flirting. In truth, her brother had an accurate read of the situation, and she knew it, but there was no way that she could admit it here, out loud. "We were just bantering about what brought two Americans to France, that's all."

"Two Americans? Did he come alone? Did you?" her father continued to give her grief.

"You know what I mean. We talked about you, too. In fact, I told him all about my wonderful father whom I adore so much." When explanations failed, flattery was always a strong second option. "I told him you were the best salesman in all of America, and that you'd brought us here as the best vacation ever."

Her mother and father exchanged a glance at the word vacation, further confirming Heather's suspicions that more was at play than a simple transatlantic family adventure. She continued on, heaping praise on her father until he could stand it no longer.

"Okay, okay, you needn't treat me a fool. I understand what you're doing," Edward said, waving his hands at her in mock annoyance.

"So, will this Jason be downstairs for dinner?" her mother asked, looking up at Heather while holding back a grin.

"I… I suppose so. I didn't ask," Heather replied, as she also wondered to herself. They'd arranged to meet later in the evening, but she hadn't even considered the fact that dinner was to be served soon, and he'd likely be in attendance. "I'm sure he will. But please don't embarrass me!"

"And why would I do that?"

"I only mean that he's just a boy. Nothing to be so worried about."

"My dear, I've worried about boys since the day I gave birth to you. I'm not likely to stop now. But I will respect your wishes and won't say a word."

"Thank you, Mom."

"I promise nothing!" her brother yelled, loud enough that every upstairs occupant could likely have heard.

Heather rolled her eyes, absolutely certain that her brother would do everything in his power to make her miserable, as usual. Feigning sweetness, she replied, "How nice of you! I sure appreciate your thoughtfulness!"

"Uh huh," he muttered, already bored with the exchange.

Surprisingly, there was no additional questioning or hardship from any of them. Her brother's silence was a rare gift. As they finished the menial tasks associated with a long stay and then prepared for dinner, they graciously left her interactions with Jason unmentioned, and she appreciated that meager courtesy.

When it was time to head back downstairs, Heather was the first one out the door. She tried not to look like she was in a rush, lest her family go back to teasing her. With deliberate delay, she walked down the narrow staircase and glanced into the room beyond. Her nose took in the fragrant smells of the soup Madame Moreau had been cooking, its richness filling the space pleasantly. She also caught a whiff of baked bread and fresh fruit. Her nostrils were notoriously discriminating.

As guests of the inn gathered around tables and talked, Heather's head panned the room, searching for the shock of red hair atop Jason's head. Scanning the room twice, she saw no sign of him. Either he was not yet here or did not plan to come down for dinner.

Heather's heart sank, more disappointed than it should be. There was no reason for her to feel so sad. Jason was no more than a stranger that she'd enjoyed a conversation with. Not to mention the fact that she'd planned to see him again not even two hours from now. *What is going on with me?* she wondered. *I'm like a love sick puppy. I need to get a hold of myself already.*

All throughout dinner Heather was distracted, and as much as she tried to hide it, that distraction did not go unnoticed by her brother.

"Love bird still not here, huh, sis?" Micah asked with a sneer, sounding almost angry. Heather nearly flinched at the words.

"That's enough Micah, no need to torture her. Enjoy your meal," her father commanded, perhaps sensing that Heather was genuinely frustrated.

The soup was delicious, a flavorful broth of potatoes, celery, onions, and tomatoes served with rouille on fresh slices of bread, all of which was delivered alongside rascasse, a fresh fish caught nearby. The stew was called a bouillabaisse, a local favorite, and Heather's family ate it eagerly. Heather merely swirled the broth with her spoon and picked half-heartedly at the fish, her mind elsewhere.

Shortly before 9PM, her family had finished the meal and sat contentedly at the table, making small talk about the city and their plans for the following day. Her father intended to rise early, no later than sunrise, to see their merchandise to market and connect with potential buyers. Her brother would be expected to tag along. Lynn mentioned her desire to visit the market as well, intending to purchase fabric that she could use for one project or another. While knitting had held her interest of late, she was also an excellent seamstress and had crafted many of her own dresses. New and exotic fabric was a calling she could not ignore.

"It's early, but I am tired, and I'm ready for bed. Lynn," her father said, turning to his wife, "care to join me?"

"Sure, I'm tired too. Come on, kids, let's head upstairs."

"I'd like to stay downstairs; maybe have another cup of tea," Heather replied, neglecting to mention her other appointment.

Her father hesitated, studying her face, and Heather read doubt in his eyes. "I'll just stay a while. The tea really is excellent," she added, attempting to persuade him.

"No, I don't think so. Besides, you'll wake us up when you enter. Come, it's time to retire."

Heather was distraught, her plans crumbling. "Just a few minutes, please? I'll be as quiet as a mouse, I promise."

"You heard your father, Heather. Now come." Her mother's voice was resolute, representing a united front against her pleas. "It's barely nine o' clock, I'm not even tired," Heather tried, reaching in vain for some possible avenue of convincing narrative.

"That's too bad. We're going up, and both of you are coming with us," Edward stated, including her brother as though he, too, were trying to avoid leaving. Instead, Micah was looking at her with a smirk on his face, clearly happy to see her miserable.

"Fine," Heather said glumly, acutely aware that she may never get the chance to see Jason again.

As they got up and walked towards the stairs, her mother put her hand around Heather's shoulders and leaned in to whisper quietly, "I'm sure you'll see him again in the morning."

Heather looked at her mother and tried to feign a smile before leaning her head into her mother's shoulder.

"Thanks, mom," she said, and proceeded to their room.

Chapter Eight

Jason had come upstairs shortly after he and Heather had parted, determined to have it out with his father once and for all. As he walked the stairs, he tried rehearsing what he wanted to say, but thoughts of the girl downstairs clouded his mind.

Her smile and laugh were both completely irresistible, he thought. *The way that her nose scrunched up when she was surprised and the easy way she spoke about her life, using her hands as commas and exclamation points. She's incredible!* Jason wasn't sure if he'd ever met anyone quite like her. The smell of her perfume had been faint but exquisite, and he caught himself thinking about it as he opened the door to their room.

"You've come back," his father said, sitting in the dark room and smoking a hand rolled cigarette, an unlit candle sitting on the table beside his chair. Although he'd been expecting his father to be there, Jason was still startled.

"Yes. I... I needed to clear my mind. I needed to get away."

"I see. I would have expected you to return sooner. I was beginning to worry. It's late now, nearly dinner. Where did you go?" his father asked, his deep voice much calmer than Jason had anticipated.

"I just walked. I went down to the beach, wandered around. Then I came back and just sat downstairs. Talked."

"To yourself?" Dean asked, unable to mask a note of concern in his voice.

"No, to a girl. An American. Just someone I met," Jason said, and his father seemed to be relieved. *Who had he expected me to say?* he wondered.

"Ah. And now I suppose you've come back to demand answers."

His father's directness caught him off guard. He had expected his father to be on the offensive, angry at him for storming out and being gone for hours. All of his mental rehearsals had been predicated on his father's anger. This calmness made him second guess himself.

"Well, no. Actually, yes. I deserve to know," he stated, finding his resolve once again while simultaneously bracing for his father's rebuke. His father said nothing, sitting silently beside the window and seemingly deep in thought.

"I'm sixteen years old, nearly a grown man. I've helped you build our home, taken care of the farm; I've done everything that has been asked of me. I'm old enough for whatever secret it is that you're keeping about why we're here." Tears welled up in Jason's eyes, the passion of his words threatening to overtake his outwardly calm demeanor.

"Yes, you do."

Jason took a sharp intake of breath. Relief flooded through him, and he exhaled audibly. Once again, his father had surprised him.

"Son, I'm going to tell you things tonight. Things you must never repeat to anyone. Not to your friends, not to that American girl, not to anyone. Do you understand me? There may be a time when it will be safe to discuss, but until then I don't even want you to bring it up to your mother or I. Do you understand me?"

When it will be safe? Jason thought, confused about what could possibly be so important that the mere mention of it could jeopardize their safety. Perhaps this was a secret that he did not want to know after all. What if it was something horrible? He had never considered the possibility that his father could be keeping something nefarious from him.

"I asked if you understood what I just said to you. Answer me, son, or I will not continue."

Jason hadn't realized that he had not responded. "Yes, of course, sir. I won't say a word to anyone. I swear it."

The lesson he'd learned in his boyhood jumped into his mind. *Let your 'yes' be yes and your 'no' be no*, he heard his father's voice say inside his swirling mind. "Yes, I mean."

"So be it. Take a seat," his father said, retrieving a match from his pocket and striking it. He held the flame to the wick, lighting the candle beside him. They had been conversing in the dark, only the light from his father's cigarette illuminating the room. Now, as his father prepared to tell him the secret of their journey, they stepped out of darkness and into the light.

It didn't take Dean very long to give a thorough accounting of everything that had happened. He didn't go into details, only providing the general outline, but Jason felt his disbelief growing at every sentence.

Afterwards, Jason struggled to wrap his mind around what he had just been told. It seemed too far-fetched to be possible; nothing like that could possibly entangle his family. They were just small town Iowans, born and bred in the middle of nowhere. It simply wasn't possible that it could be true. *Or could it be?*

His mind raced, trying to process and make sense of it all. Jason began asking his father every single question he could think of, although he was too stunned to come up with much. Some of his questions went unanswered, his father didn't have all of the answers. However, what he did know, he shared. Even so, Jason had trouble accepting the truth of it.

"Can you show me?" he asked, finally.

"Yes. Tomorrow we will return, and I will show you what I have discovered. After that we will not speak of it again. You agreed, yes?"

"Yes, I understand. Of course."

His father reached down and picked up his pocket watch off the table beside him.

"I fear we have missed dinner. It is nearly 10PM. Should we see if Madame Moreau, if Adelia, has anything leftover?"

Jason's stomach agreed immediately, reminding him that he had not eaten properly for many hours. He also remembered that he had promised to meet Heather downstairs at 10PM, only a few minutes from now. Their conversation earlier now seemed like a lifetime ago, but his anticipation of their reunion set his heart beating even faster.

"Yes, definitely," he said, rising up from his seat on the bed and heading out of the room.

Once downstairs, Jason looked diligently across the room, scanning it three times before acknowledging that Heather was not there. He was a few minutes early, however, and he set himself to locating Adelia.

Adelia Moreau was standing in the northwest corner of the room, near the rows of shoes and coats, sweeping up the day's accumulated dust and debris. Jason had paid little attention to her before, just an old lady who rented out rooms to strangers. Now, he gave her a more meaningful appraisal. She was short and slender, with surprisingly dark hair for her age. What gray she did have was complementary, making her look regal rather than weary. Her calloused hands held the broom firmly, with no sign of infirmity or brittleness.

As if feeling his approach, Adelia turned and smiled at Jason before beginning a string of French spoken far too quickly for Jason to understand. Recognizing his look of confusion, Adelia started again, this time in English.

"You have finally come downstairs! Did you and your father have a good talk? Are you hungry?" she inquired, glancing over his shoulder at Dean. Looking back, Jason saw his father give a subtle nod, seeming to signal to her that his son was now in on the secret.

Her smile vanished, replaced with a more serious expression. It could not have been called harsh, however, and Jason thought she still looked happy. Suddenly, she leaned in and gave him a hug, her embrace significantly tighter than he would have expected.

"I'm am happy to finally meet you properly, Jason," Adelia said.

"I'm happy to meet you too, aunt Adelia," Jason replied, even though grandaunt would have been more accurate. Only after he'd spoken did he realize that perhaps he should not have acknowledged their relationship. He looked back at his father, who was still wearing a weary smile, the transgression apparently not serious enough to warrant anger.

"You must be hungry, come, sit. I have saved some for you," she said, bracing the broom against a corner and ambling over to the stovetop.

The soup still simmered, and Jason was glad for it. Adelia ladled two portions into bowls and carried them over to Jason and Dean, steam still rising from each. She set them down, then returned to the stovetop to fetch two small fish from a pan left at the back. She brought those to the table, along with the necessary silverware.

"There, eat," she said simply, perhaps understanding that Jason would not need additional encouragement. Both Jason and his father began eating in earnest, not letting a scrap or drop go to waste. Adelia watched them eat, seeming to consider whether she should begin a conversation or not. Apparently deciding against it, she turned away and began the process of cleaning the dishware and utensils used by her evening's guests.

As they ate, Dean and Jason shared lighthearted conversation, the tension between them finally eased. They spoke of the work that still needed to be done on their house, of Jason's mother, Kathleen, and how she would surely be worried to death at their delay, and they spoke of home. Of their real home, not this temporary holding place.

"I'm ready to be home, son. I really am. I'm sorry that this has taken so long," Dean said quietly, his expression both sincere and complicated.

"I know. I am too. When do you think we will leave? Spring?"

"I'm not sure. I suppose it will depend on what Thomas can tell us when we return next week. He has information that will help us decide what our next steps entail. Over the years he has chased many leads. He's chased many ghosts. Now that we…," his father paused, looking around the room, "that we have something to go on, we can focus on something more tangible."

"It will be nice to have a plan. I'm looking forward to it, I must admit."

"I am too, son. Until then, we simply wait and see. A week, maybe less. Then we will have something," his father said with a weary smile. They continued eating in silence, Adelia bringing over an extra portion of fish for Jason without asking. He ate it as eagerly as he had the first.

Jason was nearly finished when he thought to look for Heather. He had not noticed anyone descend the stairs, and the front door had not been opened. A quick glance informed him that Heather was not there, she had not come. It was 10:45PM, too late to expect her to make an appearance.

Why hadn't she come? he wondered, suddenly considering the possibility that he had misjudged her interest. Perhaps she had only meant to tease him and never actually intended to come. *That would be about right*, he thought with some bitterness. He'd known that she was too good to be true.

He attempted to put that aside by returning to the revelatory conversation he'd had with his father. There was so much to think about and contemplate, but he still struggled to keep his mind off the beautiful redheaded girl that was supposed to be here. A few minutes passed, his meal now entirely ingested, and he pushed the bowl and plate towards the center of the table.

"When will we leave in the morning?" Jason asked his father, suddenly unsure about whether he wanted to see Heather again at all. *If she had meant to stand him up, why should he want to see her? But if it was something beyond her control, what then? They were leaving in the morning. He'd probably never see her again anyway,* he thought, confused and disheartened.

"First light. I am ready to be home. Your mother will be happy to see us. We'll be home before noon."

"Sounds good," Jason muttered, still letting his eyes roam around the room futilely.

"Let's go to bed, shall we?" his father asked, not bothering to wait for a response before standing and walking away.

Jason grunted, taking a few extra seconds before standing up himself. As he turned, Adelia approached him, the daily dishware and chores now completed.

"It really was nice to meet you. I hope we can talk more. Our family is so…," Adelia said, finishing the sentence by holding her thumb and finger about an inch apart.

"Yes, it really is. I enjoyed meeting you too. I'm sure the next time we are here my mother will come too."

"I hope so," Adelia said, giving Jason a gentle pat on the shoulder.

"Goodnight. We're going to leave in the morning, for real this time, so I should get to bed."

"Yes, goodnight," Adelia said, holding her hands together and watching him as he turned and left the room.

Chapter Nine

Heather eased the old wooden door open, making every effort possible to minimize the noise. It had taken her nearly ten minutes just to make it from the room she shared with her brother to the doorway. Each step was agonizingly slow. A sudden creak startled her, causing her to close the door and hope she wouldn't be noticed. Only after the door was closed did she realize that the noises were coming from outside, in the hallway. One set of footsteps passed by their door, soft creaks marking each step. *Was that Jason, or his father?* she wondered, having no way to know for sure and not wanting to bump into either one in the hallway. She waited, considering her options. If she left and went downstairs, there was a chance that Jason was still there. If, however, that had been him, a trip downstairs was a needless risk. Slowed by uncertainty, she had just decided to risk it when she heard another set of footsteps walk down the narrow hallway. Sighing, she knew that she had now certainly missed her opportunity. Even if it was Jason in the hallway, she couldn't risk opening the door. His initial reaction, or hers, would certainly be enough to wake her parents.

Her inability to honor her word weighed on her. She had wanted to be there so badly, to finish the wonderful conversation that they'd begun earlier. It wasn't her fault, she knew, but it didn't make her feel any better.

Letting herself rest against the closed door, she pressed her head against the frame and looked up at the ceiling. *Would she ever see him again? Would he even talk to her after she'd stood him up?* she wondered.

Gathering herself for the return trip, she pushed off and propelled her legs to take the first step. This time, she didn't make nearly the effort to remain silent. If asked, she would just say that she'd needed to use the chamber pot, no longer worried about the risk of reprisal.

She made it back to her own bed without waking anyone. Apparently, she could have been much less careful the first trip as well. Had she been faster, she would have made it downstairs before Jason and his father had returned to their room. She kicked herself for her caution.

She quickly changed into her nightclothes, taking off the skirt and blouse that she had secretly worn to bed, fully covering herself with blankets so that her brother would not notice. Finally back where she'd started, she decided that she would rise early. She needed to see Jason before he left, if only to apologize. It was the right thing to do.

The night passed, Heather sleeping surprisingly well. When she awoke, it was still dark outside, only the barest of light passing through the window to her left. Putting the blankets and sheets aside, she rose and looked out the window. The sun was just about to rise and make its daily appearance. Heather smiled, happy that she'd managed to awake on time.

She dressed quickly, not worrying about awaking her brother. His snoring never softened or abated, never acknowledging the rustling sounds she was making. She selected a baby blue dress that was hemmed in white. It was her favorite of all the dresses she'd brought along, accenting both her figure and her eyes.

Sitting on the bed, she laced up her brown shoes, nearly tall enough to be called boots, but much more comfortable. Made from dark, smooth grained leather, they fit Heather perfectly. Finished, she stood and quietly walked through the doorway to her parent's room. As expected, both of her parents were awake, her mother straightening bedsheets while her father sat at the table in the northwest corner of the room.

Predictably, her father's worn Bible sat open in front of him. Nearly every morning her father rose before the sun, reading from one portion or another. Lately, he'd been reading the Gospels, taking in the accounts of those closest to Jesus. He was disciplined to the task, rarely letting a day go by without the precious words found in the Good Book.

Heather smiled, loving the man that her father had become since meeting that wonderful bald man in Texas. Or perhaps she should attribute it to meeting a different man, the man that her father was currently reading about.

Clearing her throat to make her parents aware of her presence, Heather walked fully into the room and headed towards the powder room.

"My, you're up early," her mother said, continuing to carefully dress the bed.

"I like to get an early start on the day."

"Since when?" her father asked, looking up from whatever passage currently held his attention.

"Since we arrived in France, of course!" Heather replied with a laugh, intentionally misattributing her excitement.

Her parents glanced at each other, both suppressing grins. It appeared as though neither one of them were buying her story. Neither of them said anything, and both returned to their previous tasks. Heather used the mirror in the powder room to adjust her hair, adding a navy blue ribbon but otherwise letting her hair stay down.

"I'm going to go down and see if Madame Moreau has any croissants, I'm very hungry," she said, testing the waters with a plausible explanation for her exit.

"It's quite early, I doubt that anyone is awake," her mother said in reply, but she stopped short of denying her.

"Perhaps, but if not, I can come right back."

"See that you do," Edward interjected, not looking up.

"Thank you," Heather said, pleased that her parents didn't press the issue even if they suspected that she might have other reasons for leaving.

She opened the door and stepped out into the hallway. Moving towards the stairs, she took several steps before realizing that she was not alone. She turned, briefly startled. Behind her, Jason had just opened his door and had stopped when he'd caught sight of her. They looked at each other awkwardly, neither of them quite knowing what to say. Heather was the first to break from her trance, recognizing that she needed to be the one to take the first step, at least metaphorically.

"I'm… I'm sorry. I… my parents…," she stammered, still off guard and unable to adequately express her feelings. "I just couldn't make it. I wanted to, I really did," she finished, regaining some composure.

"It's okay. I'm glad that you're here this morning. We're leaving now, and I am glad that I get to say goodbye."

Heather felt her heart race. *Was this it? Was this all the time that they would have?* He would leave, and they would never see each other again. She was suddenly sure of it. While they had only known each other a single day, shared only a single conversation, she felt a connection with him unlike anything that she'd felt before.

"You're leaving? Now?"

"Yes. I was just headed downstairs to say goodbye to Adelia. Madame Moreau, I mean," he said, still standing next to his open door.

"I… can you wait? Just for a moment?" Heather asked, realizing that she had only one option if she ever wanted to hear from him again.

"Sure, I suppose. Probably only for a few minutes. My father wants to return as soon as possible."

"Okay, stay here. I'll be right back!" Heather said, opening up her own door and rushing back into the room where her parents occupied themselves.

"Daddy, your pen, do you have it?" Heather asked, trying not to let her urgency betray her voice.

"Yes, it's here. What do you need it for?" he responded, looking at her with a quizzical expression.

"I just need to write something down. Something I don't want to forget. May I borrow it? And some paper?"

Her father always kept his pen and some paper nearby when he read the Bible. He often filled pages with notes, tucking them away in a well-worn satchel for later examination. He reached down and handed her both his pen and a scrap of paper, still looking at her questioningly, but saying nothing.

Heather took the pen and paper and retreated to her own room, not wanting her parents to see what she was writing. Perhaps they wouldn't mind, wouldn't be concerned, but she couldn't risk them stopping her. Quickly, she wrote down the numbers and letters before tearing off the brief portion of text.

Returning to her parents' room, she set the pen and remaining scrap of paper on the table beside her father and hurried out of the room before either one of them could say anything. Closing the door behind her, she let out a heavy sigh of relief, happy to be back in the hallway with Jason.

She approached him, paper in hand.

"I had hoped that we would be able to talk more this morning. Or perhaps go for a walk. Or...," she trailed off, her words finishing before her thoughts had caught up.

"I would have liked that," he replied, flashing a smile before looking down at the floor. She thought he might be embarrassed.

"Well, anyway, I thought that at the very least I could give you this. If you wanted to talk more, at least you'd have a way to find me. I mean, write me. To write me," she fumbled, crossing her hopes with her words.

"I'm not sure when we will leave here. I don't think I can write from France," he said, looking glum.

"Well, when you get home, write me. I'll wait," she said, realizing that her words held unexpected weight.

"Should... should I give you my address, too?"

"No, like you said, who knows when you'll return. Just include it when you write for the first time. I promise I'll write back. No matter how long it takes."

As she finished, Jason's father exited the room, glancing up in surprise as he saw the two of them talking.

"Hello, Good morning miss."

"Good morning," she replied.

"It's time we get going, Jason. We'll grab some fruit in the marketplace on the way. I'm going to go downstairs and say goodbye to Adelia. Come down when you're ready," his father said, squeezing by Heather with a nod.

"I guess it's time," Jason said, sounding as though he wanted to say more. "I will write, I promise. I just don't know when."

Heather felt her heart jump, and she hoped that he was being sincere. She did not want this to be their last interaction.

"I look forward to it."

Closing the gap, Jason reached his hand out to shake hers. Heather smiled. Instead, she threw her arms around him, squeezed tightly, and quickly withdrew. Without another word, she turned and went back into her room, the blush on her cheeks a deep red.

Chapter Ten

The trip back to the island was routine and the water calm. A light breeze aided their travel and carried with it the scent of saltwater. Jason thought it smelled as good as anything ever had. In the last twenty four hours, he'd gone through an incredibly wide range of emotions, from anger to confusion, from outrage to complete bliss. As he sat on the boat and reflected on the previous hours, he felt indescribably blessed.

"Let's get her to shore, shall we?" his father asked, breaking his train of thought. Together they paddled the small craft into shore and affixed it to the pier, tying it down with practiced ease.

Their home was not far from the dock, less than a ten minute walk even at a leisurely pace, and they covered the distance in even less time. Jason's mother, Kathleen, was outside working the garden as they approached, and she stood upon hearing them. She raised her hand to shield her eyes from the sun, and a large smile graced her face.

"So you decided to return, did you?" she asked, seemingly not angry that they'd been gone longer than expected.

"I'm sorry for our delay, we… it was my fault. We'll talk about it later," Dean said, glancing only briefly at Jason before embracing his wife.

"It's alright, I'm just happy to have you both back safely. Did you get everything taken care of?" she asked, her face taking a more serious expression.

"I did. We did, rather," his father replied, his eyes darting sideways to Jason.

Her smile returned, even larger than before. "Is that so? I am thrilled to hear it!" she said, her words neglecting to address the underlying message within his father's comment: *Jason knows.*

"Shall we go inside? I have dinner prepared. It's just stew, but it should be ready. I made a full batch hoping that you would return today. I must confess that yesterday's food was wasted on my worry."

"That sounds great," Dean and Jason both said, nearly in unison. They laughed, Dean giving him a jovial slap on the back as they made their way inside and sat down at the small wooden table that Dean had constructed when they'd first arrived. Kathleen walked to the stove, evaluating the boiling stew before serving Dean and Jason their meals.

Jason began eating in earnest the moment that she set the bowl down in front of him. The stew was hearty and delicious, and it reminded Jason of home. Bits of carrots and onions, chunks of potatoes and beef, it was a very American dish, and it hit the unfilled spot in his stomach.

As he ate, Jason's mind couldn't help but focus on the last piece of the puzzle his father had previously described to him. He was hesitant to broach the topic, but his curiosity was welling up inside him. His father had promised to show him the proof, the name, that had spurred their trip, and he was eager to see it for himself. He vacillated between asking now and waiting, not wanting to upset the cart of reconciliation they had found last night. He continued eating as he considered his options.

"How was Thomas?" Kathleen asked, ladling herself a bowl of stew and sitting down beside Dean.

"He was fine. Eager. He is getting very old, and I think he's been cooped up in that shop for far too long. Adelia asked me to give you her best, although I expect you'll want to accompany us when we return next week."

"Yes, I think I would. It will be a nice change of pace. When will we go?"

His father paused, contemplating the question. "Soon. Early next week. Thomas and I spoke at great length, and we are both convinced that time is of the essence."

Jason perked up, listening intently. Although he'd suspected it previously, his father's comments confirmed his suspicions that his father had returned to Thomas when he'd disappeared in the morning. Mild annoyance stirred, but the reassurance of knowledge and a full stomach did much to quell it.

"Thomas told me that several different people had come by recently to ask unusual questions. There may be others that are interested. The sooner that we move forward the better."

Kathleen did not reply, simply nodding her head in agreement and blowing at the hot stew cupped at the end of her spoon. Jason waited for him to continue, but he seemed to have said his piece. He decided that now was as good a time as any to broach the subject.

"Can you show me? I'd like to see it," he asked tentatively, his voice betraying his eagerness.

"Yes, after dinner. When we are finished we will go down."

Jason had been eating with his usual vigor before, but after that declaration he practically inhaled the rest of his meal. His second portion was gone before Dean finished his first bowl, and he sat nervously awaiting his father.

"Afterwards, we must see to the animals, yes?"

"Yes, of course. I'll go right out. After."

His father smiled, grabbing a lantern sitting nearby and striking the wick. He looked over his shoulder as if beckoning Jason to follow. The gesture was entirely unnecessary, as Jason was already close to his heels. Proceeding outside, Dean walked to the southern corner of the home and extracted a small key from his pocket. Jason had always considered it strange that they kept the cellar doors locked, but his father's explanation that it kept out animals had seemed plausible enough. Only now did he realize that it had been yet another misdirection.

Dean opened the lock and also the doors, and then proceeded down the rickety steps leading to the cellar. His mother's canning work was arranged on shelves scattered throughout the space.

Tomatoes, peas, carrots, and beans were amongst her favorites, although Jason could only stand to eat the carrots. He much preferred the peppers, and they were in short supply for that very reason.

"Now you understand why I spent so much time down here, digging and reinforcing the foundation. I was worried that I would collapse the entire place with the digging I needed to do." Knowing what he did now, Jason understood completely and nodded his head in agreement.

His father proceeded to the far side of the room, the only side currently unoccupied, save for a work bench. Moving it aside, he used a spade to clear several inches of dirt. Below that was a wooden plank that was quickly removed and put aside.

"There. It's down there," his father said quietly, as though someone else was listening in. "Look, quickly. Then we bury it."

Jason was momentarily taken aback. *Bury it? After all this work to find it?* he thought.

Jason kneeled down next to the exposed hole. The cellar's door was still wide open, illuminating the cellar sufficiently to move around and perform routine canning tasks. To see into the blackness of this space, however, he needed the lantern. Taking it from his father, he peered down, surprised at the depth to which the hole extended. At least three feet below the floor's surface, a stone block was entombed within the foundation's structure. The stones immediately around it were also visible, their roughhewn faces dirty and unremarkable.

The crucial block, however, was immediately apparent. On its face were three simple words: *Eustache Dauger, valet.*

"That's it?" Jason asked, feeling as though there should be more.

"That's it. That's all there is," his father responded.

"It's just a name and a title. A lowly title at that. Are you sure this matters?"

"Thomas has assured me that it is enough. That this name, along with his documents, prove that it was him and that he was wrongfully imprisoned."

"Why didn't he show us those documents? If you two had already expected this, why not have them ready?"

"Ah, yes. Well, fate seems to have conspired against us. The documents have been stored for many years elsewhere, somewhere safer and less obvious. He would not retrieve them until we were sure. Even once we were, the place where they were being kept was occupied. By your redheaded friend, in fact," his father said, flashing a small grin.

"Heather? What does Heather have to do with it?" he asked incredulously.

"Nothing, of course. But her family was, is, staying in the room where he has hidden everything."

"Why would he hide things of such importance in an inn? In a place he doesn't own and where strangers are constantly present?"

"There's something I haven't told you, Jason. You see, you already know that Adelia is your grandaunt, but what you don't know is that Thomas is Adelia's brother."

Jason reeled, at first unsure of what his father had said and then taken aback that his father hadn't mentioned it before. *Why not tell him along with everything else? What use had it been to not mention it originally?*

"Wait,... why didn't you tell me?"

"I meant to, we just got sidetracked, and it slipped my mind. After the conversation had ended, there was simply never a good time to bring it up without strangers around."

His father's explanation was simple enough. They had, after all, been more heavily involved in other conversation. He could forgive him for a momentary lapse.

"So this Eustache Dauger, he's the reason for all this. Still, it seems so long ago. Why should we care so much?" Jason asked, the revelation having worn off and the memories of his forgotten life returning to him at full force. "Is this really worth the sacrifice?"

His father paused to contemplate. His hands were idle, and he used the moments to retrieve two shovels from their pegs on the northern wall. He handed one of them to Jason before gathering his composure and speaking.

"Eustache Dauger spent more than thirty years in prison for a crime he did not commit. He was humiliated, degraded, and his humanity was stripped from him. He spent those decades away from his family. To this day, only the few of us even know his name. It was very important to your grandfather that the world not only knows the name of his ancestor but knows that he did not deserve the punishment he was given.

"When your grandfather passed, he left all of his worldly possessions to your mother with just one single instruction. One final and solitary wish. Do you know what that was?" Jason shook his head and waited for the answer. "He said, '*Clear the name of Dauger. Clear my name.*'"

Jason paused, taking in the information. A question nagged at the back of his mind. "I still don't quite understand why anyone except our family would care about any of this. Why is such secrecy needed after all these years?"

Dean laughed before he spoke, a full and hearty laugh that boomed in the confines of the cellar. "I suppose you wouldn't understand. I haven't mentioned it only because we believe Eustache Dauger to be innocent of any crime, but the reason that others care is because of what he is supposed to have done."

Jason asked the obvious question, "And what is that, exactly?"

"Oh, nothing too much. He's only accused of stealing a fortune of gold and jewels that had been intended for the king of France."

Jason wasn't sure whether to laugh or cry. "So you're telling me that the only reason people want the documents that Thomas has collected is because they think they will lead them to this stolen treasure?"

"That's right. They don't care one iota about the legacy of the Dauger name, all they care about is a fortune of gold. They think we may have found a treasure map."

Jason nodded, the pieces of the puzzle beginning to find their places in his mind. "But we believe him to be innocent, so our motivation is simply to clear his name."

Dean nodded solemnly. "We used every dollar and deed your grandfather left to finance this trip and fulfill his final wish. Soon, the name of Dauger will be indeed be clear. Your mother's name will no longer hold the stain of the man in the iron mask."

Chapter Eleven

Heather sat up in bed, awoken by the sound of yelling. She casually rubbed her eyes, clearing away the sleep and softly stretching her arms above her head. For most people, being awoken by loud yelling would be cause for alarm, but for Heather it was a weekly occurrence. Her brother could occasionally be playful and affable, but more often he was sullen, angry and detached. In no circumstances was he a morning person. Sleeping in this undersized room for nearly a week had done nothing to improve his temperament.

"You can go to hell if you think I'm going to lug all that crap down there at eight o' clock in the morning. No way!"

"You're a part of this family, and you are going to do your part. That's all there is to it," Edward replied, holding back anger. Had this confrontation happened years ago, before her father had found redemption in the hands of a bald country preacher and at the foot of the cross, this fight would already have been physical. Escalation had been the modus operandi of her father. Now that her father was sober, he struggled to find effective methods to deal with his son.

"Now listen here, we've got to get everything down there. He wants to buy everything, do you understand? All of it. We take it down this morning and we don't have to worry about it anymore," Edward attempted to explain, growing frustrated as Micah gesticulated, mocking his words.

"So move it all yourself. Have your precious Heather help you. I'm going back to bed."

Heather watched through the doorway as he made his way past her father. When Edward didn't immediately make way, Micah used his shoulder and then his arm to move him. The move knocked Edward to the side, trapping him between Micah and the bedframe. Teetering briefly, Edward let momentum carry him downward until he met the soft mattress.

Heather was unable to see his expression, blocked by both the doorframe and her brother as he entered the room. However, she knew the pain that rested there. It was an expression full of exasperation and futility, one fueled by the feeling of failure. Edward had modeled this to his son, and he clearly felt the weight of that as Micah's behavior spiraled further and further out of control.

As he entered the room, Heather could clearly see the rage on his face, his features twisted and exaggerated. She also knew that this room was certainly not the place to be at this very moment.

"What the hell are you looking at?" Micah screamed at her, a stream of spittle flying from his mouth as the words exploded from him.

She said nothing in response, knowing that anything she said would simply be thrown back at her. As she got up, Micah thrust his head and shoulders towards her as though preparing to strike. Heather flinched and inhaled sharply. It would not have been the first time that he lashed out at her. Scowling, he withdrew slightly and let her pass without further intimidation. She kept her eyes locked on him until she was fully out of the room, just in case he changed his mind.

As she entered her parent's room she began to cry, wet tears welling up and then hurtling downward towards the floor. She immediately rushed towards her mother, condensing her body as her mother wrapped her arms around her. Lynn's look of understanding and concern said everything that needed to be said.

"It's alright, everything is fine. Everything will be fine," her mother whispered, gently stroking her long red hair as she murmured comfort and platitudes. Attempting to convince herself that her mother was right, Heather tried to hold the tears in, wiping them away with the back of her hand and standing up straight. She looked at her mother and tried to feign a smile.

"I'm okay. He didn't… he didn't do anything. Just yelled. I'm okay," she said, still shaken. Although he had not hit her, his very presence still scared her. Her brother was her father's past, and that past was one that she was loathe to experience again. Getting away from her brother was her first priority.

"Can we go downstairs? Get some breakfast or just go and walk?" she asked, turning to her father whose head was buried in his hands. Looking up, his curly hair matted and in need of a good combing, he simply nodded.

"Let's do that. Let's see if Madam Moreau has anything for breakfast," her mother said as she put her arm back around Heather and turned her towards the door that led to the hallway. "I know it's early, but I could use some more of that tea, couldn't you sweetie?"

Heather smiled weakly and nodded, leaning her head against her mother's. As they broke apart to walk through the door, Heather cast a glance backwards at her father. He had made no move to follow them, still sitting on the bed facing away from the doorway.

"Dad, are you coming?" she asked, not wanting her father to be alone with Micah. The current stormfront had passed, she didn't want the next one rolling in behind it.

"No, you two go. I'm going to stay. Make sure he doesn't trash the place."

Heather pinched her lips together, wanting to argue but unable to fight against her father's logic. Micah had destroyed more of their belongings than she could count during his fits of anger, and more than one wall had suffered holes at his hands. If he did that here, they were unlikely to have a place to stay afterwards.

Both Heather and her mother remained silent, opting to simply leave the room and head downstairs.

"Your brother will find his way, just like your father did. Just give him time," Lynn said, searching for something to say.

"Maybe he will. I… I just don't want to be there waiting for him while he does. He's exactly like daddy used to be, and I can't do it anymore."

"He is a lot like your father was, and I know that it's tough on you. Just stay the course. When he gets like this, stay away from him and let it blow over."

"That's not as easy as it sounds, especially when he drinks, Mom," Heather said candidly, looking for a way to explain to her mother how incredibly tired she was. She was so tired of the constant fights and the complete meltdowns her brother had on a regular basis.

"I know. I really do."

"What if it never changes? What if he never changes? What if this is just the way he is always going to be?" Heather asked, genuinely hoping that her mother could provide her with reassurance that change was inevitable or imminent.

"I don't know honey, I just don't know. You cannot force people to change. They either want to, or they don't."

Heather sighed deeply, looking down at the floor as they descended the stairs. *I won't stay in that house if he's there. It's not a home,* Heather thought, trying to convince herself that she meant it. That she could somehow summon the moxie to leave. In that moment she knew, however, that she could not. She loved her parents. Besides, she had absolutely no where to go.

Their breakfast was simple, but delicious. The croissants were as airy and perfect as they possibly could have been. Fresh fruit was also offered, although Heather was content with just a croissant and her tea. Madame Moreau had looked at her strangely when she'd asked for it, tea typically being an evening drink in France, but she'd dutifully prepared it without actually voicing a question. This morning's variety was menthe, very crisp, and it left her refreshed and awake.

Edward had come down to join them about thirty minutes after they sat down, informing them as he did so that Micah was asleep and had, fortunately, not created any more havoc.

"When do you have plans to meet the buyer?" Lynn asked.

"No later than eight o' clock. We are to bring everything to his shop, not too far from here. Most of the goods can be brought in one or two trips with two people's help, but by myself it will take at least three, if not four."

"I could come help, Daddy, if you need me to."

"No, honey, it's alright. I will manage, even if it takes me ten trips. I'm glad to have it all sold. I did not expect to stay more than a week, and we've already been here six days. Having one buyer take everything is also an unexpected blessing."

"How did that happen exactly?" her mother asked, taking a sip of her tea and cupping her chin in her hand to listen.

"It was the strangest thing. I was walking around the market yesterday evening, stumbling my way through the few places I hadn't already visited to inquire about their interest in our goods. I stopped at a small shop carrying various home items. The shop keep couldn't understand my French and waved me off, but a man standing there addressed me in English and asked what I had to sell."

Her father stopped to take a large bite of an apple, and then another, before he continued on with his story. He held the apple in his hands as he talked, pausing here and there to munch on it further.

"Anyway, I told him what we had, and he didn't seem particularly interested. However, when I cautiously mentioned the journal, he perked up and grew quite eager to see it."

Heather's eyebrows raised. *Journal? What journal?* she wondered to herself, but said nothing. Edward noticed her confusion.

"You see, among the items we purchased from the estate, we came across an old book full of French writings. It seemed to be some sort of journal or diary, judging by the dates on the pages. And in the back of the book I also discovered several transcripts that seemed older than the book itself, all marked with a seal. I didn't know why at the time, but they seemed important."

Her father grinned. This was clearly the real reason for their trip, and now that his plans were paying off, he was eager to share the details.

"While we were in New York, I was able to locate someone who could translate some of the text. Just a few pages. Once I did, I knew that we had to come to France. That the journal and those transcripts belonged here. This man...,"

Before he could continue, there was a loud commotion outside. The sounds of people shouting distracted everyone in the room. Madame Moreau walked over to the door, still carrying the broom she'd been using. After she'd opened it, the smell of smoke instantly hit Heather's nostrils. Madame Moreau, Jason had called her Adelia, gasped audibly and brought her hands to her mouth.

Before anyone could ask her what was happening, or look out the door themselves, she dropped the broom and walked outside, reflexively closing the door behind her as she did so.

Chapter Twelve

Their return to Cannes occurred less than a week after Jason and Dean had initially made the journey. This time they made the trip as a family rather than just a duo. Today's sea was gentle, only the slightest of breeze moved the air. The sky was calm, bright blue, and cloudless, and Jason could feel the rays beating down on his exposed skin. Jason did not tan, his fair skin's only defenses were the myriad freckles that littered his back and arms. Failing those, the rest of him was apt to burn with only the most minimal provocation.

Conscious of his animosity with the sun, Jason often carried a piece of extra cloth to tuck under his hat. It was not the most fashionable choice, but it did the job it was intended to accomplish.

Underneath the protection of the fabric, Jason was acutely aware of how warm the day had become. Sweating, he paddled the oars, the muscles of his back well developed but deceptively lithe.

"When we get to shore, we will be meeting at Adelia's. Adelia will close the inn, and we can view everything and discuss our options," his father remarked, easily keeping pace with Jason's paddling efforts.

Kathleen smiled, her white teeth contrasting with the dark tan of her face. Although he'd certainly gotten his green eyes from her, he'd received none of her complexion.

"I cannot wait to see Adelia, it has been so terribly long."

Dean glanced over at her, seeming to contemplate the timeline in his head. "We went to market in... April, was it?"

"March, the last weekend. It was miserable cold," Kathleen stated, remembering with an involuntary shiver. "And we only stayed the few hours. We didn't even have a chance to talk properly."

As they approached the docks, another small skiff passed within about ten yards of their starboard side. A deeply tanned man leaned far over the edge of the craft, his tight grip on the rigging the only thing preventing a swift drop into the blue water. He jeered at them, a snarl of a smile revealing his apparent disdain for oral hygiene. He let his boat glide far too close to theirs, seeming to have no regard whatsoever for the potential for collision. To Jason it felt both intentional and inimical. Dean yelled at the man, raising a hand and shouted.

"Get away from our boat you lunatic!"

The man's reply was guttural and totally unintelligible to Jason. Whether he replied in French or some other unknown language,

Jason had no idea. As the two boats passed and the man shrank into the distance, Jason looked to his mother and found worry written across her face.

"What is it? Did you hear what he said?"

"Yes. Not exactly. Enough," she said, bringing her hands up and across her chest. Even though it was a warm day, she squeezed herself as though she were cold.

Dean also noticed her concern and found his own anger being replaced with worry for his wife. "Honey, what did he say?" he asked softly.

He said, "You will leave or you will die. You will all die."

The temperature of the water didn't change, nor did that of the air, but all of a sudden Jason felt a cold chill pass through him. The previously calm day became a tempest, even if only metaphorically. Jason was shocked into silence, his mind racing at the implications of the man's unexpected threat.

"He threatened us?" his father asked, although it seemed almost rhetorical. 'You will all die,' was about as much of a threat as a person could fit into four words.

"Was he talking about…," Jason stopped short of specificity, but his meaning was clear. The question hung in the air, neither of his parents apparently eager to address it. Instead, they cast uneasy glances at each other, both looking increasingly worried as the moments ticked past.

"How could they possibly know anything? There's simply no way for anyone to know for sure that we…," Dean said, trailing off and trying to maintain his composure. "Jason, you didn't say anything to anyone in Cannes, did you? Tell me that you didn't."

"No! Of course not! I didn't say a word to anyone except you, I swear it."

"Not even that girl? Not anything?"

"Nothing, not a thing!"

"Then it has to have come from Thomas. He's the one who has the documents and letters we need. Come on, we need to hurry, he could be in real trouble."

Jason and Dean redoubled their efforts on the paddles, their rowing crisp and strong across the gentle water. As they got closer, Kathleen put her hand up to her forehead, squinting against the bright sky.

"There's smoke. Something is on fire."

"Fire? Are you sure?" Dean asked, not pausing from his rowing.

"Yes, I'm sure. It's dark brown, it's no chimney or cooking fire."

As they closed in on the dock, the smoke was easily visible to them all. Seeing that it was coming from the eastern part of the city, Jason cast a worried glance at his father. Dean returned the look, and the two shared a single thought, *Thomas' shop.*

They tied the boat in record time and departed the dock in a flash. They ran as fast as they were able, bounding over cobblestones and curb sides as they hurried towards the billowing smoke. Kathleen fell behind but yelled at them to go ahead. When they were within a few hundred yards of the building, Jason took off, finding a gear beyond any that his father possessed. Arriving first, Jason saw a building engulfed in flame. There was nothing that could be done. The fire's work was already nearly complete, encompassing every inch of the book filled shop.

Jason sank to his knees, unable to believe what he was seeing. His mind raced. *Had everything his family had worked and sacrificed for been for naught? Was this the end of their journey? And where in the world was Thomas? Was he inside?*

Jason frantically searched the crowd, looking to and fro for the rotund man he now knew was his great uncle. The crowd grew along with the fire, and Jason noticed that they had started a line, buckets of water being passed back and forth. Jason ran forward to join them and found that his father was already there, bucket in hand.

"Do you see Thomas anywhere?" he yelled at his father, his eyes blinking at the acrid smoke.

"No, he's not here. I don't see him." His father's eyes delivered the rest of the message.

Bucket after bucket was passed, over and over until the fire had been quenched, or had run out of fuel on its own. Jason's arms ached of use, first the panicked rowing and now the utter exhaustion of heavy water pails passed frantically, one after the other. The building was now a shell of its former self. Almost nothing remained on the inside, at least not as far in as he could see.

The buildings beside had been mostly spared, save for dark black stains adorning the outside facades. They had held firm against the fire for long enough that they would suffer no long term structural damage. Thomas' shop, however, was a complete loss.

Inside the ruined building was the accumulated knowledge of generations. Blackened books, maps, and other documents littered the floor. Most had burned away entirely, leaving nothing but ashes and dust. The few that were left were not salvageable.

"Thomas was so careful. Even though the place was a mess, he was always so cautious with the fire. Every time I've ever been inside he was…,"

"Dad, this was no accident. We both know that."

Dean only muttered, painfully aware of the obvious connection between this destruction and the threats from the unknown sailor. The only meaningful questions that remained were who had done it, why, and the most important one of all: was Thomas alright?

Instead, he asked, "Where's your mother?"

They both looked around, eventually spotting her at the outskirts of the small circle in front of the building. She was speaking with an older woman that Jason did not know. She was lost in their conversation, not even glancing in the direction of her family. She looked worried.

The crowd that had gathered during the fire's raging was dwindling, going back to their lives before the interruption. Many stayed, however, talking in smaller groups of a few people. Their French was quick and casual, a bad combination for Jason. He caught bits and pieces, words here and there, but nothing beyond what you would expect when people were discussing a fire. His mother's conversation was too far away to eavesdrop on.

"Should we go to the inn? Is that where he would go? Dad?"

Dean was still staring blankly at the charred ruins, not even acknowledging that his son was speaking to him. Lost deep in thought, Jason had to ask twice more before he got a response, and even that was barely a nod.

As they started in the direction of the inn, Kathleen finished her conversation with the old Frenchwoman and walked to meet them. They all trudged off towards the inn together, briefly silent before Jason turned to Kathleen and asked about her conversation.

"Do you know that woman? Did she know anything?"

"Yes, she has a booth in the market, just up the street from here. I purchase fabrics from her on occasion."

"Well, did she know anything?" Jason asked again.

"She said, well, she said that there was a loud sound, a crack, and then several minutes later the fire started. She said it could have been a gunshot."

"A gunshot? Before the fire?" Dean asked, clearly suspicious. "Was she sure?"

"No, she didn't seem very sure of anything, except that there was a loud sound. I don't know what else it could have been, though."

"Did she say how long ago the fire started?" Jason asked, quickly recognizing that if Thomas had been shot, they might not have much time to find him.

"Not long, just fifteen or twenty minutes."

"Let's go, then, and quickly," Dean said, upping his pace to just about as fast as he could without running. As they half-walked, half-jogged towards the inn, Jason noticed droplets of red leading the way. The droplets grew larger as they went, beginning to run together in crimson trails. They were not the first to come this way.

They had nearly reached the inn when they heard the crying coming from an alleyway. Tucked into the darkest part of the narrow pathway, a elderly woman was crouched over a collapsed man with an enormous pot belly. There was no doubt, it was Thomas.

"Adelia? Is that you?" Kathleen asked even as she ran towards the woman.

"Here!" Adelia cried out hoarsely, not even turning her head towards the question. Her voice was choked with tears.

"Oh Thomas, Thomas, que t'ont-ils fait?" she sobbed.

His chest was still rising, but only in the most miniscule of measurements. His breathing was faint, and every breath was clearly labored. There, in the middle of his chest, just below his heart, was a bleeding wound. Kathleen turned away when she saw it, falling into Dean's chest and beginning to sob.

Jason went to Thomas' side. Evaluating the wound, Jason felt his heart sink. He had no idea what to do. As he looked helplessly on, he could hear Thomas muttering through shallow breaths.

"What is he saying? I can't understand," Jason said, although no one was listening.

Thomas' eyes fluttered open when he spoke, rolling around and unable to focus on any particular thing. When Thomas spoke again, Jason was surprised to hear English. Apparently Thomas realized who he was.

"They... did not... get them. Still has. He still has... the merchant... I...," Thomas trailed off, his voice giving out completely and his eyes closing. His body shivered, fighting for air and respite. As Adelia wailed beside him, Thomas took his final breath, his body going completely still on the ground.

Adelia gasped, her sobs becoming ragged whimpers, each more desperate than the last. Dean separated from Kathleen to embrace her. As he did so he turned towards Jason and asked, "What did he say? Did he say who did this?"

"No, he said that someone didn't get something. He... still had something? I'm not sure what he meant," Jason said, struggling to recall the exact words. "Oh! He said something about a merchant! The merchant still has something, maybe?"

"I don't know who that is. It doesn't matter. This has become too dangerous. I don't know who they are, but someone cares desperately about what we are doing. Enough to kill over it. We must go, now."

"Adelia, honey, I'm so sorry." Kathleen bent down and took Dean's place, trying to give comfort to her as she mourned the loss of her brother. "We need to go. If someone else knows, this is the first place they will come looking."

Adelia blinked in surprise, uncomprehending.

"I... saw the fire... I ran and, he, was just here. His chest...," she trailed off.

Jason could see that Thomas had made it to this alleyway before he could go no further. Bloody handprints followed the southern wall as he'd tried to keep his balance. Failing, he'd collapsed here, twenty feet into the alleyway and out of view of the main road. With all of the attention being given to the fire itself, it was no surprise that no one had encountered him before Adelia had likely noticed the blood on her way towards his shop.

"You must come with us. We are leaving. It has become too dangerous," Dean pleaded with her even as he looked around, fearful of an ambush or some other hostile encounter.

"No, I will not. I cannot. My brother, he, he is all that I have. I cannot go."

At that moment, the pieces fell into place for Jason. He suddenly understood that there were multiple things happening at once. While they were here, dealing with this one, another tragedy was happening elsewhere.

"Dad?"

"What? What is it?"

"Where was that man going?" Jason asked, his voice tentative.

"What man? Did you see someone?"

"No, the man on the boat. The man we encountered on the way here." Jason's question was an obvious one, but until now none of them had given any thought to where the sailor had been headed, other than away from them.

"Dear God," Kathleen gasped, arriving at the answer a moment before Dean did. "He's going home. He's going to the island."

Chapter Thirteen

Looking out the front door of the inn, Edward frowned. The blue sky was clouded by unnatural brown smoke. Clearly there was something going on, and the innkeeper had left to see what it was. Something about her reaction gave him pause. It seemed obvious that she'd been reacting to more than just the mere sight of smoke.

"Daddy?" Heather asked, looking at the door beside him.

"Yes, honey, what is it?"

"Should we go? Maybe someone needs help?"

"I don't think there is anything we can do. The smoke is already lessening. Whatever it is, there's nothing that we will be able to help with."

"What about Madame Moreau? Why did she leave?"

"I don't know, honey. She's lived here a long time I think. She's probably worried that the fire is close to someone she knows."

The concerned look on his face did not abate, even as he tried to alleviate his daughter's concerns.

"Let's arrange our items, see what makes most sense to take first, shall we?"

Madame Moreau had allowed them the use of a small storage room to the side of her own. It was not a large space, but it was sufficient to store the items that they had brought to sell. Their textiles had the majority of the potential profit, but the buyer had not seemed interested in them. The only reason that they had been sold was because Edward had convinced the man that the only way he'd sell the journal and other documents was if he would purchase the entire lot at once.

"If I take the clothing and fabric first, that may be easiest. The lamps and that sideboard will have to go last. Hopefully, by the time I have to take, that Mike will be up and around. Or perhaps I could borrow a cart from one of the local shops. I did see one right down the street."

"Why not just go down there and ask now? Perhaps you could get everything in just a couple of trips instead of carrying it all?"

Her father pondered the thought briefly, turning it over in his mind.

"That's not a bad idea. Even if not, maybe I can find out what was going on with the fire. I'll go down and ask the gentleman I saw with the cart, then I'll come back."

Lynn and Heather nodded. As Edward left, both women walked to the door and looked out at the now diminishing smoke.

"I hope everyone is okay," Heather said, her mind always concerned with the well-being of others.

"Me too. I'm sure they are."

Lynn and Heather stared out the door at the rising smoke as Edward stepped outside and made his way towards the market.

Edward made his way towards the place where he'd seen an unused cart the day before. When he arrived, the shop was boarded shut and the cart was nowhere to be seen. Glancing around, he noticed that most of the shops were similarly boarded and closed for business. Perhaps the fire was more serious than he'd previously believed.

Vacillating between heading back to the inn and continuing to pursue his goal of acquiring a cart, he decided to walk in the direction of the fire. If he reached it without locating a suitable cart for rent, he'd return to the inn and carry the goods himself.

He walked down the uneven streets, occasionally stopping by an open shop to inquire about the possibility of renting a cart. When none of his inquiries proved fruitful, his focus shifted in the direction of the dying smoke. As he did so, his breath started to quicken.

Finally leaving the narrow alleyways he'd been walking, he arrived at a large courtyard and let out an audible gasp. The building that sat destroyed on the far end of the paved court was the very building to which he'd intended to deliver the goods. The fire itself was extinguished, although the rubble still smoldered, but from what Edward could ascertain, the building and its contents were not salvageable. The owner of the building was not in the crowd, nor was Madame Moreau, their innkeeper. His heart raced, his sale now likely in jeopardy, not to mention the very life of the man he'd made the arrangement with.

Deciding to walk a different way than he'd come, Edward started back towards the inn. He took a left when he'd come to the open court and then another left at its end. Now heading up a slight incline, he began to jog.

As he rounded the corner near the top of the hill, he nearly collided with a woman exiting an alleyway. Jumping sideways, he narrowly avoided the impact but could not keep his feet, falling head over heels on the stone street.

"Oh, désolée, est-ce que ca va?" the woman asked.

Only then did Edward notice that the woman had her arms around another woman that he recognized.

"Madame Moreau? Are you alright?" Edward asked, his concern becoming closer to panic when he saw her blouse and hands covered in what appeared to be blood. Her face was flush, blotchy with anguish and tears. "What... what happened?"

"Her brother, he was... he was attacked. We must get her back to the inn and report it to the authorities. Do you know where the inn is?" Edward was momentarily surprised as the woman now spoke to him in English.

"I'm staying there, I was heading back right now."

The woman looked at him, at first with simple puzzlement but with a growing look of suspicion.

"What did you say your name was? Adelia, do you know this man?"

Adelia looked at him with glassy eyes. She nodded slowly but said nothing. It was apparently enough for Kathleen, who still waited for him to answer but said no more.

"My name is Edward Burdett. My family is here on business and we are staying at the inn. Do you know Madame Moreau?"

Apparently still suspicious of his appearance, the woman responded simply. "Yes, I do."

Edward glanced down the alleyway where they'd come from and saw a large figure sprawled on the ground. "Is he...," he trailed off, not bothering to complete the sentence.

"Let's get to the inn. Then I must go to get the authorities. I'm surprised that no one has come to the fire already."

They walked slowly, Adelia seeming as though she may collapse at any moment. Their eventual arrival to the inn brought with it a renewed sobbing from Adelia, as if just seeing the building she and her brother owned was like losing him all over again.

Edward opened the door for them, pausing after they'd entered to shut the heavy door behind them as well. Inside, Heather and Lynn rose to their feet upon seeing Edward. They both rushed to help Adelia, having her sit at a table near the fireplace. They exchanged unsure glances with Edward, neither one wanting to be the first to ask the obvious questions. *What happened? Is she okay? Is that blood?*

"I must go and tell the authorities, can you stay here with her until I return?" the woman asked. She paused, and added, "My name is Kathleen and Adelia is family. Please keep her safe."

"Yes, of course. We will be here," Lynn said as Kathleen left the inn.

"Daddy, are you okay? What happened?"

"I went down towards the fire after looking for a cart. When I got there, I found the building where I was supposed to deliver the goods had been destroyed. It was the building that was on fire. On my way back I bumped into Madame Moreau with that woman. Apparently they know each other."

Heather and Lynn exchanged worried looks.

"Where did all this blood come from? It doesn't look like she is injured," Lynn said, searching for any wounds.

"No, it's not hers. It belongs to a man. Actually, I think it belongs to the man I was supposed to sell everything to, the man I was set to meet today. I didn't get a good look, but I'm pretty sure."

"What are we going to do?" Lynn asked in alarm, now worried about the proximity of the crime to their own family.

"What can we do? We wait here until the police come."

That did not reassure Lynn, and she began nervously pacing the floor as Heather kept her arm around the shaking Frenchwoman.

"Let's start by lighting a fire. I know it's warm, but she's shivering. We can start by doing that."

Edward nodded and began stacking the wood.

Chapter Fourteen

Kathleen hurried towards the gendarmerie, her shoes moving deftly over the cobblestones. Jason and Dean had convinced her that it was safer for her to stay and aid Adelia than return to the island with them. They were sure that something unpleasant waited for them and had promised to return the moment they could. Until then, she was to report to the police and then wait with Adelia.

The plan made her nervous, her worry amplified to the point that she was struggling to remain calm. Thomas had been killed, his shop burned to the ground, and her family's life had been directly threatened. If she stopped to consider all of the implications of the last few hours, she knew she'd be unable to go on. She'd collapse right where she stood.

As she rounded the last corner before the police station, she paused to lean on a dirty, brick building. It's exterior had clearly been neglected for many years and the accumulated grime was likely to stain her blouse. She didn't care, her only concerns were to catch her breath, do what she needed to do, and return to Adelia.

Just as she pushed away from the building, she heard faint voices coming from the alleyway next to the gendarmerie. Peeking around the corner, she saw two police officers standing there smoking from long pipes and engaged in conversation. She nearly spoke to address them, but something about their demeanor cautioned her against it.

"Le feu s'est déclaré maintenant. Je viens juste d'entendre ça aux infos," the taller man said to a slimmer and shorter deputy. The marks on his coat seemed to indicate that he outranked the man he addressed, although Kathleen could not be sure.

"Et l'homme? A-t-il été retrouvé?" the shorter asked in reply, his voice surprisingly deep for a man of his size and stature.

"Oui, il a réussi à courir assez loin, puis il s'est effondré. Nous déplaçons déjà le corps. On s'en occupe."

The shorter man simply nodded, taking a puff on his pipe and kicking at some dirt on the ground. Holding the smoke in his mouth, he finally exhaled a large puff and blew it away from his face.

Kathleen's mind raced frantically. *These men were discussing Thomas. They were not only aware but involved! They were disposing of his body? Why? For what purpose?* The questions swirled fiercely in her mind as Kathleen tried to fit the pieces together.

All of a sudden, she realized that she could be in grave danger if she was found. She eased her body completely out of view, resting squarely against the brick building. She knew she needed to leave, to get back to Adelia, but she could not help but listen as the men continued to speak.

"Et l'autre homme, sait-on où il est?"

"Il est probablement encore à la pension. Il n'a aucune raison de partir maintenant. Même s'il le fait, sa famille est toujours là. Nous irons le chercher bientôt, aujourd'hui même. Nous dirons que c'était une transaction qui a mal tourné."

Kathleen held back a gasp. *They were going to frame the man staying at the inn with Adelia! But why? What could they possibly hope to gain?*

"Et les documents, sommes-nous sûrs qu'il les a toujours?" the deep voiced asked his companion.

"Affirmatif. Il était sur le point de les vendre à M. Dauger, mais comme il n'a pas pu les lui vendre, il doit toujours les avoir. Une fois que nous serons à l'auberge, nous mettrons tout sens dessus dessous et nous les trouverons. Et si nous ne les trouvons pas, nous lui ferons dire où il les a planqués."

So that's what this is all about. The man has something, some documents, that Thomas wanted, Kathleen thought. She knew that the odds of those documents being unrelated to her own family's interests were vanishingly slim.

Before she could explore the line of thought further, a loud clang jarred her. A barred gate on the side of the police station opened. Kathleen risked a glance around the corner to see a third man lean out of the building.

"Viens maintenant. Il est temps que nous y allions. D'abord au feu, puis au corps. Ensuite, nous arrêtons l'homme."

The men nodded in response, Kathleen now realized that the taller man must not actually be in charge after all. This third man spoke with an air of authority, and his coat was emblazoned with patches and medals. Whoever he was, he was clearly the one giving orders.

The men put out their pipes and walked through the doorway. Before he passed through, the shorter man looked in her direction and she jerked her head back around the corner. Staying deadly still, willing herself to be completely silent, Kathleen waited there. She counted to five, then ten, and then decided that she had not been spotted. It was time to go.

On the way back to the inn she removed her shoes entirely. She could run faster in her bare feet, and she knew that she needed to go as quickly as possible. The distance took her nearly five minutes to cover at a full run, and when she arrived she was winded and gasping for air. She burst into the inn with more force than she intended.

"You have to go, now!" she shouted before even taking stock of who was in the room.

Heather was still standing next Adelia, her arms around the woman as both stared at the fire. Lynn was speaking to Edward just a few meters away. Another man, eighteen or twenty years old, sat in a corner. Kathleen looked at him with a worried expression, having no idea who he might be.

After her exclamation, all of them turned to look at her. The man in the corner stood up and moved next to Lynn. Their comfortable proximity led Kathleen to believe he must be their son.

"Right now, you have to go. There is no time to waste!"

"Slow down, slow down. What are you talking about?" Edward asked, obviously trying to make sense of the situation.

"I can't fully explain, there's no time and I simply don't know, but the police are coming. They are coming for you, right now."

"The police? For him? Whatever for?" Lynn asked, defensively.

"I don't have an answer for you. I overheard them speaking. They are going to claim that you killed Thomas."

At that, Adelia snapped out of her trance and stood. "Is it so? The police are involved?"

"Yes, I heard it from their own mouths. I'm telling you, they will be here within minutes. If you don't leave, they will arrest you."

All of them stood frozen for a moment, unsure of how to process the information they were being given. After a moment's pause, all of them began scrambling at nearly the same instant.

"Take only what you absolutely must, you do not have any time to spare. And Edward…,"

"Yes, what is it?" Edward replied as he headed for the stairs.

"Whatever documents you were taking to Thomas, make sure they do not find them. That's what they want, and they are willing to kill for them."

Edward nodded vigorously and ran up the stairs. The entire family arrived back downstairs less than two minutes later carrying everything that they could. The rest would have to stay.

"Go, go," Kathleen said as she motioned towards the rear of the inn.

"There's a door back there, it leads to an alley. Follow it all the way down until you hit a larger road. From there you can go towards the docks. I hope you can find a boat willing to take you. If not, find someplace to hide."

"Thank you, thank you!" Lynn said.

"It's fine, now go!"

They all hurried out the back door which Kathleen rushed to close and lock behind them. She exchanged a weary and terrified look with Adelia after the door was firmly latched.

Less than five minutes later, the police arrived.

Chapter Fifteen

When the police knocked on the door, Adelia had already returned to her seat beside the fire. Kathleen had draped a blanket over her as well. In spite of both blanket and fire, she still shivered. Kathleen had been sitting beside her, patiently waiting for their arrival. She was the one to rise, and when she opened the heavy door three officers walked in without hesitation.

Kathleen knew what they were after, the only question was how they would go about it. Would they be swift and brutal, or would they attempt subtlety?

"Ma'am, I am sorry to report that we have found the body of your brother," the tallest of the three men said to Adelia, who was still facing away from the men. They spoke in French, but Kathleen was too exhausted to do anything except mentally translate. Thinking in French was simply too much work right now.

Subtlety it was. Good, Kathleen thought.

"She knows. He was on his way here. She found him."

The men looked nervously at each other. They had not expected this wrinkle. Kathleen realized in that moment that she should not have admitted that piece of information. They should have cleaned Adelia up and pretended to be shocked rather than to admit that Adelia had found him in that alleyway. The realization shook her, but she did not let it show.

Now that it had been spoken out loud there was no going back. They would have to make do with the situation as it was.

"Yes. She found him, and then I found her. After he passed, I brought her back here. She is in shock."

"Did… did he say anything before he died?" the man with the deep voice asked. Even the rolling, baritone quality of his voice could not hide the nervousness his question contained. Kathleen sensed that their very lives could depend upon their answer. To admit what Thomas had said before he died would be calamitous. The truth, now, would likely be death or imprisonment.

"No. He could not speak. Adelia found him only moments before he passed. He said nothing."

The men exchanged more glances, their postures evidencing their relief.

"Well, you see, a travelling merchant killed him. We believe they were arguing about a transaction they had made."

Going along with their story, the one she'd already heard them conspiring about previously, Kathleen feigned surprise.

"That's awful! Are you sure?"

"Yes, completely. There were witnesses," the most decorated man said.

Witnesses who've been bought and paid for, no doubt, Kathleen thought, even while shaking her head as if in disbelief.

"Have you caught the man who did it, then?"

"Unfortunately, no," he said as Kathleen let out an audible sigh of relief, although she hoped that it passed for desperation.

"We believe he was staying here, at the inn. Is anyone here?" the deep voiced man asked.

"Here? He was staying here?" Kathleen asked, convincingly incredulous.

"Yes. We have it on good authority that he was staying here with his family," the man replied, confirming their previously stated intentions to rip the place apart looking for whatever documents that they wanted.

Adelia spoke, surprising both Kathleen and the officers. "No one is here. They left," her brevity was capped with tears.

"May we take a look around? Make sure? We want to be sure that you are safe."

Kathleen choked back a sardonic laugh, and Adelia just waved her hand dismissively. The officers took the wave as tacit permission and set about searching the inn.

It took them nearly an hour to search the building, although they didn't offer even a pretense of why they were searching so determinedly. It would have taken only minutes to confirm that no one was inside, but by the time they had finished the fire had dwindled to nothing, and Kathleen's previous adrenaline had settled into her bloodstream as nervous energy. She tapped her foot impatiently on the floor.

When the officers finally came downstairs with a delicate wooden box in hand, Kathleen looked at it with dread. Apparently Edward had not taken the documents with him after all.

"We have found some interesting items under the floorboards in the room upstairs. Was that the room that the merchant was staying in?"

"Yes," Adelia replied simply.

"I see. Well there are various documents here. Official documents. All of which are stolen. We will be taking them while we continue our investigation into this matter."

Kathleen wondered why Edward had left the documents even after she'd told him explicitly not to. Had he viewed it as too time consuming to retrieve them from wherever they'd been hidden? It didn't matter now, the police were taking them. Perhaps now that they had them they would not pursue the Burdett's further.

The men turned to leave, their ill-gotten goods in the hands of the captain.

"If he returns, you will notify us immediately, yes?" the tall officer asked, almost forgotten in passing.

"Yes, of course. The man killed my brother. I hope he burns in hell," Adelia said, her eyes smoldering. The officer who'd asked the question drew back, perhaps sensing that the target of those words was not actually Edward Burdett.

After the men had left, Kathleen knew that she needed to stay at the inn, but every instinct she had screamed at her to leave. She needed to get to her family and make sure that they were alright.

Instead, they were probably already back home and staring into the face of a killer. Her fears threatened to overwhelm her. Even if she left, she would have no way of getting back to the island.

Dean and Jason had only barely managed to convince her that she should stay in the first place. Standing there in that alley, beside the dead body of her uncle, they had told her that she needed to stay to help Adelia. To keep her safe. She knew that it was true, but she also knew that they were more concerned with keeping her there for her own safety.

If they were going to face down a killer, there was no way that they wanted her there with them. She took little comfort in their act of chivalry as she paced the floor of the inn.

Forcing herself to stop moving, she helped Adelia to wash up, carefully cleaning the blood off of her hands and her forehead where she'd rubbed her brow. Her hair, pulled tightly back in a bun, had escaped without blemish. Her blouse had not been so fortunate. They retreated to Adelia's room to fetch a new one.

After Adelia was changed, they set about restoring the upstairs rooms to their previous settings. Both guestrooms had been completely overturned. Dresser drawers pulled out, tables upset, beds taken apart. In the far room, even the dresser itself had been overturned.

They started cleaning in the first room, the room that had belonged to the Burdett's. The damage there went beyond simple relocation of furniture. Floorboards had been removed and there were even holes in the walls. As Kathleen surveyed the scene, she was shocked, both at the audacity of the police as well as the thoroughness of Edward's hiding.

The space under the floorboards was not easily accessible. They had not been loose or uneven. He'd apparently brought tools along with him. *Why go to such trouble? Did he know the importance of what he possessed?* Apparently he had.

"Did you know that those rugs were given to me by my mother? That dresser too," Adelia asked, thinking back to a less turbulent time.

"No, I didn't. They are beautiful. Truly."

"They are probably worth a fortune. They come from the 18th century. They've been handed down in our family for generations. The rugs were a gift from a nobleman to your great, great, great, grandfather, although they were not actually given directly to him, for obvious reasons."

Whatever reasons those were, they were not immediately obvious to Kathleen. Her head was still swirling from the events of the day and she was barely listening to Adelia's words. Even as she tried to process what had just been said, she fell behind.

"...and so the dresser came along too. Thomas truly loved that dresser," Adelia said, trailing off as silent tears fell from her eyes. Kathleen didn't catch the brief snippet about the dresser's origins, but right now it did not matter. All that mattered was her family.

"I'm so sorry, Adelia. I wish there was something more that I could do."

"I know, honey. Thomas died doing what he loved. He was always one to be chasing down mysteries. Even when he was a boy."

Her gentle smile lasted only a moment before grief found her once more.

"Where are Jason and Dean?" Adelia asked, as if only just realizing that they were not there.

Kathleen hesitated, initially inclined to tell her about the man who threatened them before changing her mind. There was no need to add more worry to her current burdens.

"They should be back shortly. They just went to make sure everything was okay at home."

The simple explanation seemed to satisfy her, and they moved on to the second room. Although they could not return the dresser to its correct orientation, they did manage to get most of the other accessories back into place.

There was a certain sense of satisfaction that came along with being useful, even amidst the tragedy they were facing. Keeping the hands at work helped to calm her mind and prevented her from obsessing about the whereabouts of her family.

After they had finished with both rooms, they made their way back downstairs. After restarting the fire, Kathleen took to the stove, putting on a teapot. When the water was hot and the tea had steeped, she sat down beside Adelia. Neither of them really drank much of it, both lost in their connected but independent worries.

As the hours passed, Kathleen's worry grew from whisper to exclamation. Every fiber of her being was on high alert. Twice they heard voices at the door and both times she practically jumped out of her chair. Each time she'd been disappointed, just strangers looking for a room.

It was nearly 8PM when they finally arrived. Dean entered first, and Kathleen nearly collapsed. He was covered in black soot nearly from head to toe. His hands were clean, probably having been washed in the seawater on their way back, but she could see that they were covered in cuts.

Jason entered behind Dean, his clothing similarly ruined. His red hair was filthy and almost as black as his father's. His disdain for his hair color being what it was, he probably liked the look.

"What happened? Are you okay?" Kathleen expelled the questions as though they had been fire inside her lungs.

"We're okay. We are not hurt," Dean answered.

"There was a fire, mom. Another one," Jason said, although their appearance made the comment nearly unnecessary.

"They burned it down, Kathleen. Everything except the barn. We tried to salvage what we could, but there was almost nothing left."

Kathleen started crying. Her tears falling to the floor as Dean tried to comfort her. Through her tears she could not help but ask, "Did you see the man? The one who threatened us?"

"No, just the fire. No one from the prison even ventured down. Kathleen, I think there is more to this than we realize. I don't know why they have chosen now to act, but we need to do something."

Kathleen nodded, fully aware of how right he was. "We have to go. Leave the island. Leave France. We need to go home," she said, now convinced that if the authorities needed someone to blame and could not find Edward, they would be next in line.

Dean looked surprised, as though he had expected more resistance from her.

"In the morning, first light. Until then we can stay here and rest. We need to be prepared for anything," Dean said wearily. The day had begun before sunrise, and even their first boat ride here seemed like a lifetime ago.

Adelia listened as they spoke, seeming to understand that their departure would leave her totally alone. Kathleen watched as the thought of it hit her. In spite of her cruel fate, she knew that they were right.

"You should not go by boat. If they are watching for you, that is where they will look first," she said.

Kathleen's mind flashed to the Burdett's. Had she sent them to be captured? At the time, she had thought they could leave undetected, the authorities had no reason to believe that they should know to escape, after all.

"My friend Jacques travels often to Marseille. I will talk to him tonight. If he is leaving, I know that he can be trusted to get you there safely."

"You should not go out Adelia, not now. You are not ready. Besides, you may be being watched," Kathleen pleaded with her.

"I am an old woman speaking with one of my dearest friends. If they want to arrest me for that, fine."

"I don't want you to put yourself at risk," Dean interjected.

"And how will I live if you all suffer? If something happens? You are now the only family I have. If I can help you, I must. I'll hear no more."

With that, Adelia turned and left the room. A few minutes later she returned, dressed in black. Her time of mourning had begun.

Chapter Sixteen

Edward led Lynn by the hand, following the narrow path that Kathleen had suggested. In places, the rear of buildings pressed almost entirely to the small hill to the east, leaving only a foot or two for them to squeeze through. Micah had jogged ahead while Heather followed closely behind.

All four remained as quiet as possible. They were carrying only a few items each, although Edward had managed to grab their smallest suitcase.

They weren't running, but they were moving as quickly as possible. By the time they reached the bottom of the hill where Kathleen said the path met the road, all four were breathing heavily.

"Which way did she say to go?" Heather asked, unsure of where they were in relation to the docks. She could see the water but had no idea which way would be best.

"She didn't say, moron," Micah said derisively.

"Shut it," Edward said, "we need to head east. From there we can make our way down without going through town."

Heather hesitated, waiting for someone else to take the lead. Which way was east was totally lost on her.

Edward led the way, taking a right and heading down the road. At this point they walked more slowly, having no interest in drawing attention to themselves. After several hundred yards they took a left, heading down a steep hill that led towards the ocean. They made several jogs back and forth.

As they walked they tried to blend in, although they looked almost nothing like the local population. Her mother could pass for a Frenchwoman, Heather supposed, but her own red hair was not likely to be mistaken for a native.

Most of the foot traffic paid no attention to them, attending to their daily duties and not even casting a glance in their direction. The actual shop keepers were more likely to look at them, several times attempting to get their attention in an effort to sell one good or another. The fragrance of croissants wafted from one stand. The smell was nearly enough for Heather to want to stop.

"We are almost there," Edward said glancing back over his shoulder.

Heather looked around. They were close to the water, sure, but where were they actually going? They had no boat to board and had no idea of whether they would be able to book passage on one.

"Daddy, where are we going to go?" she asked.

"I don't know. We need to find a way to leave as soon as possible. I'm going to ask around, see if there are any outbound boats with room for us."

Lynn looked around, a feeling of unease building in her stomach. The more that Edward asked around, the more likely that word was to get back to the police that foreigners were looking to book passage away from Cannes.

"Be careful. Ask only the minimum," she advised, feeling the need to say something, even if it was not helpful.

When they arrived next to the docks, a smile broke out on Edward's face. The ship that they'd arrived on was moored at one of the slips at the end of the first row. Not only that, but there were members of the crew working on deck, bringing in lines. They seemed to be preparing for departure.

"Stay here, I'll go talk with Pierre."

Micah started to walk along with Edward as he headed for the boat. "Stay here with the girls. Just in case."

"Forget that, they'll be fine."

Edward hesitated and then decided against saying anything. With Micah it was always wise to pick your battles.

"Alright, but don't say anything. Let me do the talking."

Micah mumbled a response, but Edward wasn't concerned. He didn't talk much to the people he liked, much less strangers.

As they approached the boat, the captain emerged from the innards of the vessel. He watched as two of the crew members worked, one scrubbing the deck and the other arranging lines.

"Captain Pierre!" Edward said, attempting to keep his voice calm and light.

"Ah, Edward! Bonsoir!" the captain replied, his English was minimal, but served its purpose when needed.

"We are looking to book passage back...," Edward trailed, starting again in his best attempt at French. "Nous voulons retourner à Marseilles. Avez vous une chambre?"

The captain laughed. "We have room," he said, his English better than Edward's French, seemingly.

"We leave tomorrow. Morning. Yes?"

"Yes, yes. Thank you! Merci!" Edward replied, his relief evident.

The crewman who was working with the lines shouted something at the captain, who waved quickly and then turned away, his attention now returning to his ship.

Edward and Micah returned to Lynn and Heather, both of whom looked relieved.

"Can he take us? Are they leaving now?" Heather asked, impatiently.

"Yes, they can take us when they return to Marseilles. The ship leaves tomorrow morning. We will have to stay until then."

"Stay? Here?" Lynn said, looking around.

"There are several boarding houses nearby. We will have to hope that there are rooms available," he replied, holding his hand up to his forehead. The sun was just setting, its beautiful reddish orange light sparkling on the cool blue water.

Heather looked out at the sea, watching as the waves ebbed and flowed, dancing back and forth and crashing into the moorings of the dock. Little rises of blue fire.

"There. One of those signs says 'rooms'," Lynn said, pointing to a building with yellow trim along the far eastern edge of the dock.

They walked towards the building, still very aware that they could be stopped or seen at any time. Once they arrived, Edward ushered them all in and cast a glance behind them before closing the door. There were people and activity everywhere, but no signs of the police or other foul play.

The inside of the building was loud and crowded. The main floor was filled with tables and chairs, most of which were occupied by sailors and other patrons. This was more of a bar than an inn, Heather realized. The confined space stank of old beer and sweat. Heather grimaced at the combination while Lynn located someone to ask about a room.

Moments later, Lynn began speaking with a large woman, seemingly as wide as she was tall, with coarse brown hair pulled back in a greasy bun. They conversed briefly, the woman eventually pointing in the direction of the stairs at the northern end of the room.

Lynn returned, not appearing particularly happy. "They have one room. One bed. And it's twice what we were paying Madame Moreau."

Edward cringed. "I don't see as we have much choice. Let's pay the woman and go."

After they'd paid and been given a key, they retreated away from the crowd and settled into the room where they were to stay. The single bed was shoved into a corner, only an end table sat beside it. There was nothing else in the room, although there was a dingy window that faced west, lighting the room with mottled hues of red and orange.

Heather scouted the space, noticing a cabinet door she had not seen before. Opening it, she found several blankets. They were old and smelled faintly of smoke, but they seemed otherwise clean enough. She took the smaller of the two and handed the other to her mother.

She folded hers, creating a pillow to lay on rather than the hard wooden floor. Choosing the corner farthest from the bed, Heather attempted to rest. It was early, but the events of the day had worn her down to nothing, and she soon fell into a fitful sleep.

Only Micah slept well, his deep snoring reminding the rest that he was enjoying the bed while they slept on the floor. Heather was surprised that he had not insisted on going downstairs to drink. Perhaps even he realized how serious their situation was.

In the morning, Edward and Heather were both up before the sun, and Lynn awoke very shortly thereafter.

Edward roused Micah, who offered no objection. The four of them left the room as they'd found it, leaving the key on the end table and making their way out. No one stirred outside, and they left the inn and made their way to the boat.

On and around the boat, signs of life were everywhere. The boat was fully prepared and ready to go, and the crew was active with last minute duties. Pierre waved them aboard, directing them below deck before returning topside.

Less than an hour later, the large boat set sail, heading back to Marseilles.

They had made it, they'd escaped. They were headed home.

Part Two

*"A burning ember threatens,
floating in the night,
all it needs is smallest fuel,
and it sets the world alight."*

Chapter Seventeen

The summer had come and gone, as had fall. Cold winds had blown the last of the yellow and red leaves from the trees in the front yard. The first snowfall was unusually early, coming before Thanksgiving and littering the ground with large white snowflakes. The events that had driven them so hastily from France had gone almost entirely unmentioned, as if their year abroad had never happened. It was a constant source of frustration to Jason, but his efforts to discuss it were continuously shut down.

Jason sat by the fireplace, warming his hands and thinking about the situation. He'd been attending to the animals in the barn with his father before they had decided that enough was enough and had come inside to escape the cold.

Dean's pipe, coupled with the smoke from the fire and the soup on the stove, filled the front room with a complicated but satisfying aroma. Jason breathed it in, letting it fill his lungs before he exhaled. Even in spite of the cold in his fingers, he was glad to be back where he belonged.

They'd taken longer to return from France than he'd ever wanted, and the return journey had been as nerve wracking as it had been complicated. They'd travelled to Marseilles with Adelia's friend, just as they had planned. However, by the time that they arrived, the last passenger ship had already left. They'd had to wait several weeks for another.

Staying at an inn for several weeks depleted what little cash they had available, most of their valuables having been destroyed when their home went up in flames. Fortunately, Dean had long ago hidden some money in the barn, so they were not completely destitute.

They'd used all of the money they had, down to the very last franc and dollar, to book passages home, first on the Neustria and then by train back to Iowa. Neither trip was luxurious, only being able to afford the most minimal of accommodations available.

Once they had arrived home, there had been much to do. The farmhouse had fallen into disrepair. Even though they prepared it as best as possible for their extended absence, time had not been kind to the home, and there were many things that needed to be mended. In a way, it felt like being back on Ile St. Marguerite all over again.

Dean and Jason had gone back to work, fixing windows and walls and roofs, just as they had when they'd first arrived on the island. The repairs this time around were not nearly as significant, but they still occupied their time for several weeks.

Nearly every waking moment that wasn't being spent working on the house or farm, Jason had spent with Calvin and, to an only slightly lesser extent, Heather.

They'd spent hours catching up when he first arrived, discussing all the things that had happened during Jason's absence. Even though it had been nearly two years, their friendship had picked right back up where they'd left off. Even time, it seemed, could not change what they shared.

Heather was attending high school and still hoping to attend college once she completed. Jason thought it was a waste of time, but it certainly seemed to make her happy, even if she did complain about the work sometimes.

Calvin had gone to work on his family's farm, just as Jason had expected he would. His complaints mimicked Jason's own, callouses and sore muscles. Underneath of the normal complaints, Jason sensed that Calvin wasn't completely satisfied. He wanted more than their small town had to offer.

Although he didn't see Heather as much as he did Calvin, Jason's fondness for her had not decreased. They'd spent countless hours together, and he often found his thoughts drifting in her direction. There was something about her that he couldn't quite articulate, something that drew him to her and did not let him go.

It had been this way for nearly as long as he'd known her. There had been an instant attraction, at least for him. Those feelings had never been mutual, however, and he'd done his best to push those thoughts aside. Calvin would likely argue that he'd done so poorly.

Over the last two months since his return, Jason could feel that something had changed. Although they all remained the closest of friends, he was aware that Calvin and Heather now shared a special bond, something he was not privy to. He shook away the thought as he sat next to the fire.

He was here, now, and he was thrilled. At least he tried to convince himself that he was.

"Soup is ready anytime. Are you ready to eat?" Kathleen asked Jason, her hands already reaching for the ladle. Asking Jason whether he wanted to eat was one of the more foolish questions that had ever been devised.

"Definitely!"

"Let me finish my pipe. I'll just be a minute," Dean replied, fully aware that Kathleen was going to serve Jason first anyway.

As she scooped soup into a bowl for Jason, Kathleen sang softly. Her voice carried on it a hymn, one of her favorites, the story of a cross and a sacrifice. A sweet story of redemption.

Dean snuffed out what was left of the tobacco in his pipe before getting up and joining Jason at the table. By the time he'd sat down, Jason had nearly finished his first bowl of soup. Ravenous was a word that more than one person had used to describe his eating habits.

While Dean ate his first bowl and Jason his second, Kathleen fluttered about the kitchen, decluttering and attending to other miscellaneous tasks. Rarely did she sit down for more than a minute or two during dinnertime.

"Think it'll warm up or are we going to be freezing from here on out?" Jason asked between bites.

"It'll warm up a bit. Always does when we get snow this early."

Dean had been right, which he'd say was usual. The snow that had fallen had melted only a few days later and by the time that Thanksgiving actually arrived, temperatures were a more typical middle fifties.

The following week, only a few days before Thanksgiving, Jason, Calvin, and Heather were once again sitting at the counter of the mercantile, idling away the hours of a late November Saturday.

"How's high school going?" Jason asked, not having heard as much about it as he would have liked.

"It's fine, there's a lot to do. A lot more than there ever was before. I wish you guys were there with me," Heather responded, fiddling with a bracelet adorning her wrist.

Jason sucked a lemon drop, his mouth puckering slightly at the sourness. Pushing it into his cheek, he said, "Wa-ell, I sure don't." The candy distorted his words. Rather than spit it out, he swallowed it too early, causing him to cough and grimace.

"Lovely Jason, just lovely," Calvin chimed in.

"Shut it. Anyway, I'm glad that I'm done with school. It was always too much work for too little use," Jason said.

Heather rolled her eyes. "You are so lazy. I swear, if you even tried…," she trailed off. Her annoyance with his effort, or lack thereof, was not a new development.

"She's still Mrs. Straight A's, so nothing has really changed," Calvin said with a laugh.

"That so? Good for you. I would expect nothing less anyway."

Heather cast a glance at Calvin, her lips ever so slightly upturned at the corners. She was secretly proud of her grades and appreciated that he'd brought them up.

"Stop it. Both of you!"

"Hey Calvin, did you read the last penny dreadful? Man, that was good!"

"Oh yeah, I did! It was great. That guy getting his head chopped off was pretty gruesome."

Heather shut her eyes and squirmed. The violent publications that Jason and Calvin enjoyed were not her cup of tea, and she tried to avoid conversation about the more unsettling topics they contained. "Moving on…," she said, hoping to cut them off. "Do you want to go to my house and play cards?"

The three of them often played cards late into the evening, whether it was gin rummy or euchre or one of several others. Jason typically won, although that was more due to his competitive nature than it was actual talent.

"I don't know, we played cards yesterday. Maybe I should head home anyway, I think my dad has a few things he wants me to do," Jason said, bored of their normal routine.

"I'd come. I don't have anything else to do," Calvin responded with an eagerness that made Jason feel like he was being left out.

"On the other hand, we haven't played pinochle in a while. I'd be up for that. What do you think?"

Calvin and Heather exchanged a glance that was just a beat too long. Heather was the first to break the connection, responding, "You know, maybe you were right. I probably need to get home too. I have piano lessons, and I need to work on a paper that's due on Monday."

A surprised look crossed Calvin's face but passed quickly. "Alright, well maybe tomorrow after church?" he asked.

"Sounds good. I'll see you guys tomorrow."

They watched as she left the counter and headed for the door. Just before she reached it, Calvin called out after her.

"Would you like me to walk you home?"

Heather turned and first looked at Calvin before furtively darting her eyes towards Jason. Reconnecting her gaze with Calvin, she said, "No, I'll be fine. See you both tomorrow."

The two of them sat at the counter for another thirty minutes, discussing shilling shockers and other stories they'd been reading, along with the mundane aspects of farm life that never stopped, even as winter approached. Neither one of them brought up Heather, not knowing how to deal with the sudden awkwardness that had rudely inserted itself into their friendship.

Chapter Eighteen

It was the hottest November that anyone in Sacramento could remember. Even in the last week of the month, temperatures were in the upper seventies with cloudless skies and no wind. Heather walked towards school, old Sac High, in the early morning. The high school was one of the oldest high schools in the West, having been founded in 1856.

As she approached it, she scanned the wood-clad, two story building as she did every weekday. The building was nearly twenty years old but showed few signs of wear. The mansard roof was handsome, and the widow's walk was a surprising feature for a school, giving it a distinctly elegant feel.

The choice to attend high school the previous year had been an easy one for Heather. When asked, she had not hesitated to enroll. Her grades were sufficient, and it gave her the opportunity to get out of the house, a welcome respite from the constant turmoil inside.

Since returning from France, Edward had struggled to find his balance. He had been convinced that the trip, the sale of those documents, would be enough to comfortably fund not only their return but also seed money for him to open up a shop locally. Their panicked exit had drained them financially, inserting instability into their lives and his career.

Edward had attempted to distance himself from the past as much as possible. Instead of opening the store he'd planned, he'd taken a job at the local textile mill and spent nearly every waking hour working. When asked, he refused to discuss the documents that had compelled him to travel to France in the first place. As soon as they'd arrived home he'd hidden them away, never to be brought out again. Heather didn't know whether it was the work or the failure, but she had never seen him so moody and exhausted.

Adding to the volatility was Micah. Since they'd returned, his drinking had not just gotten worse, it had spiraled into something far deeper. He'd sleep all day, drink all night, and rage about life in all the hours in between. More than once, he and Edward had come to blows.

Heather grimaced as she thought about it. The constant tension inside the house wore on her, grinding away at her sanity. These few hours at school were blissful reprieve.

As she walked down 9th street, she saw her best friend Alyssa approaching from the east, on M street. She walked with her head held high, as always, her dark brown hair impeccably combed. Cascading down to nearly her waist, Alyssa's hair had always been one of her defining features. While most of the other girls wore their hair up in curls or bows, Alyssa always wore hers down. The stark contrast made her stand out, especially to the boys.

Heather sighed. Although she loved her friend, she was often envious of her. Alyssa was the kind of girl that everyone loved and wanted to be. From her physique to her demeanor, and of course the hair, everything about her was just a little too perfect.

Heather crossed the street, waving her hand to get Alyssa's attention as she did so. When she caught sight of Heather, Alyssa smiled and walked towards her, clutching her school books to her chest.

"Hey! I didn't see you yesterday, where were you?" Heather asked, having noticed her friend was absent the day before.

"My mom was sick, and Dad is away again. I needed to stay home to help. She's feeling a lot better today, though." Alyssa's father traveled a lot for work, but even though they had been close friends for years, Heather still didn't understand exactly what her father did for a living.

"Oh, I'm sorry to hear that! I'm glad she's better. Did you need me to help you with lessons?"

"Oh no, I've got it. I've been working ahead in all the classes anyway."

In addition to everything else, Alyssa's grades were always near the top of the class, if not on the actual summit.

"Ok. Well, I took some extra notes just in case. Let me know if you change your mind," Heather offered, always thinking about what was best for those around her.

"Will do!"

The two girls walked into the high school and ascended the stairs. Their first class was English, the only class that Heather truly dreaded. The English room was to left of the stairs, and the two girls took seats side by side.

The room was long and narrow, three benches wide and four deep. The classroom could accommodate twelve students comfortably, although by the time class started there would be nearly fifteen.

Several rows back and towards the windows sat Bryce, the third part of their small social circle. Bryce was tall and willowy, with dusty brown hair and dark brown eyes. He gave them a nod and a quick smile as they sat down. The boys sat on one half of the classroom and the girls on the other, and he remained sitting with several other boys who were laughing and making jokes.

Heather felt a flutter deep inside her. Pushing it away, she adjusted her hair and made sure that her books were in order, even though she was already sure that they were.

When the teacher walked in a few minutes later, Heather had her assignments neatly prepared and her book perfectly aligned with the corner of the desk. Even though English was her least favorite subject, she would not be caught unprepared.

The hours inside the various classrooms blurred together, forming a continuous sanctuary of time that Heather cherished. School itself was nothing of particular import, but the peace and calm was truly invaluable.

As her last class of the day concluded, Heather's thoughts drifted back to Bryce. He puzzled her, his signals always seeming to vacillate without notice. She believed her own interest was clear, but his was anything but. The hot and cold nature of their interactions frustrated her to no end.

Even so, a soft smile found residence on her lips as she gathered her things and walked out alongside Alyssa. No matter about Bryce, tonight she was free.

The girls chattered as they walked towards Alyssa's home. The two of them had arranged for Heather to stay overnight to discuss the plans for a dance that Alyssa's mother, Margaret, was to put on. Although a formal ball was not something most other teenagers were interested in, they both were positively giddy with excitement.

"I don't even care if anyone in our class comes, I just want to dance. I'll dance with you if none of the boys show up," Heather said, excitement breaking the tone of her voice.

"Scandalous!" Alyssa said, giggling.

Margaret had invited the parents of nearly everyone in their high school, along with their older children. Whether any of them would come or not was a mystery to Heather.

"But, actually, I'm positive that you'll have someone to dance with, as I know at least one of the boys is coming," Alyssa said, her lips upturned at the corners in a grin. "Bryce told me earlier that he was going to come. If that matters to you anymore, that is."

Heather flushed. The two of them had alternated back and forth with their interest in Bryce. Now that it was Heather's turn, she felt the heat rise in her face. Alyssa had delivered the message with a smile, so she obviously wasn't jealous, but even the mention of the situation was often awkward. Fortunately, Alyssa moved on from the topic.

"Do you know what you are going to wear yet?" she asked.

"I'm going to wear the one dress daddy didn't sell. It doesn't fit me perfectly but mom said that she could hem it."

"Ooooh, I like that one! So you convinced him to let you keep it, huh? Lucky you!" Alyssa gushed, genuinely happy for her friend. The copper color of the dress was absolutely stunning on Heather, and Alyssa knew that she had been trying to convince her father not to sell the dress from the very day he'd won it at auction.

"Yeah, when he didn't take the dress to New York I knew he'd let me have it eventually," Heather said. Edward was enamored with his daughter and rarely could resist giving her what she wanted. "What about you? Do you know yet?"

"I think so. There's a blue dress that I've been trying to convince mother to buy for me, and I think she will."

As they continued walking and talking, Heather closed her eyes and took in the warmth of the sun above. The rays lifted her spirits and darkened her skin. She was the rarest of the rare, a redhaired beauty with blue eyes who could also tan. She'd gotten just enough of her mother's Armenian heritage to darken when she spent time in the sun.

Here in November, her skin was fair and her freckles distinct, but that didn't stop her from enjoying the moment. After she'd taken a few steps she opened her eyes. Momentarily distracted, the conversation had briefly escaped her.

"So, do you?" Alyssa asked, apparently unaware that her friend had been temporarily transported elsewhere.

"Do I... what?"

"Think anyone else from school with come," Alyssa said, head cocked slightly to the side in confusion.

"Oh, yeah, I don't know. Maybe. Polly probably will. Maybe John, too. I'm not sure."

A few moments later they turned the final corner before coming to Alyssa's home. The home was large, sitting on nearly two acres of land, and exquisite in its design. The old Victorian home was a pale blue with white decorative shutters. Eight stairs led to a large porch that faced the road, immediately below an elegant turret that housed their library. Topped with a crow's nest, the home was one of the jewels of the area and was envied by many.

The inside was equally impressive. Every room was lavishly appointed and decorated. Large bay windows on nearly every side filled the room with warm light.

"Aly, is that you?" Margaret called out as they entered, referring to her daughter by the pet name that nearly everyone used.

"Yes, it's me, mom. Heather is here, too."

"Oh wonderful!" Margaret said, walking into the foyer to greet them.

"We're just going to go upstairs, okay? We've got a lot to work on."

"Alright dear, dinner will be ready in about an hour. Nice to see you, Heather."

Once upstairs, Heather and Aly spread out all of their plans on the floor. Although most everyone had already been invited by word of mouth, formal invitations still needed to be written and delivered, along with plans for hor d'oeuvres, desserts, and other miscellanea. Most of those details would need to be discussed with Margaret, of course, but she was giving them a wide latitude to help.

The hour before dinner passed quickly, along with the hours afterwards. Before the night was over they had made decisions on nearly every important aspect of the event, and Heather was exhausted.

As they prepared to go to sleep, Heather's mind wandered back to Bryce. As usual, she had no idea what to expect from him. Would he show up to the dance and finally tell her that he was interested? Would he even show up at all? The thoughts ran together in her mind, creating a swirl of confusion and self-doubt. *Why would he even be interested in her with Aly around anyway?* she thought, instantly trying to chase away the thought. *Don't do that. Don't go there.*

Suddenly frustrated rather than tired, Heather struggled to get comfortable in the massive bed that she shared with her best friend.

"You okay?" Alyssa asked, noticing her tosses and turns.

"I'm fine, just thinking. About Bryce," she admitted, surprising even herself. "Do you think he cares for me? Am I crazy for wishing so much that he does?"

"Oh honey, I wouldn't worry about it. He's your best friend, our best friend. I think he's just nervous that something could go wrong. Besides, what about that boy you met in France? Maybe he will end up being your knight in shining armor. Either way, when the time comes, everything will fall into place. I promise," Alyssa said in a comforting voice that she had mastered over the years of their friendship.

Not responding, Heather turned on her back and stared at the ceiling.

When the time comes, everything will fall into place. Heather thought, repeating Aly's words back to herself. *I promise.*

Chapter Nineteen

Heather walked home alone the following morning, intentionally taking the long way and strolling leisurely. Her time at Aly's house reminded her of what her own home lacked, and she was enjoying the last few moments of peace. These few minutes were all she had left before she would be forced to return to her real life.

Being Saturday, school was not in session, and it was likely that both her mother and Micah would be home when she arrived. Edward was often expected to work long hours, even on weekends, so he probably would not be home. Although he'd had little previous experience in factory labor before taking the job, his dedication to the work had propelled him into a position of

Unmasked

oversight. His elevated position, however, did not exempt him from long hours and, at times, physical labor.

The house was quiet when she walked in, no voices or other sounds of activity. As she surveyed the house, she noticed movement through the rear window; her mother was working in the garden at the back of their home.

She walked in her direction, passing through the foyer and through the main living space of the house. As she entered the kitchen, she noticed a yellowed envelope sitting on the counter top. She was two steps beyond the letter when she realized that it was addressed to her.

Nearly jumping backwards, she snatched the letter from the counter while simultaneously yelling for her mother.

"Mom! When did you get this?" Heather exclaimed, attempting to shout her way through the wall and window standing between her mother and herself.

Lynn stood and took off the gloves she wore, leaving them outside as she entered through the door.

"What did you say, honey?"

"Mom, this letter, when did it come?"

"Oh, yes. The letter," the way her mother said it made Heather crinkle her forehead in confusion. "Well, I just found it yesterday."

"Found it? What do you mean, found it?"

"I was cleaning out Micah's room and I found it stuffed in his desk. I asked him about it, and apparently it arrived quite some time ago. He seems to find it amusing for some reason. I'm sorry, darling."

Heather felt her face flush in anger. She had been waiting for months for a letter that had already arrived, and it set her blood to boiling. *Of course Micah would hide it from me. Of course,* Heather thought.

"Is he here? Now?" she asked her mother, fully intending to confront him regardless of the consequences.

"No, he's not. I actually don't know where he is. He went out last night and hasn't come home. Even if he was, you shouldn't bring it up. It will just make things worse. You know that."

"Why do you always defend him, Mother? He's a jerk, and you know it!"

"Honey…," Lynn said, but trailed off without finishing. Heather held the letter in her fist, accidentally crumpling the edges as she brushed past her mother and headed towards her room. *Damn him. Damn him!* Heather thought, although she'd have preferred to scream it at him directly.

Once inside her bedroom, she turned and slammed the door, not caring if her mother didn't like it. She protected him, so she deserved it.

She sat down on her bed and put her hands to her face, breathing deeply a few times before she looked down at the envelope in her hands. Although she'd creased it, the return address was still legible, *Cedar Falls, Iowa,* she read.

She opened the envelope carefully, making sure not to tear through the address. She removed the single piece of folded paper inside and smoothed it out as best she could on her lap. She took a few more deep breaths before she started to read.

September 16th, 1896

Dear Heather,

We arrived home just a couple of days ago, and I wanted to make sure to write you right away. I've been worried about you. After my mother told me what happened, what was about to happen, I've been thinking a lot about you and hoping that you and your family are alright. I cannot believe that the police were going to say that your father murdered Thomas! It's awful, and just thinking about it makes me angry.

Did you make it back easily? We actually left the very same day that you did. A man burned down our house and threatened us. It's unbelievable. We travelled to Marseilles and then waited there until we could catch a ship. It took us nearly three weeks, and during that time we were afraid that someone would come find us. Fortunately, no one did.

Will you be going to school when you return? I won't be and neither will Calvin, but Heather is already enrolled and attending.

We returned at the end of the season, so there will soon be plenty of harvesting work to keep me occupied. We leased our fields to another farmer during the time we were gone, but there are plenty of farms that need extra hands this time of year. Calvin and I will both be busy, I imagine.

Anyway, I won't keep you any longer, I just wanted to write and make sure that you were okay and because I said that I would. I've written my address on the reverse, just in case you'd like to write back.

Sincerely,

Jason Baldwin

Heather's mind swirled; she was completely flabbergasted. The woman that had saved them was Jason's mother! In the months since that fateful day, they had discussed her on many occasions, always attributing her presence to divine providence. To think that all along it had been his mother was astounding. In the smallest of small worlds, theirs had been connected in such a profound way.

And the letter had been sitting here the entire time, hidden away by her malicious older brother. *Was his entire purpose in life to ruin hers?* she thought venomously. She stalked around her room, occasionally pausing to throw something or beat her hands against her bed. The anger inside her was fierce, burning away the miniscule reserves of patience that she possessed.

When she had calmed down somewhat, even if not completely, she stormed out of her room and found her mother in the garden.

Momentarily forgetting her anger at her brother, she revealed what the letter had told her about their mysterious rescuer.

"It was his mother? That's unbelievable! So does that mean Jason is related to the innkeeper?"

Heather paused. The thought had not occurred to her. "Well, I suppose that must be the case. Jason didn't mention it though."

"Even so, what divine serendipity. I've always said that there was a larger hand at work in our escape."

Now that the revelation had come to light, Heather's anger at her brother resurfaced and threatened to overtake her once more. Attempting to remain calm, she took a deep breath before speaking.

"Mom, something has to change. I can't deal with Micah anymore. No matter what I do, he finds ways to make me miserable," she paused briefly before adding, "to make you miserable".

Lynn looked up at her daughter and gave her a wearied look. Her face was full of understanding. "I know, Heather, I know. But there are some things that only time can change. Your brother is… working through life at his own pace. Things will get better, even if I cannot tell you when."

"That's not good enough! I need you to do something about it if dad won't. Or… or…," She trailed off, unable to think of anything to say. She was trapped and powerless. If her parents were unwilling, or unable, to reign Micah in, there was little to nothing that she could do about it. "…or I'll leave. I'll go away," she finished weakly.

The threat was hollow, and they both knew it. She had nowhere to go.

Chapter Twenty

It was the second week of December and, as usual, Jason had joined Calvin and Heather after his morning chores had been completed. Heather had wanted something new to read, and so the two boys had agreed to join her in town to pursue the available titles.

"Do you ever think you'll move away, Calvin?" Heather asked as they sat in the circulating library at the southwest end of Main St. The table in front of them was full of books they had selected from the many volumes available. Calvin thumbed absentmindedly through a volume of *A Christmas Carol* by Charles Dickens.

Putting it down and shoving it towards the center of the table, he said, "Probably not. Where would I go?"

"I don't know. You could have gone to college if you'd chosen to attend high school. What about into a city?" she responded, seemingly always looking to the future.

"The city? I suppose. I do like it there. Sure as heck is more exciting than here, and a lot more to do, besides."

"Or you could go to the normal school. It's not too far from here," Jason jested, cracking a smile and giving Calvin a playful elbow.

"Right. I'm going to be a teacher, hardy har har har."

"No really, I think you've got the disposition for it. Really suits you!" Jason joked, continuing to give Calvin an unfairly hard time for his softer nature.

"Boys, boys," Heather interrupted, playing the referee as she did so often, "don't worry, I'm sure the normal school has room for *both* of you!" At that, Jason reddened, his own medicine less pleasant going down than being given out. "You really could though. There are almost no male teachers. You'd find a job for sure!"

Jason and Calvin both rolled their eyes, making it clear that a teaching career was not in either of their futures.

"Anyway," Heather continued, her own eyes rolling back at them now, "what do you guys want to do? For real. I want to go to college, but I don't want to teach. Have you guys heard that they just opened a new college in Des Moines? It's called Drake. I think I might want to go there."

"Des Moines? That far away?" Jason said, a note of sadness in his voice. He'd known Heather for what seemed like a lifetime, and he couldn't imagine life without her there.

"Maybe. I don't know. It's a thought," she trailed off, perhaps sensing that the conversation was about to take a depressing turn.

"I think you should. If that's what you want to do, go for it," Calvin said, always one to encourage others.

"On that cheery note, why don't we go down to Kirk's and get some butterscotch? My treat." Calvin and Heather looked at him in surprise, butterscotch not being one of his favorites. Being one of theirs, however, they were happy to take him up on the offer.

They didn't talk as they walked to the mercantile, content to walk across the town in silence. The crisp December air was still, but punctuated by huge flakes of falling snow. The sun was obscured by deep clouds and all three wore coats to ward off the cold. Heather pressed her arms together, clutched her handbag closer to her, and shivered.

After they arrived, they sat down at the counter and ordered, Mr. Kelly scooping out several small handfuls of butterscotch and putting them in a paper bag. Jason had ordered some lemon drops instead, the sour candies being amongst his favorites. They were quiet for a few minutes as they warmed up, Heather being the first to break the silence.

"You know, you never did say what you wanted to do, Jason," Heather said, restarting their previous conversation.

Jason thought he'd escaped the question cleanly, in no way eager to admit that he had no idea what he wanted to do or where he might want to go.

"I think I want to leave, but I don't know. I'd be alright with just taking over the family farm, too; where I am is not all that important to me I guess."

"Don't you want to *do* something though?" Calvin asked, putting an extra emphasis on the verb.

"I don't want to do nothing, I just…," Jason trailed off. *What I want is just to get married to a woman who genuinely loves me, have a couple of kids, and live free,* he thought, but did not say out loud. His simple desires seemed too intimate for the situation, and he tried to deflect instead.

"I just don't have time to think about all that. I mean, between helping on the farm and you two, I hardly have a spare minute to myself. I'll figure it out eventually."

"What about a girlfriend? I hear that Faye fancies you. Perhaps you should pay her a visit?" Heather said, the corners of her lips rounding in a coy smile.

Jason's thoughts flashed to the other Heather, the one he'd met in France. He wasn't sure why, but somehow the thought of calling upon another girl seemed wrong. He shrugged and rolled his eyes rather than answer.

Heather took stock of Jason as he sat at the counter. He was tall, over six feet, and skinny. He wasn't puny by any means, but he could certainly stand to gain a few pounds. His arms were deeply freckled, covering his otherwise white skin with a canvas of tan specks.

He'd recently grown a small beard, and she hadn't yet decided if she liked it. Otherwise, his face was mostly clear of the freckles that adorned the rest of him, save for a few on his nose. His eyes were a pale green with flecks of yellow near the pupils. His shockingly blonde eyebrows were nearly indiscernible; he may as well not even have them. Sitting atop his head was an orange shock of hair, both wiry and wavy.

Heather glanced to her left in turn. In some ways Calvin was similar in build to Jason. Although he wasn't quite as tall, and was even more desperately in need of a few extra pounds, his face was far more symmetrical and his blue eyes matched her own. His smile was huge, rows of white teeth neatly aligned. Heather's eyes caught Calvin's, and she blushed, quickly averting her gaze and grabbing another candy from the bag on the counter.

"Are you looking forward to school starting back up after the holidays?" Calvin asked Heather, swiveling in his seat to face her.

"Not really. Don't get me wrong, I like school, but the work has been a bit much lately. I'm glad for the break."

"Who would want to go back to school?" Jason asked incredulously, although fully aware that Heather generally loved school and was consistently the teacher's favorite.

"Give me a break, I like school because I like to learn new things. If school was as easy for me as it was for you I'd never complain. You had it so much easier than you know."

Jason supposed she was right. School work had never been his favorite pastime, but it had certainly been easy for him. Reading came very naturally to him and so did math, and everything else was really just a function of those two subjects. He also supposed that was why he had found school so boring. There simply had never been a challenge to be found there.

"Well, maybe so, but I'm glad to be done. Even if I'm just working the farm with my dad, I'm happy to be finished with school."

Heather said nothing, opting to remain silent and take the very last butterscotch from the bag.

Mr. Murphy, perhaps noticing that the candies were gone, walked behind the counter in front of them and scooped out a few more pieces of butterscotch. Smiling, he handed the bag directly to Heather.

"Haven't seen your parents in a while, how're they doing? And why don't you take these to David for me, won't you? I know he loves them."

"I will, thank you! And they're quite well. Thank you for asking," Heather responded. Looking at the clock on the other end of the room, Heather sat up from the stool, clutching the bag in her hand.

"I didn't realize it was so late in the afternoon. I have chores to attend to before dinner, and my parents will be wondering where I am. I'll see you guys later, okay?" Heather said, not waiting for a response before turning and walking quickly out the door.

"Yeah, I probably should get going too. My dad said that I need to help him clean the barn. It hasn't been mucked in ages," Calvin said with a disgusted look. "I'll see you tomorrow if it doesn't snow too much more."

"I won't hold my breath, I think this one may be a big one," Jason responded as he looked out the window.

As Calvin walked out, Jason watched as he took a sharp left after exiting the store. Jason furrowed his brow, momentarily confused. *Calvin doesn't live in that direction*, he thought. He got up from the counter and walked to the large pane window at the front of the room. Painted lettering partially obstructed his view, but it was immediately obvious where Calvin was headed. He was following Heather, who was pulling a sapphire blue scarf from her handbag as she walked away.

Chapter Twenty-One

The first letter showed up on December 18th, 1896. Jason had been surprised at its arrival, always having believed that the girl he'd met in Cannes would forget about him within days of their departure. Even more so after their dramatic escape from France. *Why would she remember him after all of that?*

His mother handed him the envelope just after they'd finished dinner, a delicious favorite of biscuits and gravy. She'd picked it up at the post office on her weekly trip into town for goods and had held it all day, waiting for evening to hand it over.

"So, California? I guess that means that they made it out of Cannes safely; I'm so glad to hear it! And that Heather must have really taken a liking to you to write you after so long from so far away," his mother said, apparently taking some enjoyment from his slight discomfort. She was also unaware that Jason had been the first to write.

"I wouldn't know, I haven't been given a chance to read it, now have I?" Jason said, snatching the letter from her outstretched hand.

As he opened the envelope, he could smell the faint hint of something both pleasant and oddly familiar. The smell grew stronger as he removed it from the envelope, and he breathed it in, its presence triggering a memory of their first meeting. She had sprayed the letter with her perfume.

"I'm going to go to my room and read it. Perhaps I'll reply. May I be excused?" Jason asked, abnormally politely. Kathleen giggled slightly before waving her hand towards his room.

Jason sat down at the wooden desk tucked into the corner of his room. The desk sat next to a narrow window and even here, at dusk, it allowed for enough light to read by. He took in the smell of Heather's perfume one more time before he opened the letter fully, noting that she'd drawn several neat hearts on the outside of the folds.

Dear Jason,

I am SO sorry that I did not write back sooner! My idiot brother hid your letter, and I did not get it until now. He makes me so angry!

I was shocked to find out that it was your mother who helped us! We had absolutely no idea who she was, only that she helped us in our hour of need. Please tell her that I appreciate everything she did from the very bottom of my heart. She may very well have saved our lives!

Did you ever get a chance to see Madame Moreau again? When we left her, my heart was breaking for her. Although she told us to go and I know that we needed to, I wish that we could have done more. Losing her brother like that, so suddenly and violently, it was tragic. I hope that she is alright. If you did get the chance to see her, I hope that you gave her whatever comforts you could.

We had to leave so suddenly from Cannes that we didn't even get a chance to properly see the sights. I do wish that I had gotten the chance to take that tour you promised me. I think about that missed opportunity often.

Now that we have returned, I have once again started attending classes at our local high school. My closest friends are also enrolled, so that, too, is a blessing. Are you finished with school, or are you going to high school as well?

I guess I never did get a chance to ask, how old are you?

My best friend and I are planning a dance at the end of month, sort of a new year celebration. I know it's a little strange, but it's going to be absolutely wonderful, and I am very excited for it! To be honest, it's mostly for people my parent's age, but that's okay. Hopefully, I will have someone to dance with, but even if not, it should be very fun.

I don't know long it will take for this to arrive. I've never actually mailed a letter before, so I'm not sure if I should be asking you how your Christmas was or whether you are excited for it. I mailed this on December 10th, two days after my birthday. I suppose that you could consider your reply to be your gift to me.

I really do hope this letter finds you well, but I won't waste any more of your time. If you'd like to write me back, I would really enjoy that. If not, I will understand. I know I'm just some random stranger that you met along the way, so there's no pressure to write if you don't want to.

Thank you for your time.

Sincerely,

Heather P. Burdett

Jason cocked his head to the side as he read the last sentence. Thank you for your time. *What an odd thing to say,* he thought. *Why wouldn't I want to get a letter from a gorgeous girl, even if she does live across the country?*

He read the letter three more times before the light began to fade enough that reading was difficult. When he finished for the last time, he held the letter up to his nose once more, letting the sweet fragrance fill his lungs. He knew it was strange, but no one was around to see it, and he didn't care anyway.

Jason couldn't help but smile. Something about the way that she wrote was so simple and yet so enthusiastic. He was unable to hold back a grin even as he descended the stairs and rejoined his parents by the fireplace.

"So? What did the letter say?" his mother asked as she hovered over the kitchen sink washing dishes.

"You know, just hello and it was nice to meet you. Stuff like that. Oh, and she wanted to thank you for your help. I guess her family thinks you're an angel."

Kathleen waved her hand as if to indicate that she'd only done what anyone else would have. "It was nothing, really. When you write back make sure to tell her that."

Dean was sitting in an old rocking chair and reading the newspaper. He lowered it and looked over the top before he said, "I think she fancies you. Too bad she lives in California."

Well, at least one Heather does, Jason thought, suddenly gloomy. "I don't know, I think she's just being friendly," he said, instead.

"I think it's great that you two are writing, it will help you with your penmanship. For as smart as you are, you really shouldn't have writing that looks like chicken scratch," Kathleen said, not looking away from the pan she was scrubbing with vigor.

As the evening went on, Jason couldn't help but think back to the letter. Every time he did, that same goofy smile returned unbidden. He went back upstairs to his room early and lit his lamps. Hunched over his desk, he took out a pen and began to respond, this time trying to be more dedicated to his penmanship as his mother had suggested.

Three attempts later, he finished. There was a little bit of space left on the page, but he couldn't think of more to say. He folded the letter and inserted it into an envelope. He'd have to buy postage at the post office the next time he went into town.

He stayed up late that evening, sleep seeming to elude him no matter how many times he adjusted his pillow or position. When he finally did get to sleep, his dreams were a confused mess. He was swimming with Calvin when Heather from California joined them. Moments later, 'their' Heather came and tried to swim, only to be told that she'd been replaced. Other dreams came and went, all surrounding his friends.

He woke before the sun had even risen. Sitting up in bed, he was immediately fully awake. There would be no return to sleep for him. He dressed and made his way downstairs. As usual, his father was already up. Even when there were not early morning chores to do, Dean was an early riser.

"My, you're up early. Did you think it was Christmas?" Dean said with a chuckle.

"No, I just woke up. Knew I wouldn't get back to sleep so I didn't bother to try. Is mom up?"

Dean looked at him as though he'd asked the most ridiculous question he'd ever heard. "At 5:30AM? No, she's not." As if reading his mind, he continued, "If you want something to eat, you'll have to make it yourself."

Jason decided that he could wait for a couple of hours. Although he was as hungry as he always was, breakfast was his least favorite meal, and he couldn't be compelled to cook for himself.

The morning came and went, as did the early afternoon. Jason looked outside and decided to take his letter into town, even if it had snowed another couple of inches overnight. Even with the new snow, it wouldn't be too bad.

"Mom, I'm going out. I'll be back in a couple of hours," he called out after bundling up. "I'm going to mail that letter," he added, just in case she needed a reason.

"Alright honey, stay warm!" she responded, apparently unconcerned with his absence.

He trudged the mile into town, the snow having drifted over the roads. The walk was a little more strenuous than he'd anticipated, but he still made it to town within the hour. Being Friday, the office was closing early, and he knew if he'd waited the letter would not get out until at least Monday. Just before he got to the post office, he glanced across the square. Although he had intended to mail the letter immediately, he noticed Calvin across the way, entering the blacksmith's shop. He hurried in that direction instead.

Once inside, he waited until Calvin had finished speaking to Mr. Johnson. Calvin turned around and nearly ran into Jason, his head down as if on a mission.

"Oh, hey, didn't see you there. What are you doing here?" Calvin asked.

"In town mailing a letter, just saw you on the way and thought I'd say hello. What are you here for?"

"Nothing, stupid wagon broke an axle, just need a new one. Mr. Johnson said he should be able to get one ready by the new year."

Jason glanced outside. The snow had stopped falling, and the blue sky was starting to peek back through the clouds. It had warmed up some, too. "Want to come over? I don't have anything to do today."

Calvin nodded as he responded. "Sure, me either. I actually told my parents I might walk to your house, so they won't be expecting me back anytime soon."

The two boys started walking towards the post office. Calvin asked about the letter as they made their way in that direction.

"What are you mailing? Your parents order something?"

"Remember that girl I told you about, the one that I met in France? Well, she finally wrote. So I'm mailing my letter back."

Jason filled Calvin in on the details of the three letters so far, and he seemed to be paying surprisingly close attention.

"And you said her name was Heather, right?"

"Yeah, that's her. Heather Burdett."

"So not only is she Heather, she's also Heather B. That's too confusing."

"What do you mean?" Jason asked, not quite sure what Calvin was getting at.

"Well, you're obviously going to be writing this girl, and so you'll be talking about her. And if she shows you the slightest bit of attention you'll probably never shut up about her...," Calvin paused to let his ribbing of Jason set in, "and so it'll get too confusing to have two Heather's."

"You're a jerk, you know that?" Jason said, although there was no anger in his voice.

"So I'm going to call her...hmm. You said she's in California, right? Yep, I'm going to call her Cali."

Jason looked at him, deciding whether he liked this development. A few seconds later, he said, "Cali, huh? I think I like that. I like that a lot actually."

With that thought in mind, Jason knew exactly how to fill the extra space at the end of his reply. Once they arrived at the post office, Jason carefully opened the envelope and scribbled a few more lines of text.

From that point on, they referred to her as Cali.

Chapter Twenty-Two

Heather was unaware of the change in her name until the next letter arrived, the day before the dance was to take place. Ever since she'd learned of her brother's treachery with the previous letter, she'd made sure to examine the mail the moment her mother arrived home with it whenever possible. On days like today, when she had to wait until after school, she was always sure to question her mother about the post. When she did so today, Lynn handed her an envelope, and she snatched it away greedily. She retreated to her room with it.

December 18th, 1896

It was so nice to receive your letter, and a happy belated birthday to you as well! If you mailed your letter on the 10th then it took 8 days to arrive, which I don't think is too bad.

It sounds like you have an eventful month. Other than celebrating Christmas with my family, I really don't have any plans. I certainly don't have a dance or anything to attend. Are events at the start of the new year common in your area? Around here we really don't celebrate the new year formally, just casual greetings and expressions. A dance sounds like it would be fun though, even if I'm not much of a dancer.

You asked how old I was; I'm 17. My birthday is in August. I never enrolled in high school, always just figured I'd stay around home and run the family farm. It's pretty exciting that you are though, and it sounds like it's good for you. Some days I do wish I would have gone, if only for something to do. It gets pretty boring here in the winter.

My friend Heather is attending, she wants to go to college afterwards. Can't say that I understand why, but I hope that it makes her happy. I haven't seen her as much since I've returned because of school, plus I think she's grown closer to Calvin anyway. I guess you probably don't care about all that though.

Speaking of Heather (the one out here), Calvin feels like it's confusing to have two Heathers to talk about, so we've kind of nicknamed you Cali, short for California. He came up with it, but I hope you don't mind because I have grown fond of the name. Don't get me wrong, I really like the name Heather, too, but there's something nice about Cali. Feel free to call me whatever you want to your friends!

Heather read the last paragraphs over again. She wasn't sure how she felt about the idea of being called Cali. Something about it made her feel strange, and yet she found herself smiling in spite of the feeling. There was something about having a nickname that made her feel special. The idea of leaving everything behind was one that she had often, and she supposed that a new name was a good place to start.

She read the letter a few more times before inserting it back into its envelope. She would, of course, write back, but it would have to wait. Heather was expecting Aly over at any moment, and they had plans to attend to. In reality, all those plans would consist of was talking about the dance, but she wouldn't let that truth get in the way of an enjoyable afternoon.

"So you like this boy, huh?" Aly asked, her hands supporting her head as she laid on Heather's bed.

"He's very nice. He's obviously too far away for anything more to come from it, but I enjoy writing to him," Heather said as she fiddled absentmindedly with one of the many dolls that sat on shelves in the corner of her room, its porcelain face fixed in an eternal grin.

"You could move out there. You know, if it ever did get serious," Aly responded.

"Move? To Iowa? That's... too far away. My mother would never forgive me," Heather said, as though Aly had suggested that she move to the moon.

"On the other hand, it would get me away from Mike. Just yesterday he punched a hole in the wall right outside my room. Did you see it?" Aly simply nodded, by now used to the chaos of Heather's family life.

"Back to the dance, Bryce told me that he changed his mind, he's not going to come," Aly said, and Heather felt her heart sink a bit lower inside her chest.

"Did he say why? I thought he was planning to."

"He just said that he thought it would be too much trouble. I don't know. Whoever knows what boys are really thinking anyway," Aly added.

The two of them continued to chat and gossip throughout most of the afternoon. Just before dinner, Aly said her goodbyes and headed back to her home while Heather went to the kitchen to help her mother prepare the meal.

After the family had finished eating, Heather went back to her room to admire her dress. She stared at it as it hung on the outside of her closet. On impulse, she decided to try it on one last time before the dance.

It took her several minutes to get into, but after a slight struggle she emerged victorious. Her victory lap took her from her room and back into the kitchen where the rest of the family was still sitting.

"What do you think, mom?" Heather said with a gleeful twirl.

"It looks great, honey! And I have an idea, wait here for just a moment," her mother said as she left the room.

Heather turned to the table where her father sat beside Micah, whose head was turned away from her. They were engaged in animated, if muted, conversation. After a few moments, the previously quiet interaction grew in intensity until it burst.

"Well damn you, too. Damn all of you," Micah said, beginning to push himself away from the table.

"Now you wait here, young man…," Even as the words left her father's mouth, Heather knew they had been a mistake. Her brother did not take kindly to being referred to as anything less than an adult, and his reaction was swift and furious.

Before Heather knew what was happening, Micah swept all of the remaining dishes from the table in a violent fit of rage. Two plates hit the floor and shattered. A porcelain dish that held the last of the baked beets flew through the air and collided with Heather's knee, causing her to gasp in pain.

"I don't care what you say, I'm not leaving, do you understand me?" Micah half-said, half-screamed at their father, his eyes wide. Just as he shouted, Lynn entered the room, a pair of white gloves in her hands.

"Micah! What have you done?" Lynn yelled, dropping the gloves onto the counter as she rushed to Heather's side. "Go, now!" she shouted as she shot him a glare that could have etched glass. Apparently deciding not to test his luck further, Micah cast one more menacing look at Edward before he stormed out of the kitchen.

Heather was sobbing. Her knee was throbbing where the dish had hit it, and she welcomed her mother's embrace as she bent down around her. Only then did she notice that the remnants of the baked beets had been distributed generously across the front of her now ruined dress.

Chapter Twenty-Three

Heather sobbed into her pillow. The beautiful copper dress sat crumpled and ruined in the corner next to her dresser. Its hem poking out and reminding Heather of the loss every time that she opened her eyes.

For an hour afterwards, Lynn had done her best to salvage the dress and remove the angry, purple blotches scattered across its front. All of her efforts had been in vain; she'd been unable to make meaningful headway. After giving up on the dress, Lynn had tried her best to sooth her daughter. That, too, proved futile. At Heather's passionate insistence, Lynn had reluctantly left her alone in her room.

Several hours later, Heather had cried all of the tears that she had within her. When she looked into her mirror, the eyes that stared back at her were bloodshot, and the eyelids above were tired and heavy. Lying back down on the bed, Heather replayed the scene in the kitchen in her mind, wishing endlessly that she'd never left her room in the first place.

Unsure of what else to do, Heather sat down at her desk and took out the letter that Jason had written. As she re-read the words, she felt her sadness ebb. When she'd finished for the second time, she took out a pen and paper and began to respond.

She poured out everything that she had bottled up within her, from the dress getting destroyed, to her feelings of being trapped, the stresses of her friendship with Bryce and Alyssa, and everything else in between. Writing to her far away stranger made her feel better somehow, a type of catharsis.

When she'd finished, she returned to her bed and curled beneath the blankets. The weather had finally cooled, and it felt wonderful to be enveloped by the warmth the coverings provided. Between the anger and the tears, it didn't take long for her to fall asleep.

When she awoke the next morning, her eyes were bleary. Although she'd slept for nearly twelve hours, she still felt as tired as she had when she'd gone to bed.

She got herself ready for the day and made her way to the kitchen where both of her parents sat. She was surprised to see Edward sitting at the table, normally he'd have been off to work long before now.

"What time is it?" Heather asked, thinking perhaps it was earlier than she had realized.

"It's just a bit after eight," Edward responded, glancing first at his wristwatch. "I'm going in late today, boss be damned. I knew you'd want to talk."

Heather smiled softly. Her father's dedication to her made her feel safe, even amidst the turmoil of the house. "Thanks, Daddy," she started, "although I don't really have anything to say. Or wear, for that matter."

"Well, actually, your mother has something to tell you about that."

Heather looked at Lynn who was sitting across the table from Edward. She turned her head ever so slightly to the side, asking the question without saying the words.

"I've been so stressed ever since...," Lynn paused, apparently unsure of whether to address the situation directly, "well, ever since last night. I couldn't sleep, so I walked down to Lora's house. I must have looked frightful, banging on her door at eleven o'clock in the evening."

Heather gave her father a glance, but he was staring at Lynn as she talked. *Where is she going with this?* Heather wondered.

"Anyway, you know that her niece has been staying with her, right? Now, she's a couple years younger than you are, but she's about your size," Lynn stood up from the table and walked over to the pantry as she continued. "and she was gracious enough to allow me to borrow this," she finished with a flourish, grabbing a dress on a hanger from behind the door.

Heather gasped. The dress was not an equal to the copper gown that still sat in her room, but it was beautiful. A pale yellow with white lace, it looked as though it was precisely the right size. Heather walked over and examined the gown, running her fingers over the sleeves and fingering the buttons of the coat.

"It's... it's a miracle," Heather stammered, looking at her mother in astonishment. "I thought, surely, that I would have to wear one of my old dresses." Heather went silent as she continued to admire the dress.

"I know it's not exactly what you were envisioning, but it's beautiful, and I know that you will look exquisite in it. Why don't you go try it on?" Lynn said.

Heather's smile vanished. The last time she had tried a dress on, it had been ruined. Her sudden shift did not go unnoticed by her mother, who must have been aware of her thoughts.

"He's not here. I made him leave. He's staying at Aaron's," she said, comforting Heather's fear.

"Okay, I think I will, then," Heather said as she took the dress and walked back to her room. When she emerged a few minutes later, both her parents beamed. The pale yellow dress fit her as though it had been made for her, save for it being just slightly too long.

"You can wear your white boots instead of the shoes. I know they don't fit perfectly anymore, but they will help with the length," her mother said, still on the same wavelength with her daughter.

"I don't know what to say, thank you!" Heather said, reaching forward to embrace her mother, tears forming at the corners of her eyes.

"You don't need to say anything, dear," Lynn said, her own tears threatening to fall on the gown. Lynn quickly wiped her eyes as she broke the hug.

"I'm going to take it off," Heather said, still anxious after the events of the previous evening. Lynn simply nodded in response.

When she returned to the kitchen, Edward was gathering his things to leave. Although he'd stayed late to see the grand reveal, he still needed to go to work. He gave Lynn a kiss as he walked past her. Pausing at Heather, he said, "I love you, honey. I'm glad that you like the dress." They both smiled and exchanged an embrace before he left.

Heather and her mother spoke for a while before they parted to attend to different chores, each having things to take care of. For Heather's part, much of her work was preparation for the dance, and for that she left for Alyssa's house shortly after noon.

After Heather had arrived and told Aly all about the disastrous evening of the previous day, they spent the next hours hanging decorations, polishing and setting out glasses and dishware, attending to name cards, and various other miniscule tasks. Heather loved every moment of it.

Just after 5PM, Heather and Aly excused themselves and went upstairs to dress. After they had finished, they took to the sitting room to appraise each other and help with buttons, as needed.

Alyssa's powdery blue gown was a vision, made of silk and impeccably tailored. Its large puffy sleeves extended to her elbows. The neckline was lower than Heather had ever seen her wear, and Heather felt herself blush on Aly's behalf. Adding to the scandal, the dress ended quite abruptly just above her ankles, showing her white shoes and delicate silk stockings. *Perhaps it was better that Bryce would not be attending, after all*, Heather thought.

Heather's yellow dress was not up to the standards or scandal of Alyssa's, but it truly did fit her well and Alyssa oohed and aahed appropriately. Her mother's silken white gloves completed the ensemble, and Heather felt beautiful, nearly able to put the events of the previous night out of her mind entirely.

They made their way back downstairs slightly less than an hour later. The evening was set to begin at 6PM, with appetizers being served by white gloved waiters and piano music being played in the background. The dance itself would start later, although the exact time had not been planned. Unlike the formal Victorian balls of decades ago, this was more of a social evening than one dictated by rules.

Heather and Aly drifted through the sparse crowd, taking in the sight of the home at its most beautiful. Fully decorated, it looked better than Heather had dreamed that it would. While the Christmas tree had been removed, many of the other Christmas decorations had been incorporated. Colorful banners had been hung from the ceiling, lace and garland woven through bannisters, champagne glasses gleamed, and the hearth celebrated alongside with a hearty fire. The grand chandelier in the front parlor was adorned with a single strand of mistletoe at its base, and its light cast a brilliant glow across the entire room. The smile of satisfaction on Heather's face was every bit its equal.

As the hour wore on, the majority of the guests arrived, all dressed impeccably. Heather and Alyssa made it their goal to greet every newcomer as the unofficial hostesses. It was only when several of their classmates arrived that they finally relinquished their duties to Margaret.

Of the classmates that came, none were particularly close to Heather, although Debra Feldham was quite friendly with Aly. The only boy that showed up was Tollinder Müller, and unusual young man that had immigrated from Germany only a few years prior. Heather attempted to make small talk with him, along with a couple of the other girls who stood nearby. As the appetizers finished, the sound of the piano began to grow, and the crowd began to take notice.

One by one, people found their way to the larger front room that had been prepared for dancing. The piano had been placed in the alcove created by the home's largest bay window, its music fast and upbeat. The group joined in, taking partners where they could find them and dancing to the music. None of them were particularly good dancers, but all of them seemed to enjoy themselves.

The evening passed quickly. Heather and Aly danced and socialized, taking in every moment. Eventually, they grew tired of dancing and took to the parlor, where the fire still burned brightly. On their way, one of the waiters offered hot cider, and both girls accepted gladly.

The parlor itself was actually two large rooms separated by pocket doors, so the music was quieted but not snuffed out entirely. Heather found herself tapping her foot with the rhythm in spite of herself, making it hard to drink without spilling.

In this room, many guests sat in comfortable chairs and sipped champagne or cognac, discussing the topics of the day or other matters. Heather recognized only a few of the people and simply smiled when she caught the eye of strangers. Even though the room was crowded, they found themselves a place close to the fire.

"It's so perfect, don't you think?" Alyssa asked, taking a sip of the warm cider.

"It is, it really is. Everything turned out just how I hoped it would. And so many people came!" Heather responded. "I didn't actually think that anyone from class would come."

"I thought Debra would. She and I have been talking about it quite a bit. But I'm surprised the others did."

"I wonder how your mom is enjoying it," Heather said, casting a glance back towards the door, beyond which couples were still dancing and music was playing.

"Oh, you know her, she's eating up every moment of it. She's been fluttering back and forth all night long; I don't think she's sat down for a moment."

Heather knew that she was right. Margaret might complain tomorrow about how much work would be needed to clean up or how many people she'd needed to talk to, but it was all a show; she was thoroughly enjoying the attention.

As they sipped their cider and continued to chat, Heather marveled at the difference between one night and the next. Just yesterday, she'd been crying herself to sleep, sure that everything was ruined. Tonight she was sitting here with her best friend, surrounded by the most celebratory atmosphere of her life. What a difference a day can make.

Aly excused herself and headed for the bathroom that was located opposite the dining room. Heather sat and sipped her cider, enjoying the warmth from the corner fireplace. By the time she'd finished, she was beginning to wonder what was keeping Aly. She stood and walked through the dining room, leaving her empty cup with a waiter that passed her along the way.

The dining room was sparsely populated, only a few people stood around, picking from the various food spreads that remained. The bathroom in the corner was unoccupied. Left without other options, Heather proceeded through the door to the south towards the entryway and staircase. As she rounded the corner, she stopped cold. The front room was still filled with dancing couples, although the previous rag music had been replaced with a slower, more traditional sound. There, near the center of the dance floor, was Alyssa, dancing closely with Bryce.

The sight made her heart wrench. Something about the way that he held her told her that this was no simple chance encounter or dance between friends. She wasn't sure how she knew, but she was certain that this had been his plan all along. As Heather watched, the dance carried them to the very center of the floor, directly beneath the intricate glass chandelier. Bryce glanced up at it and smiled; Alyssa followed his gaze. The two of them looked at each other for a moment before they kissed, their lips parting ever so slightly as they met.

Chapter Twenty-Four

Jason felt his heart ache as he read through Cali's letter for the third time in the two days since it had arrived. There was something about her words that resonated with him; her problems suddenly seemed like his problems. His anger at Micah, someone that he'd never even met, came swiftly, and he wished that he could deal with the situation himself.

As she wrote about her friendship with Alyssa and Bryce, Jason again felt a tug at his heartstrings. Her situation felt uncomfortably like his own.

He tried to write a response but found himself stymied. The thoughts and emotions that he wanted to express wouldn't arrange themselves on paper. After nearly thirty minutes of effort, he crumpled up the sheet he'd been writing on and threw it in frustration.

He put Cali's letter aside and rubbed his eyes. The day had only just begun, but he felt as though he should already be returning to bed. Instead, he got up and went downstairs. He looked around but didn't see either of his parents anywhere. Glancing out the window, he noticed a path in the snow heading towards the barn.

Jason put on his heavy coat and laced up his boots before making his way outside to follow the footsteps of his father. The snow was high, several inches of fresh powder having fallen overnight, and Jason felt it swish as he walked.

The barn was warmer than the outside air. The body heat of the various animals, cows and horses mostly, helped to warm the space even in January; the smell was just an unfortunate byproduct. Huddled in a corner was Dean, his gloved hands working on something that Jason couldn't quite see.

"Come over and help me with this," Dean said, not even bothering to turn around.

Jason shuffled over and stood beside his father who was struggling with their seeder.

"Here, hold this," his father said, handing Jason a set of pliers and a lamp.

Picking up a larger wrench, his father grunted with effort as he attempted to loosen a seized nut. "Give that a pull, would ya?" Dean asked rhetorically. Jason set the pliers down and pulled on the seeder's arm. The tug lessened the tension on the nut and, with another grunt, Dean was able to spin the wrench.

"Good. Been meaning to do this for a while. Figured today was as good a day as any," Dean said as he wiped his sweaty brow with the back of a stained work glove.

"Do you need help now?" Jason asked. He hadn't originally intended to work, but he knew it was better to offer than be told.

"No, now that I've got this off I just need to file the post down a bit and then lubricate everything. Nothing that needs two people to get done. Did you want something?"

"Nah, I was just thinking about going into town, and I didn't see you or mom anywhere. Where is she, by the way?"

"She went into town, too. I guess she forgot something when she went yesterday. Anyway, I don't want you going today, I don't need any help with this, but I may need some help with the wagon a bit later. I want you around just in case. Besides, your mom will be home soon, and then she'll get lunch for us."

Jason sighed. He didn't actually have a reason to go into town, he was just bored of the house. Between the snow and the work he and his father had been doing on the farm equipment, he hadn't gone anywhere outside the farm for nearly a week, and he was going stir crazy.

"Alright. Well, if you don't need me now, I'll be back inside. Guess I can clean out the fireplace. mom's been bugging me about that. Yell if you need me."

Dean looked impressed. "Will do. Come get me when your mother gets home. I'm starving."

Jason returned to the house, attempting to track in as little snow as possible. After he'd taken off his coat and boots, he set to the task of the fireplace, a chore he particularly loathed. It was nearly an hour later when his mother arrived. Jason was just finishing up when she walked in, hanging up her coat and dusting off her shoes at the door. When she looked up, she smiled, clearly happy that Jason had finally attended to the task she'd been bothering him about for weeks.

"I'm glad you finally found time to do that. Are you hungry? I'm going to make lunch."

Jason was hungry and nodded in the affirmative. After he'd cleaned off his filthy hands, he shouted out the back door at his father and then sat down at the table and waited patiently.

"Your friend wrote you again," Kathleen said as she prepared several sandwiches. "I put the envelope on your desk yesterday, did you see it?"

"I did, thanks. I've actually been meaning to write my reply all morning but haven't found the right words. I think maybe I'll try to go finish it now."

"That can wait, here, eat your lunch," Kathleen said, setting a plate with a sandwich filled with meat on the table. As she did so, Dean arrived in from the barn and made his way to the table.

"Hey! Take your shoes off, I just cleaned," Kathleen admonished. Dean gave her a look that said, 'yes, dear', and complied. He took a seat beside Jason, and the two ate in relative silence. Jason consumed his sandwich in record time, suddenly eager to respond. When he'd finished, he hastily brought the plate to the counter, wiped it off, and said, "Thanks Mom!" before making a beeline for his room.

Once inside, Jason read her newest letter one more time, soaking in every detail.

Dear Jason,

I know that this letter will come off as emotional, but I just don't know who else to talk to. I feel like everything is going wrong, and I just don't have anywhere else to go. I hope that you won't read this and think of me as a silly girl because of it.

I'm so trapped here. Last weekend, my father and brother got into an argument. Micah was furious that my father had suggested he move out. In his anger, he threw beets across the room and ruined my exceptional copper gown. It happened the night before the ball that Aly and I have been planning for months.

My mother miraculously found another dress for me, and the dance went on as scheduled. Even in spite of my brother, everything turned out so wonderfully. It seemed like it was meant to be, at least at first.

My friend Bryce told us that he wasn't going to come, and I actually felt slightly relieved at that. I have had some feelings for him for a long time, and lately it's seemed like he's ignoring me. Like he doesn't want to be around me. Anyway, he showed up to the dance even though he said he wasn't going to.

I guess the whole reason he did was so that he could tell Aly how he felt about her. I walked in on the two of them dancing and kissing. It was humiliating! She just kissed him, right out there in the open and in front of everyone. I feel completely betrayed, and now the one real friend I thought I had doesn't even feel like a friend anymore. I don't know what to do.

I don't think I can watch them together. I really can't. I just want to leave and start over.

She'd left the letter, clearly marked with tear stains, unsigned. Jason hated to hear her hurt, even from thousands of miles away, but he knew there was nothing that he could really do to help her.

Writing a letter wasn't going to solve her problems even if he could think of something encouraging to say. He paced the room a while, debating internally about what to say. Still uninspired, his eagerness to respond faded. Deciding once again to try later, he returned to the dining room where his parents sat side by side at the table.

"So, how is she doing?" Kathleen asked, picking at a few green beans she'd taken from one of her canning jars.

"She's...," Jason didn't know what to say. He didn't feel as though it was his place to share her struggles with anyone else, even his own family. "working hard in school. You know, normal stuff." It wasn't completely a lie, but it wasn't completely the truth, either, and he felt bad for saying it.

"I see. I forgot to mention, I saw Calvin and Heather today, they were walking towards the library. I didn't know that they were together."

Jason looked up at her comment, unsure of her meaning. "Together? What do you mean?"

"Together, you know. They were holding hands. Looked quite happy. Good for them," she said, surprisingly unaware of the effect of her words on Jason.

Jason felt like the air had been sucked out of his chest. The revelation was, while not entirely surprising, confirmation of one of his deepest emotional worries, and he felt empty because of it.

"I... I didn't know either," he said, completely lost for words.

Chapter Twenty-Five

As time moved on after the dance, Heather still struggled to cope with the new changes in her relationships with her friends. She knew that neither Bryce nor Aly had intended to hurt her, but knowing that did little to help. She was the third wheel, and she knew it.

Even when she was alone with Aly, the closeness they'd shared their whole lives felt strained. There had been a change in their friendship, and it was painfully obvious to both of them. She found herself making excuses to avoid spending time with her best friend, something she would never have done previously.

When they were together, Heather made it abundantly clear that she had no interest in discussing Bryce in any capacity. Aly had tried to breech the subject early on, to apologize and attempt to make amends, but Heather had shut her down. As far as Heather was concerned, Bryce no longer existed.

She found herself spending more and more time alone, and her thoughts inexplicably drifting to the boy in Iowa. Although she was initially hesitant, fearful that she would scare him away, Heather began to write to him on a near daily basis. Even though most of the letters were short, she felt as though the very act of writing them helped her to escape from her surroundings.

One of the letters she'd received in return held a special place in her heart, and she re-read it often. It had arrived shortly after the catastrophe at the dance and had been one of the few things able to make her smile in the weeks afterwards.

Dear Cali,

I am saddened to hear about all of the terrible things that you have been going through. As I read your letters, I feel such a strong connection to your life, and I truly wish that there was anything I could do to help you. I know that I am a stranger who lives far away, but I've grown to cherish hearing from you.

Is there anyone else that you are close to that you could talk with? I think you need to find other friends that care about you and who value you for who you are. Even though you have been friends with Alyssa and Bryce for a long time, it doesn't seem like they took you into account whatsoever. They could have handled the situation with so much more care.

If you were my friend (although I do consider you a friend) and they treated you like that, I would have very strong words for them.

If you were here, I would be happy to help you in any way that I could.

Have you given any thought to what you would like to do after you complete high school? When I feel down, I like to think about how the future will be better.

Around here there's not very much to do, although we do have it better than many I suppose. Cedar Falls is within walking distance, and it is nice to have a larger town nearby. If you lived here I would suggest that you go to the Normal School there. It's supposed to be a great school for teachers. You've never mentioned a desire to teach, but I think you'd be a really good one. If you move out, I'll be sure to give you a tour!

The rest of the letter faded away as Heather focused on that last sentence. Although she didn't believe Jason had been suggesting that she move, the very thought of it had taken residence in her mind. She found herself thinking about what it would be like to move across the country and start afresh.

Over the course of the next few months, Heather felt increasingly connected to Jason, and, she liked to think, he felt the same way. She'd also started to think of her home in a different way. Although she still adored her parents, she began to think of her home as a temporary situation. That change in thinking helped her to cope with Micah, even as his behavior grew increasingly violent and disruptive.

As the months had passed by, they continued to share their most intimate details with each other, as well as supporting one another as they each struggled through friendships that were undergoing radical changes. On May 1st, 1897, a letter arrived that took Heather's breath away.

Dearest Cali,

Over the course of time I have grown to care deeply about you. I've come to realize that you are truly one of my closest friends. Although I spend a significant amount of time with Calvin and Heather, it's you who I truly wish was by my side.

I have been saving for a long time. Initially, I was saving money simply because I didn't have anything to spend it on, but now I have a purpose. I would like to come and visit you in California. I have not yet told my parents about this desire, but as I am now of age, I don't believe they will object too strenuously.

I wouldn't be able to leave until planting season has finished, but by early July I think I could come out for a week or so without difficulty. I have saved just enough money to cover a roundtrip ticket, so I would need to locate lodging during my stay. Is there somewhere nearby with reasonable rates?

I will understand if you find this to be too presumptive, although I presume nothing other than some time in your company.

I appreciate your friendship deeply and hope that you will write back with welcome news.

Sincerely,

Jason Baldwin

Heather could not believe what he had written. His desire to visit her was the most welcome news that she had ever received, and she immediately began planning the details. The first step was to convince her mother. She waited several days for the perfect opportunity to present itself. When it did, she took full advantage.

"Mom, I had a question for you. Do you think that a friend could come and stay with us for a few days next month?"

Lynn was in a particularly good mood that day. Her best friend had been over to visit, and they had enjoyed a wonderful morning. In addition, the previous day Edward had been promoted once again, and Lynn was happy for the additional comforts. "A friend, hmm? Would that friend be Jason, by any chance?"

"Well, I don't think it would be a problem. We do have that extra room after all and...," Heather was cut off as Lynn began to speak.

"My sewing room, you mean? That extra room? The one that is right next to yours?"

Heather blushed, feeling her heart start to beat faster. She didn't want anything to get in the way of Jason coming out. "Yes, but it's also right next to yours and Daddy's."

"What would your father say? Do you think he'd be alright with that arrangement?" Lynn asked, but Heather had already thought through this line of argument.

"Well, he wouldn't have to know. We could just call Jason 'a friend', we wouldn't have to mention anything more. Besides, he works so much that he's hardly ever home."

Lynn cast her daughter a sideways glance and tried to hold back a smile. "I don't see why not. I'm going to have to think about how to tell your father, though," Lynn said, hardly getting the comment out before Heather surged forward and embraced her.

"Thank you! I love you! Thank you!" Heather said, releasing Lynn and running from the room to write back to Jason immediately.

Chapter Twenty-Six

Jason told his father of his intentions to go to California shortly after Cali's letter had arrived. His response had been predictable, "Not until we finish in the fields you're not," he'd said. Beyond that he voiced no objections.

Kathleen had been a different story entirely. Even though he was of age and fully capable of taking care of himself, Kathleen worried deeply about the trip, agonizing over every possible thing that could go wrong. Fortunately, with Dean's measured support, Jason knew that his mother wouldn't attempt to stop him.

In the following weeks, Jason planned for the trip as best he could and continued to save what little money he earned. He hadn't mentioned it to Cali, but the majority of the money for the trip had come when he'd sold his small coin collection. It hadn't been much, but he'd been collecting for years and the sale was nearly enough to cover the ticket on its own. The additional money came from doing odd jobs for Mr. Murphy or Franklin Lovell down at the mill.

When he wasn't busy working at home or elsewhere, Jason still spent time with his friends. Both Calvin and Heather seemed happy, and Jason tried to be happy for them, although it continued to be a struggle. He'd done his best to shift his focus away from their affections and simply enjoy the time that he had with them.

"Did you hear?" Heather had said, one particularly hot day in the middle of June. Jason shook his head. "I made it in! I got accepted to Drake!"

Jason smiled and hugged her. He knew that it meant she would be moving away, but he couldn't help but be happy for her.

"That's fantastic! When did you find out?" he asked, breaking their embrace.

"The letter came yesterday, I could hardly wait to tell you both. I need to be there in late August to get registered and set up in their dormitory."

Jason looked over at Calvin, who stood just a few feet away. It felt like Calvin wanted to say something more, but instead he simply grinned and said, "Isn't it great? She's going to be the best student there, I can tell you right now."

"I agree with you, Calvin," Jason said, still looking at his friend. There was something there, but he couldn't quite place it. Deciding not to press the issue further, Jason started asking Heather questions about the move, about whether she was nervous, and generally passing the time by discussing everything to do with the college.

Once they had covered every topic Jason could think of, he decided that it was as good a time as any to inform them of his own journey.

"So, I have some news, too," he started, "I'm going to California in about two weeks."

"California?" Calvin burst out, "Why?"

"He's going to see Cali, that's why. Isn't it obvious?" Heather said, slapping Calvin playfully as if he was an idiot for missing it.

"Yep, that's right. I'm going out to see her for about a week. I've been saving up for a while and…,"

"And I think it's great," Heather said, interrupting. "It's about time that you made a move with her. Everyone knows she's special to you. You talk about her all the time."

Jason blushed. He didn't think that he talked about her as much as Heather made out. "I just want to see her in person. After all these months of writing it feels like I should, you know?"

Calvin was the next to speak, giving him some words of dubious worldly advice. Heather just rolled her eyes.

"Ignore him. Buy her flowers, compliment her dress. You'll do fine," Heather said, not letting Calvin completely finish.

The three of them spent the rest of the afternoon swimming in the farm pond at the back of Heather's property. It was about the most casual interaction that they had enjoyed in months, and Jason was loathe for it to end. Even though Heather would be leaving at the end of the summer, it felt like things would still work out just as they were meant to.

Jason was planning to stay overnight with Calvin, and after they'd finished swimming, the two boys left and made their way west toward his house.

"So, are you nervous?" Calvin asked. "I've always wanted to go out West, just never actually had a reason to. I'm kind of envious."

"Only a bit. I hope her parents like me. It was so nice of them to agree to let me stay with them; that'll help so much with the cost."

"Do you have any idea what you are going to do while you are out there?"

Jason laughed, "None at all. I genuinely have no idea whatsoever." Jason shook his head as they continued walking. "Am I crazy for going? I've only met this girl once, and I'm going across the country to see her and stay in her parents' house. Is that nuts?"

"It is kind of nutty, but if you really like her, who knows?" Calvin said, slapping Jason on the back as he did so. "I mean, we do crazy things for the people we love, you know?"

Jason frowned. He didn't know why, but something about the way he said it made Jason feel annoyed. He tried to shake it off, but it persisted. Unable to put it aside, Jason decided to address it more directly.

"My mom said she saw you and Heather the other day."

"Oh? When was that? I never saw her."

"A couple days ago. Said that you two were headed towards the library. Mentioned that you two looked like you were comfortable together. Holding hands and everything," Jason said, staring pointedly at Calvin who refused to meet his gaze.

"Umm, yeah, I guess so," Calvin stuttered, not offering any further explanation and instead kicking at a pebble as he walked. He missed and swore under his breath. Jason continued to stare at him until Calvin finally raised his eyes. "Well, you know, it just kind of happened. We've been meaning to mention it to you, but it just hasn't come up."

Half a dozen reactions passed through Jason as he broke eye contact and looked straight ahead. One Jason wanted to know all of the details, to question when it started, to know exactly how. Another Jason wanted to simply turn around and go home.

Instead, he simply said, "You didn't have to hide it from me. You could have just told me upfront. I'm a big boy; I could have handled it."

"I know. It's my fault really. Heather didn't want to sneak around, but I didn't want it to be awkward. Everyone knows how you feel about her and...,"

"It's fine. Really," Jason cut him off. "I want you both to be happy. All that other stuff is the past. Besides, anymore it's not even a romantic thing, I just don't want to be the second best friend, you know?"

Calvin looked a little confused, or perhaps just uncomfortable, Jason couldn't quite tell. Continuing, he said, "Well now you two are dating, right? So when she treats us differently that's fine. You don't treat your friends the way you treat your love interests. It's all okay."

Calvin looked at him, apparently trying to decipher whether or not Jason was telling the truth or simply putting up a front. After a few moments, he averted his eyes and stared at the road ahead of them.

"Well, I hope you mean that," Calvin said, eventually.

"I do, I really do," Jason responded, his voice firm and resolute.

"There's something else I have to tell you. I guess there is no better time than now. Like you said, no sense in hiding anything, right?"

Jason was suddenly worried. The calm that he'd experienced just a few hours ago, the sense that everything would go as it was supposed to, had been replaced by a sudden anxiety.

"The thing is, well, Heather is going off to college," Calvin paused to glance at Jason before continuing. "She's going to college, and I just kind of want to see what more is out there and…"

"And you're going with her," Jason interrupted, his voice tight in his throat.

"Well, not with her, exactly. But my uncle offered me a job working at his restaurant and… and I'm going to go. Not right away, but…," Calvin trailed off.

"So you're leaving? Just like that?" Jason said, anger flashing.

"Like I said, not right away. After the harvest. But yes, I'm moving to Des Moines."

This time, the second Jason won. He spun on his heel and walked away, never once glancing backwards.

Chapter Twenty-Seven

The chatter of wheels as the train moved past a crossing woke Jason from a light sleep. He felt like he had not slept at all the night before. One of the men sharing his sleeper car had snored so loudly that even the methodical rhythm of the train could not keep Jason at rest. He regretted spending the extra money on a sleeper car for the last leg of the journey; he should have simply travelled by day coach as he'd done for the previous three nights.

The process of making it to California had been easier than he had expected. After catching a train south to Cedar Rapids, he'd been able to go directly to Council Bluffs and pick up the Pacific Railroad. From there, he had been able to travel straight to

Sacramento with just two connections. He'd only splurged for the sleeper car on the last leg, hoping to be fresh for his arrival. The other two days he'd hired day coaches and slept in the stations.

The train's whistle blew loudly as it approached the terminal. Jason was glad that the journey was finally coming to an end, but he was even more excited to finally be reunited with Heather. It had often seemed to him that this day would never come, and now that it had, he could hardly hold back a grin.

He collected his belongings as the train slowed and prepared to stop. The squeak of the brakes sounded briefly before the train rocked and then settled beside the platform. He made his way down the row of cars until he came to the exit where he waited his turn. Finally stepping down, he glanced around, looking for the red haired beauty that he knew was waiting for him. As he scanned the platform, he wrinkled his nose, recoiling at the pungent aroma of diesel and body odor.

He heard a squeal and jerked his head towards the sound. A flash of red caught his eye amidst the crowd. Turning in that direction, the sea of humanity suddenly parted, leaving him to stare at the woman he'd travelled all this way to see.

She was dressed in a long red gown that was trimmed around the collar in white with puffy sleeves. A bow was tied around her waist, accentuating her figure. The dress seemed exceptionally formal for the occasion, but it was exquisite nonetheless. She also wore a matching hat topped with a single black feather. Jason smiled broadly, completely dumbstruck.

Heather returned his smile, although her own made his look feeble. She was one of the most gorgeous sights that he had ever seen, and her dress made him feel shabby and unworthy. Even so, she ran up and embraced him, not even pausing to speak first.

In that moment, Jason felt something shift within him. It was as if the world had fallen into place, and the pieces that had previously been missing were suddenly restored. His heartbeat slowed, and he felt as though he may lose consciousness.

He took a deep breath, his lungs filling with the fresh version of the scent he'd now breathed in from so many envelopes. It was exhilarating in a way that he could not have explained, even had his life depended on it.

Although he hated doing so, Jason broke their embrace and looked down at Heather. She was shorter than he remembered, although that observation made her no less physically appealing to him. If anything, her height made her seem cute and delicate, and his smile returned as he looked at her.

She returned his smile and was the first to break their silence.

"I'm so glad that you are finally here! It seemed like it took forever. How was the trip?" Heather asked.

Jason was so taken aback that he didn't immediately respond. His head felt as though he were intoxicated, and his chest thumped one beat after the next. He instinctively reached out and took her hand, realizing only later how forward that was. Fortunately, Heather didn't hesitate, taking his hand in hers gladly.

"It was fine. A bit longer than I'd have liked, but no real problems, unless you count snoring strangers." Heather laughed at that, and Jason felt a flutter in his stomach at the sound. It sounded the way that happy felt.

It was only then that Jason looked over Heather's shoulder and saw a woman watching them from about ten feet away. She was about the same height as Heather but dressed far more modestly. Her long brown hair flowed nearly down to her shoulders, and Jason could tell that it would be difficult to brush for its abundance.

Her skin was darker than Heather's, but she shared the same facial features. Although he had never actually met her, Jason knew that this must be her mother. The woman noticed Jason looking at her and walked over to where he and Heather stood.

"Hello, I'm Lynn. It's nice to meet you," she said, and extended her hand. Jason shook it and nodded. "It's a pleasure," he added.

The three of them chatted as they left the platform and then the station. Much of the conversation was about the trivial details of his trip, the weather, and other pleasantries. Jason felt himself distracted by the hustle and bustle of the city.

Bicycles were everywhere, and men and women alike rode them down streets and sidewalks. Jason wondered how so many people could have so many places to go all at the same time. Although he had travelled with his family on their way to France, their time in cities larger than Cedar Falls had been almost entirely limited to Cannes, France, which was no more than a third of the population of Sacramento.

"Do you like to ride?" Heather asked, noticing his interest in the many bicycles.

"I do, but I broke a wheel a few months ago and haven't been able to replace it yet, so I haven't ridden in a while," Jason said, neglecting to mention that the reason he hadn't been able to mend the bicycle was because he'd been saving for this trip. "Do you?"

"Oh, I love to ride! I would ride absolutely everywhere if I could. Mom says that it's not proper," Heather said, casting a sideways glance at Lynn, who gave her a reproving look, "but I think it's wonderful. And all the new dresses that are being made to make it easier are beautiful!"

Jason wasn't well informed about the changes in women's attire, but he had noticed an increasing number of short dresses back home in Cedar Falls. He was surprised to learn that the two concepts were intertwined.

"Maybe you could use Edward's bike, and you and Heather could go for a ride?" Lynn suggested, as if to counter her daughter's rebuke. "I know that he wouldn't mind. He works so much anymore that he never has the opportunity to ride it anyway."

"We should! Maybe we could do that tonight before he gets home," Heather said before another thought occurred to her, "or are you too tired? I'm sorry, I didn't even stop to consider that you've been travelling. Maybe we should just take it easy today."

"No, no, I'd love to, really. It would be nice to properly stretch. After four days of sitting on a train, I need the exercise."

"Great! We can pack a basket and ride down to the river. There's a beautiful little park there, and we can have lunch. You didn't already eat, did you?"

Jason shook his head. It was nearly noon, and he felt himself suddenly aware of how hungry he'd become.

"It's a plan, then. I'll pack a lunch as soon as we get home while you drop off your suitcase and change if you need to," Heather said. She then cocked her head slightly to the side as though something had just occurred to her.

"When is daddy going to be home? Do you think he is going to be alright with… everything?" she asked her mother.

"I think he'll be fine. I was planning to speak with him today as soon as he got home," Lynn said, with only the slightest trace of uncertainty in her voice. "But maybe the two of you should stay out a bit later to make sure that I have the chance. What do you think?"

Jason wasn't sure what to make of their exchange. *Had Heather not told her father that he was coming?* he wondered. He was just about to ask when Heather turned back in his direction.

"Sorry, you must wonder what we're talking about," she said.

"Well, yes, a little. Does your father not know that I'm here?"

"Oh no, he knows that you are coming," Heather said, doubling Jason's curiosity and apprehension, "it's just that he doesn't know you are...," she trailed off and looked at Lynn.

"What my daughter means to say," Lynn started, "is that he doesn't know that Heather has invited a boy to stay with her underneath our roof."

Chapter Twenty-Eight

Jason couldn't believe that Heather had not told her father that he was coming. Or rather, that she'd neglected to mention that he was, in fact, a 'he'. *What is he going to do? Will he kick me out?* Jason wondered as they made their way back to the Burdett home and then started the bicycle ride together.

His concerns were quickly forgotten as he rode alongside Heather, the sweet smell of her perfume distracting him from all other thoughts. As they rode towards the park, he couldn't help but think about how lucky he was to be there. He was two thousand miles away from home, but he felt as though home was right beside him, riding a faded blue bicycle with a basket on the front.

The food, a few plain sandwiches with slices of apples, was modest but filling. As they sat there beneath the branches of a large oak tree, they discussed the plans that Heather had for his visit, which were much more extensive than he'd realized.

"I thought that we'd take the train into the city for the day tomorrow. It's really exciting and incredibly beautiful. If you think there are a lot of people in Sacramento, just wait until you see San Francisco!"

"That'd be great. I love to see new places," Jason replied.

"The city is busy, but there is so much to see and do. The last time that we were there, mom and I were able to walk through the Bonanza Inn and...," she trailed off as she saw the confused look on Jason's face.

"Bonanza Inn?" he asked, amused.

"It's actually called the Palace Hotel, but it's such a spectacle that I guess people were looking for a more impressive name. It's really something; there's a grand court in the middle of the building where you can look up at the balconies above. All of them have these white columns, and they are truly stunning. It even has rising rooms, although we weren't guests so we couldn't actually use them."

"Sounds amazing. Is that all we are going to see?"

"Oh, heaven's no! There's also the Ferry Building which we'll see right away, the hills, and the Sutro Baths! I haven't been yet, but I hear that the baths are extraordinary. Hopefully you like to swim."

"That sounds pretty exciting, and I love to swim. I'm sure we will have a great time together," Jason's voice faltered a bit as he said those last words, somehow the word 'together' carried special significance.

"I know we will, although I think my mother will insist on coming along with us to San Francisco. There are a lot of less pleasant things that go on there, too," Heather said, some of the excitement dampened.

"Your mom seems pleasant. I really like her," Jason said, trying to perk her back up.

"I know, I'd simply rather it be just be the two of us, you know?" Heather said, and smiled. "Anyway, let's go for a ride, shall we? We can ride all the way down to the courthouse and then walk a bit. There are some cute shops there; I can show you the dress I like, too."

And so they did. They spent the afternoon riding, walking, talking, and generally having a wonderful time. Although he restrained himself, Jason had the urge to take her hand nearly every time that he walked close enough to do so. The looks that Heather gave him led him to believe that she would have found the gesture to be more than acceptable.

They returned home shortly after six in the evening. Edward had returned home before them and was sitting near the front door in a large wing back chair. As they entered, he put down the paper that he was reading and stood to face them.

"Heather, why don't you go help your mother with dinner," his tone was that of a command even though his words indicated a question. "I need to have a chat with this young man." Heather looked back and forth between Jason and Edward before nodding her head and leaving the room.

"Sir, I just want…," Jason started, but paused when Edward raised his hand.

"It's fine. Lynn has filled me in on the details. Although I'm not happy with the way that it was handled, I am not angry."

Jason felt his heartbeat slow and the anxiety he'd carried lessen. *He's not going to kick me out*, he thought in relief.

"You are welcome to stay here, in the far room, during your stay. All I ask is that you treat my daughter with the respect that your family has already shown to us. Any woman that would risk what your mother did to help us has surely raised a young man who will treat Heather well."

"Yes, sir, I will. Thank you," Jason said, and Edward simply nodded, returning to his seat and his paper.

Jason stood there awkwardly, unsure of whether he should stay with Edward or find Heather. He decided to sit down on the sofa opposite Edward, who did not look up from his reading as he did so. A few minutes passed before Lynn entered the room and told them that dinner was ready. She looked both Jason and Edward over, pressed her lips together in a smirk, and then returned to the kitchen.

The meal was delightful, a mix of vegetables served alongside roasted game hen. Jason knew that he risked making a fool of himself, but he couldn't help but ask for seconds, and then thirds. Lynn took his requests as a compliment and served him gladly.

"So, how long are you staying?" Edward asked after he'd finished the last bites of his meal.

"Five days. I wanted to stay a bit longer, but my father was adamant that I return. He actually wanted me back even sooner," Jason said, still finishing up the remaining scraps of his third helping.

Edward didn't reply and just nodded. Heather continued instead. "We're going to go into the city tomorrow, Daddy. Don't worry, Mom is going with." Edward looked over at Lynn who cocked her head slightly to the side and gave him a warning look that apparently meant not to argue.

"You'll be home before dark, I'll hear nothing else," Edward said, not breaking eye contact with his wife. "The city is still a rough place. You'll be careful, yes?"

"Of course we will, Edward," Lynn said. "We're just going to go for a few hours. See the Palace, visit the Baths. We'll be fine."

They continued talking about the coming days, making plans and discussing the details of his brief time there. By the end, Jason felt somewhat overwhelmed. The sheer volume of activity that Heather had planned for their time together was staggering, and he felt as though he were being treated like a prince. It was discomforting and made him feel self-conscious.

He sat in his bed that evening thinking about what a wild change of pace this was from his normal life. Rather than long days of work, he was able to simply concentrate on enjoying himself. No decisions to be made, no awkward interactions with friends, just quality time with someone he cared for very much. He drifted off to sleep with a smile on his face.

Heather woke Jason with a rhythmic knock on his door. Her voice was soft as she spoke.

"Breakfast is nearly ready if you'd like to join us," she said.

"Umm, yes, of course. I'll be right there," he said, tossing the covers off and searching for something to put on. "Just a minute!"

After he'd hurriedly dressed, he opened the door and headed for the dining room. The windows that faced the backyard were bright with sunlight and Jason realized how late he'd slept. *I hope they didn't hold breakfast for me*, he thought.

Heather greeted him as he entered the room. She was dressed in a dark blue dress, hemmed in a lighter blue lace. Her long red hair flowed down her back and was illuminated by the sunlight spilling in from the east. Jason felt his breath catch in his throat.

"As soon as we're done eating we need to leave to catch the train, is that alright?" Heather asked.

"Sure, that's fine. Sounds wonderful," Jason responded after a moment, still recovering from his initial reaction at seeing her.

They ate quickly and made small talk, most of which revolved around their upcoming trip into San Francisco. Jason felt a flutter in his chest as he listened to Heather talk through their agenda. Everything sounded so large and so exciting, and Jason was eager to start moving.

The train ride was unremarkable, a gentle southward plod from Sacramento to the west side of the Bay. As they waited for the ferry to arrive, Jason and Heather found a bench that faced the city, although a dense fog obscured the view almost entirely. Lynn stood a ways off, apparently cognizant of their desire for some time to themselves.

"It's beautiful, in a strange sort of way," Jason said as he stared across the water. Acutely aware of Heather staring at him instead of the view, Jason added, "and so are you."

"I'm strange?" Heather asked and Jason felt heat rise in his face.

"I meant," he stammered, "I meant you are beautiful. The strange part was just for the city. Two different things."

Heather attempted to look serious, but before she could hold her stern expression for long, she broke down in laughter. "You should see the look on your face!" she said, still laughing, a cute little snort escaping right at the end. Heather looked mortified, but it caused Jason to break down right beside her. She may have thought it was embarrassing, but Jason thought it was one of the most adorable things he'd ever heard. They sat there, both red-faced and laughing, until the ferry parted the fog and began to dock.

Chapter Twenty-Nine

The Sutro Baths were a spectacle unlike any Jason had ever seen. There were six saltwater pools spanning hundreds of feet and another freshwater pool equally as large. There were slides, rings for swinging, and even a large springboard at the far northern end of the complex.

It was a wonder that people didn't drown, the pools were a swarming mass of splashing bodies and flailing arms. The commotion was sufficient to create whitecaps on the pool's waves, and, in fact, the pool itself looked more white than blue. It was truly a spectacular display.

Both Jason and Heather had gone down each of the seven slides at least a dozen times, although only Jason had been brave enough to jump off the high springboard. Lynn had paid for them to get in and then gone to the gigantic amphitheater to watch a show. Jason had felt bad about letting her pay until he realized that the cost was only twenty-five cents.

"Jason, what do you think? I'm exhausted and a bit sore," Heather said, breathing hard after exiting the pool and sitting on the edge beside him.

"Yeah, I think I'm ready too. This is the greatest place ever, though. It's amazing," Jason said, looking at Heather. She was dressed in one of the provided bathing suits, but it seemed as though it had been made uniquely for her. It was tighter at top and bottom than any bathing suit Jason had ever seen a girl wear, somehow both covering her entirely and simultaneously revealing more than he had ever seen. He knew that he'd been staring too long and quickly turned away.

Heather didn't seem to notice. She simply nodded, and they looked over the facility together for a few more moments before heading to separate dressing rooms. When they'd finished dressing, they met back up and headed towards the amphitheater to look for Heather's mother. Not finding her there, they continued to the attached museum and wandered through the exhibits featuring stuffed animals, historical artifacts, and artwork. Browsing casually, it took them nearly thirty minutes to find Lynn, who was looking at a particularly enormous stuffed bear.

"Mom, there you are! We've been looking everywhere," Heather said as she gave her a hug.

"Hello, you two. Did you have fun?" Lynn responded with a smile, showing no signs that she was disturbed at how long they'd been swimming.

"It was incredible, Mrs. Burdett, really something special."

"Great, I'm glad to hear it! Are you getting hungry?"

"I'm starving, mom. Let's go eat," Heather said, picking up her mom's bag and digging through it to evaluate their dinner options. Lynn had packed sandwiches and carrots, along with a few shortbread cookies.

"Well, I think it's too late to see the Palace, but we can take a railcar to South Park. The last ferry leaves at 5pm, so we need to head back right afterwards," Lynn said, casting her eyes on the large grandfather clock standing near the museum's exit. It was nearly 2PM; they'd been swimming for almost four hours.

Their dinner was delicious, and South Park was absolutely beautiful. A large oval, the park's lawn was surprisingly well manicured. The morning fog had largely lifted, and the crisp air felt exhilarating as Jason inhaled the smell of the city. It wasn't exactly pleasant, but it was still invigorating.

They finished and returned to the ferry, arriving back to the train station with only a few minutes to spare. Although their trip to the city had included fewer stops than anticipated, Jason felt satisfaction rise in his chest and escape through a smile he couldn't seem to contain.

"What are you thinking about?" Heather asked, sitting close beside him and briefly touching her head to his shoulder. The momentary contact sent a wave through him, as though she were the largest static shock he'd ever felt.

"Oh, nothing, just thinking how nice of a day it was. I really had a lot of fun. It was… something I'll never forget." As he said it, Jason wasn't sure whether it was the grand experience itself, or the company, that inspired him to phrase it that way.

That evening, Jason and Heather spent the night in the backyard. Both of Heather's parents thought they were in their separate bedrooms asleep, but they'd snuck out and met to lay underneath the stars together.

For a July in California, the weather was surprisingly crisp. The blanket that Heather had brought for them to lay on was soon used for its original purpose, warming them both from the chill. As they shared the blanket, Jason felt anticipation flow through him. This was the closest that he'd ever been to another person, much less a girl, and that closeness made his chest tighten and his heart beat fast.

"Are you cold? We could go inside if you'd like," Jason said, although he wasn't entirely sure why.

"No, I'm plenty warm. As long as I'm next to you," Heather said and shimmied even closer. Jason could feel her warmth pressed into him, passively urging him to get closer still. He risked it, pressing himself fully next to her. She answered with a slight movement of her buttocks, and shivers ran up Jason's spine.

"It's beautiful back here. Do you come out a lot?" Jason asked, trying to distract himself from the beautiful woman invading his personal space. He didn't expect that any conversation could possibly make that a reality.

"Not as much as I should. For some reason, it never seems like a priority. When I have extra time, I usually end up spending it buried in a book, not looking up at the stars."

"It's gorgeous. Truly, uhm, something special," Jason said, his words momentarily catching in his throat as Heather shifted her weight back and forth against him. Jason thought that she may be doing it on purpose.

"Yes, I can tell that you are enjoying it," Heather said, shifting again. Jason felt his face flush and embarrassment rise in his chest.

Jason felt his mind swirl, unsure of what he should do in the face of such a brazen come on. Up until now, he'd always felt rejected by girls, but this girl was giving him every signal that she was more than just a little interested.

Jason started to speak, then closed his mouth instead. He closed his eyes, took a deep breath, and started again.

"Can I kiss you?" he said, realizing only after he'd asked how awkward that must have sounded. He stared into Heather's eyes as she processed his question. She didn't reply audibly, just nodded and leaned her head in close to his. Determined to do everything right, Jason put his hand gently behind her head and pulled her lips into his own.

Her lips were intoxicating, soft and wet. They kissed deeply for a few moments before parting, Jason's heart now hammering inside his chest. As he looked at Heather again, he started to say something, but she silenced him by leaning in for another kiss.

Any words he'd been contemplating fled, swept away by her lips and a rush of blood and adrenaline.

Chapter Thirty

"I can't find my shoes," Jason said to no one in particular. Heather was just leaving her bedroom and watched Jason scour the room, apparently for his shoes.

"Where did you take them off?" Heather asked, and Jason jumped with surprise. At that same moment, Lynn walked in through the rear door, her hands dirty and a trowel in her hand. "Mom, have you seen Jason's shoes?"

"Where did you take them off?" Lynn asked, echoing her daughter's question from moments earlier.

"Right here, at the landing last night after we, uh," Jason paused, risking a quick sideways glance at Heather, "after we got home."

"Well, I haven't seen them, maybe you left them in the backyard before you came inside," she paused, "for the second time." Lynn said as she headed for the kitchen, before the full meaning of her words could sink in.

Heather blushed furiously, unsure of how her mother knew that they'd spent the previous evening in the backyard together. Before the blush had faded, her brother Micah walked in the front door, slamming it behind him and barely looking up.

Heather couldn't help but notice that Micah looked awful, his hair was dirty and askew, as though it hadn't been washed in weeks, and none of his clothes seemed to have fared much better. She watched as Jason looked him over and was suddenly embarrassed, ashamed that her brother couldn't even bother to look presentable. She also saw a look of surprise cross Jason's face. Jason nodded as Micah passed by, but her brother didn't acknowledge him.

"I'm sorry about him," Heather started to say after Micah had retreated from the world and into the cave he called a bedroom, "he's just…,"

"Got my shoes," Jason interrupted, making her blink in surprise.

"What?"

"He… he was wearing my shoes," Jason said, as though the words were so bizarre that he didn't believe them himself.

"Why would he…," Heather said, almost to herself. The obvious explanation hit her before she could finish the comment. Her brother had been drunk when he'd left the house late last evening, and he'd taken the wrong shoes. She was more surprised that he'd worn shoes at all, half the time he left without. Barefoot Mike, people called him.

"Uhm, well, don't worry about it. I'll have my mom get them back. I'm sure it was an accident," Heather said, now both angry and embarrassed.

"Okay, sounds good. It's no big deal," Jason responded, now chuckling to himself. Heather supposed that was better than the alternatives.

The yelling started shortly thereafter, followed immediately by the sounds of a scuffle and broken glass. Lynn had gone into Micah's room to retrieve the shoes and all hell had broken loose. She returned to the living room with one shoe in hand and clutching her side.

"I'm okay, he just bumped me. It's okay," she said before either Jason or Heather had the opportunity to ask. "The other shoe is outside,… he threw it." *That accounts for the broken glass,* Heather thought to herself. Just one more thing for her father to fix.

Heather looked to Jason and apologized. "He's always crazy when he drinks. I'm really sorry. I'll go get your shoe, and then we can go out. I thought maybe we would go downtown, and I could show you what Sacramento really looks like."

Jason just nodded, seemingly unsure of what to make of the whole situation. He opened his mouth to say something, but before he could do so, Micah came storming down the hallway, another slammed door announcing his arrival.

"Where is it? Who took it?" Micah said, his voice threatening. "Was it your precious boyfriend? Huh?" Micah continued as he advanced towards Jason.

"What are you talking about? I didn't take anything," Jason said. Knowing her brother, Heather started to warn Jason that it was best to let Micah burn out on his own.

"Who else would have done it? Tell me that, who? Who?!" Micah was yelling now, spittle flying from his mouth and his voice cracking as he screamed.

"I don't even know what you're talking about, what am I supposed to have taken? I don't even drink, man," Jason continued, unaware that he was provoking a confrontation rather than avoiding one. It was at that moment that Heather realized that her brother wasn't simply drunk, he was high.

"Jason…," she implored, searching for the words to convince Jason to stop talking, "let's just go. Now."

Lynn was trying to calm Micah as he continued to shout and wave his arms, still holding Jason's shoe in her hand. Heather reached out and took the shoe, briefly making eye contact with her mother. An unspoken understanding passed between them, *let me weather this storm*, it said.

Heather took Jason's hand and guided them both around the large cream colored couch that sat between the two of them and her brother. Heather quickly grabbed her shoes, and they left. Heather could hear her brother's shouts even through the closed door behind them.

As soon as they reached the sidewalk, Heather sat down on the curb and buried her head in her hands. She didn't want Jason to see her cry, but she struggled to hold back the tears.

"Are you okay?" she heard Jason ask, as if such a question could be answered in a sentence or a paragraph or a book.

"I'm… I'll be fine. It's just my brother is…," *a constant reminder of our past*, she finished the thought internally.

"Kind of a jerk?" Jason finished for her, and they both laughed. "It's okay, really. I promise, he doesn't bother me."

Heather wiped away the tear that had formed at the corner of her eye and gave him a soft smile.

"Shall we go and locate your shoe?" Heather said with a quiet chortle. A few minutes later they'd found the shoe, made sure that it was free of glass shards, and were on their way towards downtown. Heather felt her heart lift as they glided down the hill leading away from her house. Away from the stress. Away from her past.

There was something about being beside Jason that felt like the future.

Chapter Thirty-One

The next morning was remarkably different than the previous one. The house was quiet, shoes were easily located, and Edward was even sitting at the kitchen table.

"Sit down and have some breakfast, Jason," Lynn said while pouring coffee into Edward's cup. Heather was sitting to her father's right and Jason couldn't help but notice that she was just as stunning today as she had been the first time he'd ever laid eyes on her in France. She momentarily took his breath away.

"Will Micah be joining us?" Jason asked after regaining his composure, wondering whether or not there would be another incident this morning.

"No, he's going to spend the next couple days with a friend of his. Sorry about yesterday morning, by the way," Lynn said.

"It's okay, I was just wondering if I needed to hide my shoes."

Lynn laughed, "No, I don't think that will be necessary!"

Jason and Heather finished their breakfast while discussing their plans for the day. They were slated to visit Heather's grandmother, someone clearly dear to Heather's heart. Her grandmother's farm sat on the outskirts of Sacramento, no more than a hobby farm by Iowa standards. According to Heather, the farm was more of a passion project than a meaningful source of income. Her grandmother loved horses, and her grandfather loved his wife.

As they discussed the farm, Jason found himself distracted by thoughts of their evening in the backyard.

"Jason, are you ready to go?" Heather asked, breaking him out of his reverie. He straightened his shirt and nodded. "The bicycles are out back, my dad said that he made sure that the tires had air."

The ride to grandma Gail's home was pleasant, albeit somewhat warmer than Jason would have preferred. Shortly after they started riding, he felt sweat forming under his arms and on his back; he would need the new shirt he'd packed in his knapsack by the time they arrived.

"So how long are you in town?" Gail asked as she prepared a carafe of tea. Jason had grown up drinking unsweetened tea, stealing sips from his mother's glass from his earliest memory. After the long ride, his mouth was parched and he'd gladly accepted Gail's offer to make up a batch when they had first entered the house.

"Only for a few more days. I've got to get back to help my father on the farm. He wasn't very happy that I left at all."

"Well, I think it's wonderful that you would come out and see Heather, even if it's only for a few days. You must be a remarkable young man," Gail said. Jason cast his eyes towards Heather who simply smiled.

"Isn't Grandma the best?" Heather asked rhetorically, the matter already firmly decided. Grandma Gail was, indeed, the best.

They made small talk and played games until lunch, sitting around an ancient farmhouse table and listening to the sound of chickens cluck and crow as they did. There was something about the entire situation that made Jason feel warm and secure.

Gail's husband, Ralph, sat in the living room while they chatted. Heather had previously mentioned to Jason that Ralph's health had been in decline for years; he simply wasn't able to move around or help around the property. He was content to sit and smoke his pipe as they gathered around the table.

They took lunch out to him around noon. Heather told Jason he should sit and eat with Ralph, "I think you two will really get along," she said, and she was right. It became clear very quickly that although Ralph's body was failing him, his mind was still sharp. Jason was unusually informed about politics for his age, and he and Ralph spent considerable time discussing the relative merits of William McKinley as president. Both Ralph and Jason were optimistic about the man. Jason couldn't remember the last time that he'd shared such excellent conversation with an adult.

After they'd eaten, Heather took Jason to see the horses, which were stabled at the top of a hill at the rear of the property. They crossed a wooden bridge over the creek at the base of the hill leading up to the stable. As they did, Heather warned him not to leave the narrow path. "The whole hill is rotten with poison oak," she intoned. Jason nodded, the thought of poison oak a sufficient deterrent against straying.

The horses were well kept, which was apparently a problem. "Grandma is getting too old to walk up and down this hill so many times every week. I know she loves the horses, I love them too, but she needs more help out here," Heather said as she stroked the mane of the smaller grey mare. "Did you know that she fell and broke her arm last summer?"

"No, I…," Jason started but was quickly interrupted.

"Of course you didn't. You couldn't have. I'm sorry, I didn't mean to get so serious all of a sudden, I just care about her so much, and I'm worried."

Jason nodded in understanding, although he had little to add. It was clear that Ralph could not do anything more to help.

"It's okay, I understand. You love her, and you don't want her to get hurt."

Heather rolled her shoulders and sighed, as if she was trying to shake off the negative thoughts. "Do you want to ride?" she asked to change the topic.

So ride they did. Jason had grown up on a farm, but had only ridden a horse on one other occasion. The feeling of riding along on the larger brown mare was exhilarating. The two of them bounded along the edge of the property, slowly at first and then faster and faster.

Eventually, they slowed back to a mere trot, content of speed and in search of conversation.

"So, what do you think?" Heather asked.

"About what?" Jason responded, not sure whether she was asking about the farm, or the horses, or anything else.

"I don't know, about everything. About your trip so far, about California, about… whatever." *About me, that's what she's really asking,* Jason thought.

"'Whatever' is great," he said, not breaking eye contact. "'Whatever' is more than great. In fact, this is probably the best 'whatever' that I've ever seen."

Heather blushed and attempted to keep the grin on her face from growing into a full smile. She failed. Something about the way she smiled made Jason think about the previous evening when they'd lain entwined for hours. All of a sudden, Jason was blushing as brightly as Heather was.

They dismounted a short time later and made their way back inside. After another hour, Heather said that they should head back. It was a long bike ride, after all.

The ride back took them nearly twice as long as the ride there had, primarily because much of it was uphill. By the time that they arrived, both of them were eager to change into clean clothes and relax.

"Did you two have a good time at Gail's?" Lynn asked. Jason realized for the first time that everyone referred to her grandparent's house as though it belonged solely to Gail, rather than to both of her grandparents. *How unusual,* he thought.

Heather answered for both of them. "We had a wonderful time," she said as she helped her mother with the last of the evening dinner preparations. "We rode the horses and had an excellent afternoon."

"I'm glad to hear it," Lynn said, "I worry about Gail sometimes. Those silly horses she loves so much."

"I'm going to go over there soon, have a chat with her," Edward chimed in from the dining table. It was the first time that Jason had seen him since breakfast. "It may be about time that she finally gives those horses up."

Much like the night before, they spent the remainder of the evening chatting together and playing cards. Both Lynn and Edward were surprisingly willing players, although Jason felt as though Lynn may only be playing as a social activity; her strategy wouldn't win any gamesmanship awards any time soon.

After they had retired for the evening, Jason and Heather once again snuck outside. It was a much warmer evening that night, and body heat was not required to keep anyone warm. Without that pretext, the two of them simply sat side by side, although Heather did take his hand shortly after they sat down.

"Do you think we'll ever see each other again after you leave?" Heather asked abruptly, rendering Jason momentarily speechless.

"What? Why… why wouldn't we?" Jason said, the thought never having crossed his mind. *Will I ever be able to make this trip again? Would she ever come out to Iowa?* Jason thought suddenly. *Maybe this is the last time…*

"I only mean, it's a long trip. I can't imagine you being able to just jump on a train anytime that you want," Heather said, more than a touch of melancholy in her voice.

"Why don't you come out to see me in Iowa? I'm sure that my parents wouldn't mind."

"Mine would, at least my dad would. There's no way they'd let me go two thousand miles away from home without them."

Jason mulled over that thought. *What if this was all there was? What if, from here on out, the only thing that could happen between them was scribbled ink?*

Chapter Thirty-Two

Nearly eleven months after that unspoken question, Heather was preparing to answer it as she rifled through the timeworn desk tucked into the corner of her room in Sacramento, California.

The letters poured out from the desk as she searched for the one that she was looking for. Since that fateful visit, the count of letters had increased to the point that they were corresponding multiple times per week. They had become precious to her in a way that she couldn't quite describe, and right now she needed the reassurance that one of them had contained.

The disfunction of their house had only increased in the months since Jason had visited the previous July. Micah's drug abuse had spiraled to a point where nothing was ever stable, and fights were apt to break out at any moment. They might go weeks without a problem only to wake up to the smashing of windows or the slamming of doors. In one particularly dangerous outburst, Micah had set their kitchen on fire. *Had I not awoken when I did, the entire house could easily have been engulfed.* She shivered at the thought.

Aha! There it is! she thought, finding the letter at last. She had read this particular letter at least a dozen times, and the corners of the paper were bent from wear. Now that she stood at the precipice of change, she needed one last boost of confidence.

Dearest Cali,

I miss you in a way that I struggle to express completely. The feeling wells up within me like an untapped spring, always threatening to burst into my life in unexpected times and places. Yesterday, for instance, I was walking to the post to see if I'd gotten a new letter from you, and the mere thought it if caused my breath to catch in my throat. There I was, walking down a roadside, totally unable to take a breath.

I wouldn't admit it to anyone except you, but just moments later I had to hold back tears thinking of the possibility of you coming to live in Iowa. Even if you were two hundred miles away I would be overjoyed, but to have you here in walking distance? The very thought of it fills me with a kind of joy that defies description.

So I must ask, are you truly considering such a drastic move? I know that you said you were, but is that comment just casual musing or is it something that you have given true thought to?

If it is the latter, and you are seriously considering attending the Normal School, I would be more than happy to go and meet the superintendent in person and inquire about any particulars that would be required for you to do so. The last that I knew, attendance had dipped slightly, so I am sure that they would be more than happy to add another teacher to their roster, regardless of her point of origin.

Even if your consideration is nothing more than passing fancy, you should know that just the idea energizes me.

I think back on our brief times together with the fondest of memories and truly hope that we can add to those experiences one day soon.

I love you.

Jason Baldwin

She breathed a deep sigh as she finished, the words a sort of catharsis for her. Jason had become very dear to her, but the decision she was about to make wasn't solely about him. Nonetheless, his words reassured her that it was right.

After she'd found her way to the living room where her parents were sitting, she found herself wishing that she could read the letter just one more time. Edward was smoking his pipe and reading a newspaper, just having returned from another long day. Her mother sat beside him, content with a book that she'd begun several times but had never quite finished.

"Hey," Heather started, unsure of exactly how best to begin, "I wanted to talk to you both about something. It's important," she finished haltingly.

Lynn closed her book. Heather got the feeling that she already had her suspicions about what was coming next. Edward finished the paragraph he'd been reading and lowered his paper as well.

"Well?" he asked.

Heather steeled herself. If she didn't start talking now she didn't think she'd ever get it out. "I'm moving to Iowa," she blurted. "I...,"

Before she could continue, her father interrupted. "Excuse me? What are you talking about? We're not moving to Iowa."

"Daddy...," her eyes searched for her mother's, somehow knowing she'd find more understanding there. When she did, she saw the tears already welling up. "I'm moving to Iowa. Not us, me. I've applied for, and been accepted to, the Iowa State Normal School."

For a moment, Heather didn't think that her father had heard her. He stared at her blankly, as if she'd told him something so incredibly complex that he couldn't comprehend its meaning. He opened his mouth to say something but closed it before a word could escape. Lynn was the first to find her voice. "You've been thinking about this for a while, haven't you?" The tears that had been holding back now fell, landing heavily on the pleats of her dress.

"I've been thinking about this for years. Well, not about the destination, but about moving. I... I love you both so much but this house is... it's...," she couldn't finish, small sobs choking out her words and her thoughts.

Edward still hadn't said anything, and Heather wondered if he was going to. Would he just stay silent as she cried in front of him? Would he throw a fit and try to stop her?

He stood, setting his pipe and paper aside. He walked over to her slowly and put his hands on her shoulders, looking down into her eyes. "Are you sure that this is what you want? Are you absolutely sure?"

225

Heather didn't speak, just nodded, more tears joining their fallen compatriots on the floor.

"When does the term start?" he asked, startling her. She had been sure that a protest was coming.

"Ear…early September," she stammered, "I need to be there in late August to move in and get acquainted."

It was Edward's turn to cry. He was not a man that you expected to break down, and at his first tear the three of them all lost their composure completely. "Well," he said, "I guess we'll just have to enjoy our last few months together, now won't we?"

The feeling of relief that swept through Heather was blissful, so utterly complete that she felt as though she may collapse. She had been agonizing over this conversation for weeks, reading Jason's letter over and over again to convince herself that it was the right choice.

It was as if her parents understood the call of her heart. Not only to join Jason, but to establish a life of her own apart from the tumultuous nature of their household. A life that could be crafted from the beginning rather than rebuilt from the wreckage of the past.

Chapter Thirty-Three

Jason was trying to keep himself busy. No matter what he tried to occupy his mind with, however, he always found it doggedly returning to all of the terrible news of the last few months.

It had started with Heather leaving for college, which had been expected but was sad nonetheless. It was always hard to be separated from a friend you had spent much of your life with. Next up had been Calvin, who had gone to work at his uncle's restaurant in Des Moines. Although they had patched things up after Jason had returned from California, the last three months before he left just hadn't been the same, and watching him leave had been another sorrow. He'd felt as though he was completely alone in the world.

Cali's letters (when he'd returned to Iowa he'd immediately reverted to thinking of her as Cali,) had kept him going. That had been true through the long, desperately cold winter and through the soggy, wet spring.

In January, Kathleen had started to cough. The coughing had grown worse and worse over the next months. Eventually, it had grown into a deep fatigue that limited her ability to live a normal life. By March she rarely left her bed. The doctor called it cancer, and it was spreading.

Jason had spent countless hours by her bedside, talking with her and reading to her. As her condition worsened, she talked more and more about France. Even though his father had sworn them all to silence, Kathleen talked at length about how she felt she had failed to fulfill her father's last wishes. Jason came to realize that he'd misunderstood all those fights he'd half overheard long ago. He'd always believed it was his father that had been determined to go to France when, in reality, it was his mother's persistence that had landed them there.

"My father," she had once told him, "would talk for hours about Eustache Dauger. It felt like he was obsessed with him. He was convinced that all of the family gossip was true, that he was imprisoned for a crime that he didn't commit."

Jason had listened as she'd told him far more than his father ever had about why they'd gone, about the real reasons. It hadn't been because his parents cared about the reputation of some long dead family member, it had been for the deep love that his mother held for her father.

"He was such a wonderful man, so caring, he…," she trailed off before she'd started coughing. Jason saw blood on the handkerchief she held to her mouth.

"Did I ever tell you why we live here, in Iowa?" she asked, letting her previous thought go uncompleted.

Jason shook his head. To be honest, he'd never really considered why they lived where they did. It was just their home to him.

"We moved here because my father wanted better for us. He hated the city, always said that it was full of crime and vice. Once, when I was very young, I heard him tell my mother that the city was no place for a young girl."

Jason nodded along, knowing that his mother was their only daughter.

"My mother ruled the roost, you see. Anything that she wanted, my father got for her. He loved her so much that he could not refuse her anything. But on this, he put his foot down. Said he'd had enough. Two weeks later we moved. I don't remember much from back then, but I remember the look in his eyes as he told my mother. She knew not to argue with him."

Jason had pondered that for several weeks. He wished that he'd been able to meet his grandfather more than a few times when he was very young. He must have been a special man to be willing to uproot everything he knew just to protect his family.

As the months had worn on, Kathleen had started speaking increasingly in French. She'd also started to request that he read to her in French, though the amount of available material was minimal. He'd taken to visiting the library at the Normal School in search of more. Although it was supposed to be for attending students, Bill Veech had arranged for Jason to be given some access.

Mr. Veech, although he insisted that Jason call him Bill, was Jason's employer.

Bill had opened a photography studio on Main St. in Cedar Falls shortly after he'd graduated from the Normal School. One day the previous fall, Jason had been walking his bicycle down the street when he'd noticed a help wanted sign in the window. On a whim he'd gone inside, fascinated by the idea of turning the momentary into the permanent. Bill must have seen the wonder in his eyes because he'd offered Jason the job on the spot. He was a grunt mostly, carrying equipment and keeping records, but he got to spend a lot of time learning from Bill. Bill was well connected on campus, and when Jason had mentioned his desire to use their library, Bill had made it happen nearly overnight.

He'd used that opportunity to check out the few French books the library contained, several of them multiple times. The majority were textbooks on the subject of teaching French, but the content didn't really matter to his mother. When she felt particularly horrible, she just loved listening to the language itself. As Jason read, he also learned. He never expected to use French again, but there was something satisfying about learning. As something of an autodidact, Jason absorbed more during those months than he likely would have with instruction from a teacher.

When his mother passed away in April, Jason felt like his world had temporarily collapsed beneath him. He spent hours helping his father on the farm, the work never ended on a farm in the spring, but his mind was never fully invested. Every hour he could spare from the farm he spent buried in paperwork or film at the Veech studio. It had become his home away from home, and he was desperately glad for it.

It was late June when the letter arrived. Jason had been waiting anxiously for several weeks for news about Cali's decision. In fact, the few weeks between the letter he held in his hands and the last had been the longest stretch without communication that they'd experienced since their correspondence began.

As he examined the envelope, he noticed that the postmark was several weeks old. It seemed as though the letter had been temporarily lost or delayed. He breathed a sigh of relief that it had arrived at all and began to tear at the edge of the envelope, his hands shaking slightly as he did so. His heart was beating quicker than usual as he began to read the words.

Love,

I finally did it! It took me longer than it should have to muster up the courage, but I finally discussed my plans, our plans, with my parents. They took the news surprisingly well, although I still don't think that it has fully sunk in. Nonetheless, they have agreed and will not stand in the way.

I am nervous to move but more than that I am excited beyond belief! I cannot wait until we can finally be together. Have you told your...

There was a portion scratched out. Jason couldn't make out what it said, but he knew anyway, 'parents'. *Have you told your parents yet?* Jason took a deep breath before he began reading again.

father yet? I'll bet you haven't. You always wait until the last minute to tell anyone anything, not that I have much room to criticize.

I know that you are still hurting; I'm so sorry about your mother. She was truly an amazing woman and I am heartbroken for you. I wish that I could be there even today so that I could help and comfort you.

Although I cannot be there today, we have arranged travel details. I will arrive by train on August the 15th. It's a bit earlier than I need to arrive, but I thought it might be worth coming a few days early to celebrate your birthday with you. Hopefully you won't mind having me around a few days early.

My parents are planning to accompany me. They would like to see the place that I'll be staying and visit the campus. I suspect that they would also like to meet your father properly. They will only be staying a few days and will depart on the 19th.

I love you.

Heather Burdett

Jason was smiling uncontrollably by the time he finished. Although he had been reminded of the grief of losing his mother, he was filled with a new hope for the first time since her passing. There was something about the situation that felt like pieces of a puzzle coming together. If he was honest with himself, it felt like providence.

Chapter Thirty-Four

The next three months passed in a blur. There had been far more preparations and goodbyes than Heather had been completely prepared for. Some of those goodbyes had taken everything she'd had within herself. She had cried desperately as she'd hugged her grandmother for what could be the last time. Saying farewell to her friends had also been difficult, but not to the depth that she would have expected. Saying goodbye to them somehow felt right, as though it was finally time to move on. She'd cried in spite of that.

Now, as she prepared to step off of the train and into her new life, she felt nothing but excitement. She couldn't quite see Jason through the dirty train windows, but she knew that he was there waiting for her. She took slow breaths as she gathered her belongings and stood.

"Are you ready?" Lynn asked, clutching her bag in one hand and holding Heather's in the other.

"Yes," her voice wavered nervously, "I'm ready."

Lynn smiled and nodded as the train slowed and came to a complete stop. The whistle made both of them jump. Edward laughed.

"Well, I guess we're here. Let's get our luggage, shall we?" Edward said as they moved towards the door. Heather didn't hear a word that he said. Her focus was fixed on the door, and world, in front of her.

There was a mass of people waiting on the platform. It was not the crowd that Jason had experienced in Sacramento when he'd come to visit her, but it was still large enough that Heather couldn't immediately spot Jason.

Her eyes scanned the crowd, not even looking for faces, just for that flash of orange among the tallest heads. A few moments later, she saw him. He was walking towards them, apparently having spotted her more quickly than she'd located him. A huge smile adorned his face.

Heather practically leapt into his arms and nearly knocked him from his feet entirely. His strong arms caught and held her close instead. She kept her eyes closed as they embraced one another, as though if she opened them she'd awaken from a dream. She gathered her courage and looked around as he broke free. When she did, she saw a man that she presumed was Jason's father looking at them.

"Heather, this is my father, Dean. You've never had the opportunity to meet," Jason said and Heather shook his hand. His hands were large and calloused, clearly the hands of a working man. She smiled.

"It's wonderful to meet you. I've heard so much about you," she said.

Heather then introduced her parents to Dean, and the five of them made their way to the rear of the train to collect their luggage. Heather had packed every scrap of clothing she owned, and a few things she had borrowed from her mother, in addition to nearly every book in their house. They needed all five of them to gather and remove the luggage from the train's storage compartments.

When they'd finally collected everything, they walked down the platform and to the front of the building where a worn black buggy waited curbside.

"It's not much, but it will get us to the farm. Might need to squeeze a bit," Dean said and began loading the luggage into the rear. They climbed into the cab, Heather sitting between Jason and his father and her parents sitting in the back seat. It was a tight fit, but Heather did not mind. She pressed her side closer to Jason and shot him a coy smile. He blushed.

When they'd reached the farmhouse, Jason and Dean helped Edward to carry the suitcases inside. Heather knew that her parents had been planning to rent a room during their stay, but Dean wouldn't hear a word of it. He'd insisted that they save their money and stay with them. Shortly after they'd arrived, the suitcases were all moved to their respective rooms. As Jason carried the very last one in, he asked, "What did you pack in here anyway? Cannonballs?"

Heather laughed, both at his comment and as she watched him struggle with the heavy case. "No, books mostly. I suppose that I could have spread them out, but I just put them all together in one case."

"Well they weigh a metric ton," Jason said, letting out a grunt as he set the suitcase down in the living room downstairs. "No need to take them upstairs, we'll just be moving them again in a couple weeks."

Heather nodded. As he said, she'd be moving into the school's female dormitory in two weeks. The thought made her melancholy. She wished that she could stay here with Jason, instead. She shook off the thought and helped her mother as she unpacked the clothes.

"Do you all want to stick around here and relax or would you like to take a tour of the town?" Jason asked after they'd finished everything.

Lynn was the first to speak. "Let's go see the town! Yeah, that sounds good."

"Can we see where you work, Jason?" Heather asked.

"Sure, I don't see why not. It's right on Main Street anyway, so it's not very far from everything. We'll go by the college and then head down there."

They chatted for a while before leaving, mostly small talk about the weather and the farm. None of them seemed interested in breaching the deeper topics right away, although Lynn did offer some very sincere condolences for the passing of Kathleen.

"She saved our lives, truly. I wish that I would have gotten the chance to thank her in person," she'd said at the end. Tears wavered at the corners of her eyes, threatening to fall. She choked them back before they did.

Heather felt the room grow somber. Determined not to let despair ruin their day, Heather suggested that it was time to leave.

"I think I'll stay here. I've got a few things to do and the buggy is pretty cramped with five anyway," Dean said, although Heather heard the waver in his voice. Heather started to say something, but Jason cut her off with a wave of his hand.

They made their way into town on the same road they'd used to come out to the farm. The corn was high; it would be a very good harvest. As Jason guided the horses, he made idle chatter with Edward about the crops. Heather wished that she was upfront beside him, but instead she'd sat in the rear beside her mother. There would be time enough to be close later, she supposed.

They reached campus a short time later and spent an hour or two walking around and taking in the sights. Edward slowed them down, walking through every building in a more leisurely fashion than Heather would had preferred.

When they'd finished with campus, they visited Main St. and walked down the streets lined with shops, including the photography studio where Jason was employed part time. Jason introduced Heather and her parents to Bill, who was nice enough to give them a tour of the building.

Afterwards, the four of them made their way back to the buggy and began to ride home.

"So," Jason started, "what did you all think?"

"It's such a quaint little town. Everyone seems perfectly pleasant," Lynn said, this time sitting in the back beside her husband.

Heather didn't say anything, she just smiled and took Jason's hand in hers. Edward spoke instead.

"It's smaller than I expected, but I like the school. I wish all of the buildings had been open." At this, Heather softly rolled her eyes in the direction of Jason. *How much longer would we have been there if they had been?* she wondered.

Lynn talked about the shops they'd visited and Jason about the things they'd do in the coming days. Heather heard almost none of it. She was perfectly content as she sat there beside Jason and thought about the day so far. Heather was more excited now than she ever had been. The school was perfect, full of everything she could possibly need, and the few staff members that had been on campus had been thrilled to receive an out of state student. Everything was falling into place.

Suddenly a thought hit Heather, one that she couldn't believe was just now occurring to her. She blurted out the words in a rush.

"Oh! Happy birthday, Jason!"

Chapter Thirty-Five

And fall into place they did. After her parents had left, Heather and Jason spent the next two weeks exploring every nook and cranny of Cedar Falls, Iowa. They walked up and down the banks of the Cedar River, had picnics on campus and in Overman and Seerley parks, visited every shop on Main Street a dozen times, and spent nearly every waking moment together.

Whether it was on campus, on the street, or on a walking trail, they could be found strolling hand in hand, laughing and smiling, talking about everything and nothing all at once. Jason told Heather that before she had arrived he had spoken with Bill, letting him know that he would not be working much during the two weeks between her arrival and the beginning of her semester. Bill had been more than understanding, and Heather was forever grateful. Brief as they were, those two weeks saw their relationship grow and blossom.

They found a quiet comfort in each other's presence, one that exceeded anything that either of them had ever known. Day after day it grew stronger, and before long each of them questioned how they had ever gone on without it.

Although they each had separate bedrooms in the large farmhouse, after the first few days they rarely used more than one. Instead, they spent nearly every night sharing each other's company.

The first time had been as natural as anything that Heather had ever experienced. It had been the second night after her parent's departure, and they'd been outdoors all day, biking from one edge of Cedar Falls to the other. When they'd returned home, they had decided that swimming in the pond at the edge of the property would be the best possible way to cool off.

They had biked directly to the pond, not bothering to stop at the farmhouse first. They didn't talk about that decision, but each of them knew exactly what it meant. Heather felt a shiver of nervous excitement creep up her back at the thought.

They parked their bikes at the edge of the water, pausing momentarily to survey the pond and the area around it. Heather walked out to the edge of the short dock while Jason remained near the shore, a distance of less than ten feet between them. Except for the dock itself, the water was surrounded almost entirely by cattails. With no wind to move it, the pond's surface was mirrored glass. Heather turned back to face Jason.

"I guess it's time to swim," she said, a nervous jitter apparent in her voice. She tried to calm her nerves but struggled, her heart beating too quickly in her chest.

"I guess so," Jason said, his voice sounding as nervous as her own. They stared at each other, both aware of their current impasse.

Heather took a deep breath and began to slowly remove her shoes and garniture, setting them gently aside. She could feel the blush rise in her cheeks as her hands moved to loosen the strings of her corset. She let her corset fall to the wooden dock below and stood there in her undershirt and bloomers. When her courage reached its peak, she shimmied out of her knickers and kicked them off to one side, nearly knocking them into the water. Now only her long chemise stood between Jason's eyes and her nakedness. Acting before fear could overtake her, Heather pulled it over her head and tossed it directly at Jason. Although the flying undershirt partially obstructed his view, Heather could see his eyes fixed on her, his mouth slightly agape. Even before the clothing hit the ground, she had turned and jumped into the cool water.

She watched from the pond as Jason followed suit, noticing that her decision to go first had clearly affected him. Although she felt flush, she did not turn away, letting her eyes gaze on him just as he had watched her. It took him only a few seconds to remove his clothes, but during those few she, too, got an eyeful.

They swam lazily for nearly an hour, occasionally splashing or engaging in other horseplay. On more than one occasion they got close enough to kiss, although each time it happened they broke away immediately. Each of them seemed to be afraid of what may happen next if they did.

As time wore on, it became clear to Heather that neither of them wanted to be the first to exit the water. Every time that it seemed one of them had gathered the courage to lift themselves up onto the dock, they retreated back into the safety and privacy of the dark water. Jason was the one who finally ended the standoff.

Perhaps feeling that it was his turn to go first, he swam to the edge and hoisted himself out onto the dock. It seemed rickety to Heather, but it held his weight without problem. She glanced at his backside as he walked away, once again feeling her cheeks redden. By the time she'd mustered up the courage to exit, Jason had retrieved two old towels from the small structure at the end of the dock.

She quickly grabbed one from his outstretched arm, noticing that his head was turned away in what seemed an attempt at chivalry. Although it was a small gesture, it had a deep impact on Heather. All of a sudden the mood had changed. Instead of being embarrassed, she felt invigorated. As if someone else were controlling her arms, she let the towel drop from her hand and wrapped her arms around his neck. As he turned to face her, surprised, Heather extended onto her tiptoes and kissed him deeply on the lips.

Heather's body raced, every heartbeat alive with energy. The first kiss became a second, and a third. Before she knew what was happening, Jason had carried her to the grass beyond the pond. He'd somehow kept hold of his own towel, quickly tossing it down and laying her upon it.

His hands were shocks of current, static electricity magnified by a thousand. She gasped as she felt them travel the length of her body and returned his passion with her own. As they explored each other, she felt his muscles tighten and heard soft groans escape his lips. The entire experience was an intoxicating, magnificent entanglement.

They moved onward like a force of nature, nothing standing between them and the raw passion driving them forward. They could no more help themselves in that moment than a butterfly could resist a hurricane. Wave after wave hit them, compelling them to the inevitable rush that comes at the end of all good things.

When they had finished, they continued to lay intertwined, each unwilling to let the moment completely pass away. It was as though, for as long as they lay there together, nothing could ever touch them. The outside could never harm them. In that moment, only the two of them existed in all of the world.

Chapter Thirty-Six

The ceremony had been less than a year after Heather had moved from California to Iowa. It had become clear to everyone that there were some things that were meant to be, and the marriage of Jason Baldwin and Heather Burdett was certainly one of those things.

They'd travelled back to California for the ceremony, Heather's family being far larger than Jason's. The ceremony was nonetheless small, comprised only of those family and friends closest to each of them. It had been a surprise, but Jason's friends Calvin and Heather had both made the trip, and Alyssa had come as well. It was a wonderful and joyous occasion.

The church had been dressed with flowers, and tulle lined the aisles. Jason had never seen anything quite like it. In Iowa, wedding ceremonies were typically boring affairs with cake and simple finger foods served afterwards in the church basement. Here, however, everyone was dressed in their finest clothes and every aspect was meticulously planned, including a photographer to capture a few select images of the event. Jason had insisted on that.

As he prepared for Heather to walk down the aisle with her father, Jason felt sweat in his palms. He wasn't nervous, just anxious. Today felt like the culmination of so many separate threads being woven together.

When she rounded the furthermost pew, he gasped audibly. She was the most singularly beautiful thing that he had ever laid eyes on. A strong light entered through a stained glass window at the rear of the church, illuminating Heather in a way that could only be described as heavenly.

The ceremony went by in a blur. Several times he caught himself staring at his bride with such focus that he failed to hear the words of the pastor. Eventually, they made it through, saying their vows and their 'I do's'. Their kiss at the end lingered longer than most of the audience likely thought it should, but Jason didn't care.

They left the church and returned to the Burdett's home, having planned a four course meal to be served to everyone that had attended. It was extravagant beyond Jason's wildest expectations. They had started with hors d'oeuvres of deviled eggs, followed by a crisp green salad with a vinaigrette dressing. The main course was a perfectly cooked filet of sirloin. They finished with obligatory slices of the cake that he and Heather had cut when they'd arrived.

"Hear, hear! I'd like to make a toast!" Edward said, raising a glass of punch above his head. Everyone turned their heads to listen, and Jason put his arms around Heather as Edward began to speak.

"When our family decided to travel to France, the last thing that we expected to find was a fiancé!" There were chuckles throughout the crowd as Edward continued. "Heather, my dearest daughter, I am so glad that God saw fit to give you to us, and I'm so glad that He worked to bring the two of you together. The road will not be easy, but it will be worth it. I wish the two of you all the happiness in the world, may God bless you and keep you!"

Everyone clapped and raised their glasses in toast. Jason looked over to see tears forming in Heather's eyes. There was no doubt that Heather loved her father deeply, and his words had touched her.

As the day went on and guests left, Jason couldn't help but feel as though it had all gone too quickly. As they were saying their goodbyes to family and friends, Heather leaned over and whispered in his ear, "It's already over. Where did all the time go?" Jason looked at her and nodded in understanding.

Once everyone had gone, Jason and Heather prepared to leave as well. They were headed for a nearby tourist home. Edward knew the proprietor and had arranged for them to be the only guests tonight. The house wasn't overly lavish by any means, but it was still beautiful. Before they'd finished, Edward found them.

"I have something I'd like to give you both. Call it a wedding gift," he said, handing a wrapped bundle to Heather. As she unwrapped the plain brown paper, Edward continued talking. "The way that I look at it, this is what is responsible for the two of you finding each other. This is what God used to make it all happen and to tie it all together."

Inside the paper was a timeworn book, bound in frayed leather. Both Jason and Heather looked surprised, immediately understanding what Heather held. "The journal. I thought you'd gotten rid of it," Heather said, turning it over in her hands.

"No, I just put it away. After what it nearly cost us, I never wanted anything to do with it. But I think the two of you should have it, now. Even though I don't know exactly what it says, it's still the story of you."

Jason took the book as Heather handed it to him and he watched as she embraced her father. "Thank you, daddy." Jason shook Edward's hand, and they both nodded, not needing to say anything. It was the perfect gift at the perfect time.

After the moment had passed, Jason and Heather headed outside. A jet black carriage waited for them, and Jason loaded their two handbags into the back before helping Heather into the cab. Jason and Heather sat close together in silence, enjoying the calm after the hustle and bustle of the day.

When they arrived, a man and his wife greeted them warmly. "Hello to you both, and congratulations! I'm Benjamin and this is my wife Beatrice. You can call us Benny and Betty, everyone else does," Benny said as he reached out to shake Jason's hand. For her part, Betty gave Heather a hug.

"Oh, don't you look so beautiful! Young love is so special!" she practically squealed, a huge grin on her face.

"Don't mind her, she's a bit on the emotional side," Benny said with a smile of his own. "Let's get you settled in, shall we?"

The home sat on one of the highest points in town, overlooking the Sacramento River. Although it was one of the older houses on that side of the river, it had been meticulously maintained. A wraparound porch provided expansive views to every side. A large patio sat at the southernmost part of the property, covered by an ivy covered trellis.

As they walked inside, Jason couldn't help but notice the sun nearing the horizon. It was going to be a beautiful sunset before long.

Benny and Betty showed them to their room, a large and well-appointed stateroom on the second floor of the Victorian home. The room was decorated in shades of blue with wallpaper of a light cream. A roaring fireplace sat at one corner of the room, and directly opposite was the bed, a large four-poster made of oak.

Having only brought a few clothes and basic toiletries, both Jason and Heather only needed to set down one bag each. After doing so, they were escorted back downstairs.

"We've arranged to stay elsewhere for the evening, you'll have the place to yourselves. We'll arrive back in the morning, and Betty will be up to make you both breakfast," Benny said, and Betty nodded her head in agreement.

"You dearies have a good time. You should head on down to the patio. We've got just a couple of things down there for you," Betty added before they left.

"Shall we?" Jason asked, extending his elbow for Heather. Heather took it as they walked down the manicured stone path leading to the trellis covered patio. Two chairs were arranged facing the river. Between them sat a wooden table and a bottle of wine. Jason picked it up and raised his eyebrows.

"Do you want to try some?" he asked. Neither of them were drinkers, but Heather nodded and Jason poured a portion into each of the two glasses that had been placed beside the bottle. They each took a few sips. The wine was still cool, so it must have been placed outside only shortly before they'd arrived.

"Jason, isn't it beautiful?" Heather said, staring westward at the setting sun. Just as he'd expected, the sunset was spectacular, an explosion of red and orange spread across dimpled clouds.

But Jason wasn't looking at the sun. Instead, his eyes were fixed on the woman who was now his wife.

"Yes, it really is. It really, truly, is."

Heather looked over and caught Jason's eyes. She smiled and blushed.

"Come on, let's go upstairs. Leave the wine, it's not very good anyway," Heather said, and stood. She extended her hand and Jason took it. They walked hand in hand back into the house and up the stairs into their bedroom.

What happened then was beautiful, too.

Part Three

"That which ends must first begin,
in the darkness or the light,
and if it's meant to last beyond,
prepare yourself to fight."

Chapter Thirty-Seven

"Jason! Have you seen my school book? I had it here last night, but I don't see it anywhere," Heather said, frantically searching their living room for the missing book. "I could have sworn I…"

"You feel asleep with it last night. I put it in the bookcase, beside your others," Jason said, cutting her off before she could complete her vow.

Heather looked up at him wearily. In the last few years, Heather's workload had steadily increased until it was nearly all she could handle. Although she loved teaching, there were days when it seemed like the burden was too great.

"I have to go or I'll be late," Heather said, walking over to the bookcase and retrieving the missing volume. "Today should be a shorter day than usual, I may even beat you home for once. Donald Bremer won't be there, his father informed me. That should make the day run a bit smoother than usual, too."

Jason listened passively, the words crossing his ears but failing to penetrate very far. To him, it had all become nearly identical. Grammar, mathematics, lazy students, feebleminded ones, it was all just school talk. Jason was desperately tired of work being the only thing that they ever talked about.

Four years after they had been married, Jason had taken over the photography studio at 312 Main Street. Bill had sold it to him for less than it was worth, for which Jason had been indescribably grateful. He'd wanted to follow other pursuits, namely teaching, and told Jason he wanted to see the studio go to someone who loved it.

Jason did love the studio, that was certainly true. From the charm of its old brick interior, to the smell of the developing chemicals, Jason rarely went to work without a smile on his face. There was something about capturing images of people that he found not only fascinating but incredibly satisfying.

"Did you hear me, Jason? I have to go."

"Oh, yes, I'm sorry. I'll see you when you get home."

Heather collected the rest of her supplies and headed out the door. She taught nearby and, at least on days when it was warm enough, usually chose to walk to her classroom. Jason would usually ride his bike to the studio, although he wished that they could afford an automobile.

Shortly thereafter, Jason also left. The studio rarely opened before 9AM, but Jason still had plates that needed to be developed from the day before, and he wanted to complete those before his first sitting at noon. The bike ride was pleasant, a cool breeze taking the edge off the August heat.

The odor of chemicals filled the dark room. To some, the aroma would have been considered overwhelming, even nauseating, but Jason found it relaxing. There was something about the smell of the chemical fixer that he found especially pleasant. Although his hands would smell for hours afterwards, there was nothing quite like watching images be created from the ether.

A knock on the door interrupted his work. He had not yet unlocked the building and had not been expecting customers. Hopeful that whoever it was would go away, Jason continued working. Less than a minute later, another knock hammered the door, this one louder than the one before. Jason sighed, quickly removing the paper from the fixer and hanging it to dry on the line running across the room. He wiped his hands and turned to address the persistent individual banging on his front door.

Through the glass he recognized Harold Miller, the owner of the building. Jason supposed he should be grateful that Harold had not simply used his key to enter on his own.

"Well good morning, Harold, I wasn't expecting you," Jason said as he opened the door and welcomed him inside.

"It is morning, indeed. Do you usually wait until 11AM to open your doors to potential customers? It's no wonder that you are late on your rent if that's the case."

Jason sighed again, although this time he did so inaudibly. Harold's monthly reminders that his rent was past due had grown tiresome long ago.

"Yes, well, not normally. But today is a slow day and I thought…,"

"Thought you'd turn down any business that might show up?" Harold said, his face stern. Jason felt as though he were being lectured, and he did not like it. Annoyance flashed across his face.

"Thought I'd be productive and finish the work I did have. It doesn't pay to keep clients waiting, after all," Jason finished, as amicably as he was able.

Harold grunted. "Regardless, you are still late. This is the fifth month in a row. Where is my money?"

Jason felt his muscles tighten and his countenance darken. He was tempted to tell Harold exactly where his money would be placed if he ever lectured him again, but he thought better of it. Instead, he walked to the desk at the rear corner of the studio and took out his keyring. Selecting a small copper key, he unlocked the drawer and pulled out an envelope.

Surveying the contents, Jason sighed for a third time. There wasn't nearly as much money inside as he would have liked. Truth be told, there was only just enough inside to pay for the rent that Mr. Miller was demanding of him. Not that he could do anything about it at the moment, he supposed.

"I have most of the rent for you today, and can get the rest to you by Friday," Jason said, optimistically.

"That's not a problem, I can easily have all of your things cleared out by Friday," Harold responded mockingly and with equal enthusiasm.

Jason glowered at Harold, barely restraining himself from saying something that he would regret. He fingered the bills in the envelope until he'd counted out the full portion of rent that was due. The meager amount left over was depressing. He handed the bills to Harold without saying a word.

"Well, look at that, you did have the money, after all," Harold said with a sly grin. "See that you have next month's rent ready in full and on time. If you don't, I swear I'll evict you, I don't care what excuse you come up with."

"Yes, Mr. Miller, I'll see to that," Jason replied, clinching his fists.

"Good, see that you do. I'll be back in three weeks for it, not a day later. Don't test me on this."

After Harold had left, Jason closed the door behind him and leaned against it. *There is no way that I will be able to pay it*, he thought as he slumped to the floor. *No way in the world.*

Just as he thought that his day couldn't get any worse, he felt a jiggle at the door handle. His noon appointment had arrived early.

Chapter Thirty-Eight

Heather slumped down into her chair, completely exhausted. What she'd believed would be a shorter than usual day had turned into a nightmare. It had started off much like any other, the usual order of reading, arithmetic, and grammar before lunch and then geography and spelling afterwards. Nothing had been out of the ordinary. After the last lesson of the day, Heather had moved the class into general lessons where she concentrated on helping students who were having difficulties. It was during that lesson where everything had taken a turn for the worst.

One of her students, a sandy haired and rotund boy by the name of Samuel, had started a fight with another student named Marcus. Heather wouldn't have admitted it to anyone except Jason, but Marcus occupied a special place in her heart.

Marcus was a small boy. Even for ten, he was shorter than usual, and his body had developed none of the muscle that many farm children displayed at his age. His parents were well known in the community, and not in a good way. They treated Marcus as though he were an unwelcome guest in their home, worth only what he could provide them in household labor. Based on the bruises she often saw on his arms, their treatment of him had passed beyond simple neglect long ago.

Heather had witnessed the beginning of the altercation from the corner of her eye, seeing the half eaten apple launched across the room and striking Marcus directly in the eye. Marcus had shouted pitifully. He rose to his feet, as if to get even farther away from the danger Samuel posed, but that had been mistaken by Samuel as a challenge. Before Heather could stop him, Samuel had launched himself across the room to continue the assault.

It had taken every ounce of her strength to separate the two boys. At twelve, Samuel outweighed Heather by at least twenty pounds, and was a full inch taller as well. Once she'd finally pulled him off Marcus, she couldn't help but gasp at what she saw.

Thinking back on it now, the vision still haunted her. Marcus' nose was almost certainly broken, now fixed at an odd angle. In addition, his left eye had swollen completely shut by the time she'd managed to find some ice and tend to him. She'd sent the other students home early so that she could treat him properly. His only friend, a young girl named Hannah, had stayed and promised to walk the short distance home with him after Heather had finished.

This was not the first time that the two boys had fought, nor was it likely to be the last. There were two bullies in her class, Donald and Samuel. For whatever reason, both had come to believe that Marcus was their personal punching bag. Heather had done her best to separate them, going so far as to insist they sit as far away from each other as two people could while still being within the same room. It had done little to stop the problem.

As she sat there, Heather felt her chest begin to heave and tears well up in her eyes. No matter how hard she tried, she could not protect Marcus. Not from Samuel, not from his parents, not from life. Even though he spent most recesses sitting inside with her, there was still so much time that she could not be around. It broke her heart as she thought about it, and the tears that had threatened now fell heavily upon her desk.

She spent a few minutes there by herself, crying until the tears stopped and her head cleared. She knew there was nothing more that she could do, but that knowledge didn't make her feel much better. She quietly gathered the school papers she'd intended to grade and stuffed them into her satchel. She'd make time to do them at home instead. She knew Jason wouldn't be pleased with that, but it was either that or miss dinner, again.

As she finished, she heard the door open and footsteps approach. Startled, she turned quickly on her heel. A rush of relief flooded through her, it was only Herbert Pfeiffer, the superintendent.

"Oh, you surprised me, Mr. Pfeiffer. What can I do for you today?" Heather asked, suddenly aware that she probably looked completely dreadful. For his part, Mr. Pfeiffer either didn't notice her blotchy face or did not care.

"Yes, I'm sorry, I certainly did not intend to give you a fright. I simply stopped by to collect the grades for the quarter," he said, his hands folded behind his back. Heather felt her heart begin to race once more.

"The grades? Why, it's only mid-October, I haven't completed them yet. They usually are not collected until November," she said, trying to keep her voice calm.

"It's the 26th of October, Mrs. Baldwin. Are they not close enough to complete that you could finish them?" Herbert asked, his face pale and stern.

Heather stammered, unsure of what to say. "I suppose, I mean, I could have them to you tomorrow. I could bring them by your office before school. Just need to tidy up a couple of things first. Would that be alright?"

"See that you do, I'll make sure to be on the lookout for you in the morning. Have a splendid evening, Mrs. Baldwin," he said as he turned to leave, not leaving room for any additional conversation.

After the door had slammed, Heather sat once more into her chair, now aware that in addition to grading the individual assignments tonight, she'd also need to do a class summary and finalize all of the grades to date. She felt overwhelmed.

There was a knock at the door, once again startling Heather. "Mr. Pfeiffer?" she called out, thinking he may have forgotten something. The door opened and a timid voice answered instead.

"No, it's me, Mrs. Baldwin. It's Marcus."

Heather felt her heart well up to bursting. "What's wrong? Are you okay?" The question was foolish, but it came out reflexively. Of course he wasn't okay.

"Can… can you take me to the doctor? My nose, it hurts a lot and…," he trailed off. Starting again through his tears, he muttered, "and my parents wouldn't take me. They said, it'd just, just,… cost them money and…," he broke down, unable to finish as sobs wracked his little body.

"Oh, honey, darling, of course. I'm sure Dr. Gibson is still in his office. Let's go," Heather said, grabbing her things in one arm and putting the other around the young boy.

"Mrs. Baldwin?" Marcus sputtered, tears still falling and nose running. "Can you... afterwards, I mean, can I go home with you tonight?"

And with that, both of them were crying.

BRANDON BOOTH

Chapter Thirty-Nine

It started to rain as Jason peddled his aging bike towards home, and the streets quickly became treacherous. The tires on the bicycle were worn with age and needed to be replaced, but the money never seemed to be there for something that could be lived with. The thinning tread did Jason no favors, and nearly caused him to crash while rounding more than one slick corner.

By the time he arrived home, he was both frustrated and sodden. He brought the wretched contraption under the sagging porch at the rear of their home. Once under the cover of the porch, he stripped off as many of his clothes as could be considered decent.

He was late, and he knew it. His last sitting of the day had arrived nearly twenty minutes late, and then had insisted upon a drawn out accounting of the process of developing the photograph. Normally, Jason would have simply locked up the shop if an appointment arrived so late and with such disrespect for his time. Things being what they were with his landlord, however, Jason felt unable to decline any business that he could get.

It was after 6PM, and Jason braced himself for the inevitable argument that would ensue when he walked inside. Heather had been quite clear that her day was to be a short one, and Jason had honored that declaration by being over an hour late. His tardiness would not go over well, he knew.

"Heather, I'm home," he said as he entered the rear door, still dripping. No answer followed. "I'm sorry I'm late, it couldn't be helped. I...," he trailed off, still hearing no response or noises whatsoever. "Are you here?"

Jason stopped and listened, there was still no response. The house was quiet. He walked quickly from room to room before verifying that, indeed, Heather was not here. Jason wasn't surprised that she had left. She often did when he arrived home late, although it was unusual that she'd chosen to go out into a downpour such as this. That thought caused a flash of alarm to course through him. *Where is she? Is she alright?* he wondered silently.

Heather walked in the door only moments later, calling out as she did so. "I'm home! I'm sorry I'm late!"

Jason rounded the corner to greet her at the door. She had evidently brought an umbrella along with her this morning, because she was dry. Standing there in only his underwear and soggy shirt, Jason also noticed that she was not alone. He jumped back into the kitchen.

"Oh, well hello there, Marcus. I see you'll be joining us for dinner again this evening?" Jason shouted as he retreated to the bedroom to dress himself more adequately. If they were to have company, even the company of a ten year old, he should at least be wearing trousers.

If Marcus had said anything in response, Jason did not hear it. When he returned, Heather was ushering the boy towards the dining room.

"Sit there and relax while I rustle up something to eat, shall I?" Heather said.

Jason could hear through the falsetto cheer in her voice. There was stress and strain beneath the words, and Jason knew it was only a matter of time before they came out. He sighed and rubbed his temples. He could feel a headache beginning to bleed out from behind his eyes.

"So, early day, huh?" he said, his irritation evident. He knew it wasn't the right thing to say, but he couldn't seem to hold it back. His volley was returned with a look that could have shattered glass. He knew he had little right to be upset, after all, he had arrived late as well. Even so, he felt justified. Another late day, another evening with Marcus, another example of her priorities.

"He begged me. He's hurting, and he's hungry. What would you have had me do?"

"Hurting? What do you mean?"

"Did you even look at him, Jason? Did you take even two seconds to actually see him?" Heather said, her voice quiet but insistent.

Jason had not actually looked at the boy. He'd just assumed that it was yet another night where Marcus had begged to come home with Heather, as he so often did. The boy's parents were delinquents, happy for one less mouth to feed anytime that they could get away with it. Lately it seemed that Marcus joined them at least once a week, if not more.

Jason stuck his head into the dining room, evaluating the boy. He looked like he'd been kicked by a mule. His eye was bandaged, but even with the covering, Jason could tell that it was badly swollen. His nose was darkly bruised as well.

"What in the world happened to him?" Jason asked, suddenly distracted from his annoyance by the miserable appearance of the boy.

"Samuel happened. Again. I guess he decided that he needed to make up for Donald's absence," Heather said, leaning up against the sink. "If I hadn't stopped him, I think he'd have really hurt him this time."

"Why is he here and not at home?" Jason asked, realizing only after the words had left his mouth how insensitive they sounded. Even so, it was a valid question. *What kind of parents would let their child be elsewhere after they'd been injured so badly?* he wondered.

"He went home. His parents told him that he'd be fine and that they weren't going to take him to see the doctor. Said it would just cost them money. I had to take him, what else could I do?"

Jason felt his blood begin to rise and his heart beat faster. "Are you telling me that we paid for his treatment as well?" He did his best to keep his words even and his voice calm. He wasn't sure whether he'd succeeded.

"Just the materials. Dr. Gibson understood the situation, donated his time. It wasn't much." Heather answered, and that calmed Jason a bit, although any added expense was unwelcome.

"Don't worry, I'll walk him home right after dinner. I promise."

Jason nodded. After all, she was right, what else could he have expected her to do? Her heart was in the right place; it always was. Over the course of the last few years, he'd become increasingly aware of how much she cared about her students. Asking her to care less would be like asking the sparrow not to fly or the sun not to rise.

"Sounds good. Then, afterwards, maybe we can spend some quality time together? Just the two of us? It's been a while…," Jason said, a sly smile on his face.

"Oh, Jason, I'd love to, I really would. But I have reports to grade, and now I have to finish up the quarterlies, too. Mr. Pfeiffer dropped that on me today, and I have to get them completed before tomorrow morning."

Jason couldn't help the look of disappointment that ran across his face. Heather looked at him with a small, sad smile.

"Tomorrow, honey, I promise. Tomorrow."

Chapter Forty

Heather had done her best, but her promise had gone unfulfilled. Instead of finding time together the next evening, they'd ended up fighting. The fight itself had been about nothing, as most of their fights usually were. *How can two people get so upset about the proper way to put away dishes?* she wondered.

It hadn't been about the dishes, of course. For Heather, the problem was here, at school. The stress of her day had overwhelmed her sensibility, pushing her to the point of explosion at the slightest perceived wrong. On that particular evening, the perceived wrong was cups which had been placed in the wrong cupboard.

Heather berated herself internally. She knew that it wasn't important, but she couldn't seem to help herself in the moment.

She'd let her anger flair, and it had ended up derailing the entire evening. Jason was not without his fair share of blame, of course. He'd gone out of his way to impress upon her how immature she was being, scolding her exactly as he would have a child. That had stoked a flame he should have known to avoid.

Not that it mattered now. As she sat at her desk, she knew it was just one more infraction on her record, one more strike against her. Another broken assurance. Jason would view it as indefensible, regardless of how much stress she felt or what other excuse she could conjure up. Jason was many things, but understanding would not have topped the list.

That had been nearly two weeks ago, and things were only just now beginning to go back to usual. It had taken days for them to say their apologies and reconnect in the ways that both of them needed. It was a vicious and mentally exhausting cycle that they could not seem to escape from. Heather needed to mend their emotional fences before intimacy could occur, and Jason needed that intimacy before he was willing to let down his guard emotionally.

Heather sighed and looked up as her students started to enter the schoolhouse. As they filed in, she couldn't help but look for Marcus in the crowd of students. Not finding him, she frowned. He'd been absent two days already this week. Although he'd returned the very next day after his altercation with Samuel, his attendance in the following two weeks had been spotty. Heather wasn't sure what she should attribute those absences to. She made a mental note to walk to his house after school and have a conversation with his parents. Again.

"Alright, class, listen up," Heather began. "Today we will be breaking up into our groups and reviewing our lessons. I will be around to help each group in turn. Be sure to stay on task; I will tolerate no horseplay," she said, looking directly at Samuel and then Donald as she did so.

Both nodded slowly, not daring to meet her eyes. After the last incident with Marcus, Heather had become an authoritarian unlike the class had ever seen. Both of her troublemakers had found her new persona to be especially oppressive, although Samuel had born most of the burden. He could hardly cough in class without receiving an admonishment. Heather knew he felt mistreated, but she did not care.

"Alright, gather your books and begin. I will be around presently."

She allowed them a few minutes to get started before she made her rounds. She started with the most gifted students, giving them only a few notes before moving on. She felt bad that she could not spare more time for them, but they needed her help far less than the others. As she proceeded, she was happy to note that the class at large was doing exceptionally well. It was only her lowest academic students that were truly struggling, and even most of them had made progress.

The day proceeded smoothly, without interruption or significant distraction. It was a welcome change of pace, and Heather felt herself relaxing as the day wore on. *It's almost as though I'm less stressed when things run smoothly,* she thought to herself with a chuckle. Sometimes it was the obvious thoughts that were the most amusing.

School typically dismissed at 3:30PM, but Heather let them go a few minutes early, hoping to check on Marcus and be home in time to cook dinner before Jason arrived. It had been a while since she'd prepared a proper meal, and she knew it would be appreciated. She grabbed her jacket on the way out, mere moments after the last student.

It was a brisk afternoon. The air had begun to cool as November had arrived. Even so, the walk towards the Wilson farm was a pleasant one. The leaves on the trees were a brilliant display of orange and red painted against a bright blue sky. She smiled as she walked, taking in the few moments that she had all to herself.

"Get the hell in here, what are you doing?" Heather heard someone yell as she approached the edge of the dilapidated farm. As she walked closer, she evaluated the white farmhouse for what felt like the hundredth time. The paint was still chipped and peeling, the porch still drooped precariously to one side, and the roof still needed immediate attention. To her surprise, she did see some evidence that work had been done on the barn, new boards propped along one side and several men working near the door.

"And what n'you wantin', huh?" Melinda Wilson said, giving Heather a start. She stood at the open door with one hand on her hip, the other clutching a pale yellow shirt that had seen many better seasons. "Well? Whatchu want?"

"I...," Heather started, momentarily distracted by the woman's sudden appearance. "I came to check on Marcus. He's been absent this week and I...,"

The woman interrupted, "was worried. You was worried about the kid. How terribly sentimental. Anyway, he's been busy. Out'n the barn help'n the menfolk. We're sellin', ya see. Need to clean the place up a bit first."

"You're selling? The farm?" Heather's question was met with a raised eyebrow, as if it were the dumbest question that Melinda Wilson had ever heard.

"A-yep, sure is. We're broke. Going ta live with my sister down south til we can pick ourselfs up a bit."

Heather reeled. The idea of Marcus being forced to move made her feel like crying.

"When are you leaving? I mean, will Marcus…," she left the thought unfinished.

"Coupla weeks I 'spose. The Berkemann's next door are going ta buy the place, just need to get a few things repaired first. They don't care 'bout the house, just the barn and the land ya see."

"So you're going to stay with your sister, you said. I suppose that will be nice, to be with family," Heather said, trying to sound more upbeat than she felt. Melinda chortled.

"Hardly! Their house is smaller than this dump. We'll be crammed in there like sardines in a can. The littluns will stay in the bedroom with us a-course, but Marcus'll have to sleep downstairs on the floor with his brother and tha dogs," Melinda said, seemingly unaware of how terrible it sounded.

Heather gasped. She couldn't help herself. Melinda noticed and began talking before Heather could say anything more. "Oh, twon't be that bad. Kids can sleep anywhere. Now, if he just didn't have to eat we'd really have it figured out."

At the thought of Marcus going without food or even a bed, Heather felt her heart race and her blood boil. Knowing that these were the same people responsible for the bruises on his arms, Heather couldn't help but say the only thing that came to mind.

"We could take him. You know, until you get back on your feet. Just until then, of course."

Melinda looked as surprised as Heather felt. She hadn't planned to actually say the words out loud, and she wasn't prepared for what would happen if Melinda took her up on the offer.

"Ya serious? You'd take the kid? Ya know he eats like a horse, right?" Melinda said, clearly more concerned with how much her son ate than whether or not he was actually living with her.

If she hadn't been certain before, she certainly was now. Any parent that beat their child, any parent that didn't care whether or not their child was living with them, did not deserve them anyway.

"You better believe I am," Heather said, mustering up every ounce of conviction she could.

"Well, alright then. Take him. We'll send for him when we're stable," Melinda said, looking as though she'd struck a particularly good bargain.

Heather gulped. *What have I just done?* she wondered as she listened to Mrs. Wilson yell for Marcus to come into the house.

Chapter Forty-One

Things were starting to look up for Jason. In the two weeks since Mr. Miller had threatened to evict him from the studio, Jason had landed four new portrait clients. In addition, he'd finally managed to secure an updated contract with the Normal School to photograph all of the current members of the faculty. That contract alone would ensure that he could pay the rent through the rest of the year, and much of the next.

Jason could feel himself smiling as he attended to the last few details of his day. It had been a long time since he believed that things were heading in the right direction, and he let himself delight in the moment. After he had finished cataloging the week's films, he tidied up the main room and headed out the door. His first stop was an unplanned visit to Harold Miller.

He knocked firmly on Harold's door before entering but did not bother for an invitation before opening the large mahogany door at the entrance to the office. He knew the bold entrance would rankle Harold's feathers, and his smile returned at the thought.

"Well, look who we have here. If it isn't Mr. Baldwin," Harold Miller said as Jason entered the room. He was leaning back precariously in his chair with his legs extended onto his huge desk and a cigarette perched between his lips. If he was flustered by the unplanned intrusion, he did not show it.

"In the flesh," Jason answered before Harold could say more. "I've come with the rent for next month."

The look of surprise that flashed in Harold's face was a sight to behold, transforming his previously dour expression into something almost comical. Harold's cigarette trembled in his mouth, threatening to fall. When Jason added, "And the next month's as well," Harold's mouth opened just enough for it to escape. Harold tried reflexively to catch it, but only succeeded in batting it halfway across the room. Jason took a step, picked it up, and then smashed it out on the ashtray on the desk. He couldn't help the smirk that crossed his lips.

Harold was so delighted to be getting his rent money that he didn't even notice. Jason pulled an envelope out of his coat pocket and handed it over to Harold, who greedily counted out the bills inside. Jason didn't wait for him to finish, just turned on his heel and headed back through the door. "I'll see you next year, Harold," he said as he crossed the threshold and headed out.

He finished a few other nearby errands before he returned to the studio and grabbed his bike. It was nearing the end of bicycle riding season, and Jason was going to take advantage of every favorable day remaining. Today was warm for November, at least by Iowa standards, and the ride home was as pleasant as the rest of his day had already been.

As Jason wiped his feet on the doormat on the porch, he could hear two voices, one of which was Heather's and the other belonging to a child. At this point, Jason had heard that voice often enough to know that it belonged to Marcus. He sighed, but even the presence of Marcus couldn't dampen his spirits. He walked into the house and greeted them.

"Well, hello Marcus, how are you doing today? Good day at school?" Jason asked as he embraced Heather, giving her a peck on the cheek as he did so. As he broke the embrace, he saw a peculiar expression on Heather's face, her brows furrowed and lips tight. *Not angry, she looks…* Jason's thoughts were interrupted.

"We, well…," she hesitated, "we need to talk. Marcus, can you give us a few minutes? There's some books in the sunroom, why don't you pick one out and practice, hmm?"

Jason did not like the sound of that. There had never existed a positive conversation preceded by the words, 'we need to talk', and Jason was sure that streak would not be broken today. It was then that he noticed the glass on the table, filled with what he knew was bourbon and garnished with a cherry.

"Here, I made you a drink. Why don't we sit down for a minute, okay?" Heather asked as she handed him the Old Fashioned. Jason grimaced. *Alcohol served unasked for before dinner?* he wondered, now expecting their conversation to be even worse than he'd originally predicted.

"I got word that the Wilson's are going to be moving and…," Heather started, but Jason cut her off.

"The Wilson's? You mean Marcus' family?" Jason felt his spirits lift at the news. He knew Heather loved Marcus, that she truly cared for him, but he was also ready to go back to having their home feel like their own again. Marcus was there so much recently that it often felt as though they had adopted the boy. What Jason didn't immediately understand was why Heather had served him a drink to tell him. As he looked at her, watched her brows furrow and lips tighten, realization dawned. "Wait, you don't mean to," he stammered but pressed on, "you aren't trying to tell me what I think you are, are you?"

"It'll only be for a little while. Just until they get back on their feet, you know. Then they…," Jason interrupted again, too angry to hear her out.

"The Wilson's have never had a bucket's worth of stability between them. That boy'll be living here 'til he's a grown man if we're waiting for the Wilson's to get back on their feet!" Jason said, his voice raising. He realized that he was starting to shout, but he could barely contain the anger that had swelled inside his chest. "Now look, you didn't even talk about this with me first. You didn't even ask whether or not I wanted…," Jason let the comment hang as he saw Marcus round the corner. Tears ran down his face, and Jason knew those tears were on his shoulders. Heather ran to the boy, hugging him close to her. The look that she propelled towards Jason made him think twice about trying to continue the argument.

"I… I know ya don't want me. I know. But my parents don't want me neither and…," Heather squatted down to the boy's level and brought her face to his.

"I won't hear another word of that around here, do you understand me, Marcus? You are wanted here. Now, my husband just doesn't like surprises, you understand? That's all there is to everything that you just heard," Heather encouraged the boy. "When the time is right, you'll go back to your parents. Until then, we've got an extra room and it'll be yours. You're one of the family, you got that?"

Marcus nodded his head and wiped his tears with the back of a dirty hand. The anger that Jason felt still burned deep in his chest, but it was temporarily overcome by the compassion he was witnessing. He knew that Heather's intentions were not only right, but undeniably good hearted.

She should have talked to me; we should have made the decision together, he thought bitterly. He also knew that if she had done that, if she had consulted him, he would have rejected the idea out of hand. There would have been no chance whatsoever that he would have given her permission to take the boy in. He couldn't decide whether that made what she'd done better or worse.

"Now, head upstairs and get cleaned up. I won't have you looking like that for dinner. Off young man, and make sure to wash those hands!" Heather said, and shooed the boy away before turning back to Jason.

"It will be fine, I promise. It won't seem like much of anything has changed," Heather said, her voice soft and her eyes pleading with him to be understanding.

"That, my dear, is exactly the problem. Nothing will change," Jason said, scorn in his voice. He saw Heather flinch at his words. He hadn't intended for them to come off as scathing as they had, but nothing could be done about that now. Once words had been loosed, no lasso could ever bring them back.

"Honey, don't…," Heather said, but it was too late. Jason had already put on his coat and opened the door.

"I'll stay at the studio tonight. I've got work to do anyway," he said as he left, slamming the large door as he did so.

Chapter Forty-Two

Heather found herself ever more involved in school work as autumn faded into winter. The superintendent, Mr. Pfeiffer, had taken quite ill, and Heather had been asked to help with some of his normal workload. His previous request that she finish midterm grades early now made sense; he'd wanted to complete as many of his duties as possible before his illness grew worse.

Heather, for all the doubts she had about her new role, thrived under it, although she would not truly admit that to herself. The workload was daunting, but Heather found herself being looked to by other teachers as an example. It was an exhilarating change of pace in her life.

Having Marcus at home with them felt incredibly natural to her, like the passing of one season into another. However, as with any seasonal change, there had been difficulty and discomfort. She knew that Jason had found the adjustment to be more burdensome than she had, and she saw the signs of stress line his face.

Just the previous evening, they'd had yet another disagreement. Heather had stayed at school late to work, and Jason had arrived home to find an empty house. When she'd finally arrived, she could tell that he'd been stewing over it.

"Please tell me what was so important that it couldn't have waited until tomorrow?" Jason had asked the moment she'd entered the house. She sent Marcus away quickly before sitting down at the table.

"Could we not do this right now? I just got home and…," Heather said, but Jason cut her off.

"That's what you always say. It's always better to talk about it later, not now, maybe next week. Now is the time. So tell me, what was so important?"

"Well," Heather paused while she considered how best to explain to him, "it's not any one thing. You know that I've been taking on some of Herbert's work while he's sick. That's been occupying a lot of my time lately."

"Ah, yes, the extra work. The work that you aren't even being paid for. I do remember that," Jason scoffed. It was not the first time that he'd brought up the fact that she was not being paid extra for the new work she was doing.

"Jason, don't be like that. It's just something we're all coming together to do. Just for now."

"Sure, just for now. Just until the next thing comes along. And then the next. What about time for us? Where are we in all of this?"

There hadn't been much that she could say to that, so she'd relied on her fury to make it stop. When cornered, Heather had never been afraid to fight back. She had felt the anger bubble inside her, and she'd let it spill out like a pot left too long to boil. She'd yelled, and so had he, but that wasn't where it would end. She knew exactly where to poke if she wanted to finish it.

"Fuck you, Jason," she'd said, throwing the words as though they were darts. Jason loathed being sworn at, and she knew it. His reaction to it was predictable and desirable, silence. As always, Jason had gone quiet afterwards, waiting only a few moments before leaving the room.

She'd known, even in the moment, that it wasn't the right thing for her to do, and she regretted it now. Even so, she couldn't take another second of petty conflict, and she felt she had no other way to regain control. That was two days ago, and she told herself it didn't matter; she couldn't go back and change it now anyway. Instead of worrying about it, she put her nose back to the grindstone and went back to the task at hand, a school finance report that needed to be completed.

She lost herself in the work, only stopping once she had finished. The sun had set outside, and Marcus still sat quietly in the back of the schoolroom, doodling on a piece of scrap paper.

"Are you ready to go?" Heather asked wearily as she put on her coat. The boy smiled and nodded, and the two of them walked out together towards home.

When they arrived, Heather was surprised to be greeted with the smells of a warm meal.

"There's a roast in the oven. Should be done by now," Jason said even before she could comment. "I also tossed in some potatoes, so we'll have that, too."

Heather was impressed, but also somewhat annoyed. It was admirable that Jason had decided to cook, but she got the feeling that this was his way of apologizing without actually having to address the issue. He was over it, so she should be too, that was the message. It prickled her in a way that she did not care for.

"Thanks, Mr. Baldwin!" Marcus said enthusiastically. Marcus was happy to eat almost anything that you put in front of him. Heather sometimes thought that was Jason's closest connection to the boy; they shared the same appetite. Putting her mild annoyance aside, Heather retrieved plates and utensils from the cupboards and set the table while Jason removed the meal from the oven.

"It may not be very good, I've never cooked one of these before. I looked for your cookbook, but I didn't find much. Just kind of threw everything together the way I thought you did it," Jason said as he cut the beef and served it.

"So you went shopping, too?" Heather asked, still genuinely surprised at the fact he'd chosen to cook. Jason nodded.

"My appointment this afternoon cancelled, so I dropped by the butcher's and came home for a few minutes."

"You really shouldn't have left the house with the oven on. That's how the fire started at the Friedman's, you know," Heather said as she started cutting up her potato. She realized that sounded harsh, so she added, "but thank you." It was half-hearted, but it was something.

Jason looked at her for a moment, perhaps deciding whether or not to voice an alternative position. Apparently deciding not to, he simply nodded. They ate in relative silence, only occasionally broken by idle chit chat about their respective days. With little for each of them to report, the conversation was minimal.

After they finished, Jason left the table and headed for the living room. Heather noticed that he didn't bother to return his plate, or anything else, to the sink. She sighed and started cleaning up after all three of them. As she washed the dishware, she glanced over her shoulder to see what was occupying her husband's attention. Unable to see what he was doing, she called out, "what are you doing over there?"

"Nothing much, just trying to read," he said, as if she was interrupting his ability to do so. She chose not to respond, and after the dishes were complete she went outside to retrieve the clothes that had been put out on the line. It wouldn't be long before it would be too cold to hang the clothes outside. After she retrieved them, she retreated to the bedroom to fold them and put them away. She quickly completed that task as well, and she decided that she would take the rare opportunity to catch up on some of the sewing projects she had accumulated.

She worked with the old sewing machine for nearly two hours before it occurred to her that she should be getting Marcus to bed. Jumping up, Heather exited the room and went on the hunt for the young boy. She found him sitting beside Jason, who was still reading, this time out loud.

"La nourriture a été terrible ces derniers temps, ce n'est rien d'autre que du bouillon," he said in French, surprising her. "That means, 'the food has been bad lately, just broth', at least I think it does. My French still isn't perfect and this is an extremely old book." As he finished, both of them finally seemed to notice that Heather had entered the room.

"Oh, hello. Mr. Baldwin has just been reading to me from this funny book. It doesn't really have a story, and it's written in another language, but I like it anyway," Marcus informed her.

"Well, that's because it's not a book, it's a journal, and it was written in another country," Heather said, wondering why in the world Jason had decided to get that old thing out. "Anyway, off to bed. Make sure you brush your teeth!" she said as the boy ran off to obey.

"I've been thinking about old times recently, so I thought I'd read this. Well, try to read it. A lot of the French is beyond me."

"Very old times," Heather responded, sitting down on the loveseat across from his chair, "it feels like another lifetime."

"Well, in a sense, it really is. This was written a hundred and fifty years before either of us existed. Another lifetime, indeed."

They both sat there silently, pondering the weight that rested on those words. The air itself felt heavy around them.

"What are you looking for in there, Jason?" Heather asked with a deep sigh. She felt a twinge of heartache as her mind drifted to the past.

Jason paused for a few long moments. "I don't know, Heather. But I will let you know if I find it."

Chapter Forty-Three

Jason had started reading the journal every time that he found himself frustrated, using it as a distraction. It took a lot of effort to translate the old French, and while doing so he had no room left for the irritations of regular life.

In addition, Jason found some catharsis in reading the words a wrongly accused man had written so long ago. Although most of the text was banal, there was something about it that endeared Jason to Eustache Dauger. So much of the man's life had been taken away from him, and all he could do was take each day as it came.

In the first half of the journal, Jason had learned very little about the circumstances of Eustache's imprisonment but had learned quite a bit about who he was as a person and what he'd done prior to being locked up.

Eustache Dauger was the son of Ercole Dauger, a lifelong servant to Michel Le Tellier, a powerful and well-connected French official. It was through his father that Eustache had entered employment as a valet to a man named Louvois, the son of Tellier. Although it had not been a glamorous job, it had afforded him a comfortable life, if a modest one.

He had taken a wife at only nineteen, a beautiful girl named Josephine, who bore him two children in the two years immediately following their marriage. It was apparent that Eustache loved the children a great deal; he spent a large portion of his writing talking about how much he wished to see them again, if even for a moment.

He also longed to give them more than what they had and described his growing discontent with their status. The family had the things that they needed to survive, but his salary did not allow for anything beyond those basics. This did not sit well with Eustache, whose daily interaction with the wealthy clouded his view on what he, and his family, deserved.

In between his bittersweet recollections of his past, Eustache would often describe the prison in great detail. Jason was astounded by how much freedom Eustache had actually been allowed, commonly strolling the grounds alongside Bénigne Dauvergne de Saint-Mars, the jailer. The two of them had developed a friendship over the many years of his imprisonment, and Saint-Mars allowed him luxuries not afforded other inhabitants.

What surprised Jason most of all was how infrequently Eustache had been required to wear the mask, which had actually been made of cloth rather than iron. The mask was truly only worn when Eustache was in the company of other people, excluding Saint-Mars and one other trusted jailer. When he was in his cell, Eustache was not required to wear the mask, nor was he required to wear it when he and Saint-Mars walked the isolated island.

Though Eustache described Saint-Mars as his friend, he was also distrustful of his motives, wondering in several passages about whether or not he could speak freely with him. However, having been imprisoned for so many years, he was loath to do anything that would jeopardize the very few joys his life contained, and chose to think of Saint-Mars as a comrade.

He'd asked for the journal when he had been moved from his first imprisonment at the fortress Pinerolo, but Saint-Mars had denied him. It was not until Eustache had been moved again, this time to Île Sainte-Marguerite, that Saint-Mars had allowed him paper and pen.

Eustache described it as, "having life breathed back into him," although Jason thought it sounded better in French. Being able to write seemed like it had awoken the spirit of Eustache, and he'd set to it with passion. Although it was old French, and much of it was beyond what Jason could effectively translate, Jason still got the sense that Eustache had poured out his life in these pages. Even the most trivial of things was described meticulously. It was fascinating in a way that Jason struggled to describe.

The portion that he was reading currently related to another prisoner who had been transferred to the island. This man screamed constantly in his cell, keeping Eustache awake and garnering the irritation of prisoner and jailer alike. Eustache described the conversation that he and Saint-Mars shared concerning what should be done. Throwing the prisoner off the nearby cliffs was not an option, apparently.

Jason sighed as he finished the page. It was late and he had been reading for hours, although he'd only managed a couple of pages during that time. He enjoyed the work, but it was still tedious, and his eyes were red with strain. "Time for bed, I think," he said to no one. He wasn't alone in the house, but it felt as though he were.

Marcus had been in bed for hours and Heather was still at work in the kitchen, books and papers spread over the table top.

Or, at least that's how she had looked when he'd come upstairs to the bedroom a few hours ago. He could only assume that she was still there, plugging away at the increasing workload that had been piled on her. Although the sickness of the superintendent had affected all of the teachers, it seemed to Jason that only Heather was getting the additional work. "And for no additional pay," he muttered absently to himself.

Jason hadn't slept well in a long time, often up late and rarely sleeping through the night. After hours of reading, his eyes were tired and sleep came easily. Nearly the very moment his head brushed the pillow, he was out.

"Jason, are you awake?" The voice drifted into his dreams, changing things. He'd been dreaming that he was staying at a strange hotel, and now a maid was suddenly knocking at his door. "Jason, we need to talk, it's important," Heather continued, breaking him out of his imaginary hotel stay.

"What is it? Couldn't it have waited until morning?" Jason said, leaving his eyes closed.

"Jason, please, look at me."

Jason sat up and rubbed his eyes. Whatever was coming apparently could not wait, which meant that it was likely to be unpleasant. "Okay, okay, I'm awake. What?"

Heather sat down on the edge of the bed and took his hand. "I've been waiting to tell you for a while, but I couldn't wait any longer. It's been a couple of months now," Heather said, and Jason's mind raced. *A couple of months? What had been a couple of months?* Heather stopped, reached over, and turned his face to hers.

"Jason, relax. This is good news. I'm trying to tell you that I'm pregnant. We're going to have a baby."

Chapter Forty-Four

Back in late September, Heather had started feeling slightly sick in the mornings, but she'd initially written those off as a byproduct of working too much and eating too little. It had been the start of a new school year, and it was always a stressful time for her. However, as the days and weeks had passed, it soon became clear that she was more than simply overworked.

Her first reaction had been fear. *How in the world am I going to be a mom?* she'd wondered many times in those first days. Between her work and watching over Marcus, Heather already felt as though she was strained to the breaking point.

Her next reaction had been joy. No matter what hardships they would face, there could be no greater blessing in the world than that of a child. *Would it be a boy? A girl? Would their child have their red hair? What would they name it?* Heather's mind had been frantic, running back and forth with questions that could not yet be answered.

She had wondered, too, about how Jason would take the news. She knew that he wanted children, but she wasn't sure that he wanted a child right now. The timing wasn't exactly ideal, and she knew it. That was a big part of why it had taken her so long to tell him, waiting nearly until she had started showing to let Jason in on the secret.

Breaking the news to Jason had gone better than she had expected. Although she'd made the mistake of waking him up to tell him, Jason had been overjoyed. He seemed more excited than she was, at least after he had been given the opportunity to fully wake up. That had eased many of her early concerns, even if it did not erase them entirely.

The months had passed by in a blur after that. Once she'd told Jason, it had become real, and everything now revolved around the little one to come. Every conversation, every interaction, all underpinned by the knowledge that they were soon to be parents. It was both nerve wracking and exhilarating.

Their Christmas celebration had been a blissful reprieve from the rest of the stress in their lives. The three of them joined Dean and they all celebrated together, exchanging simple gifts and enjoying the warmth of the season, even if not the weather. Marcus was still with them, but his presence made Christmas feel, somehow, more complete. There was something about the excitement of a child that brought out joy that could not be found elsewhere.

Jason and Heather had spent the weeks after Christmas painting the room beside theirs. It wasn't much, hardly larger than two closets pushed together, but it would be just fine as a nursery. The paint had transformed it from a forgettable sewing room into a warm space much more suitable for a child. The pale yellow paint made it feel as though sunshine were ever present, even in the gloomy Iowa winter.

Dean had volunteered Kathleen's old rocking chair, and they had accepted with gratitude. As Heather thought back on that moment, she remembered how Jason's eyes had gone cloudy at the offer. She knew that he missed his mother fiercely.

They had also been able to locate an inexpensive, secondhand, bassinet for the first few months. Jason had made it clear to her that he did not want the baby to sleep with them, but Heather knew that she wouldn't feel right having a newborn sleep in a separate room, either. A bassinet at their bedside was the perfect solution, and Heather smiled as she rocked it idly back and forth.

She was sitting on their bed, quietly staring out the window. It was now nearly April, and the typical spring showers had started early this year. It seemed as though all it ever did was rain. Combined with her round belly, she felt trapped inside. It felt like all she ever did was teach and sit at home. She couldn't even ride her bike to school anymore; she had gotten too large.

Jason had encouraged her to stay home full time and give up teaching, but she'd resisted him at every turn. She felt called to work, to teach, to be a part of the society. Staying at home simply wasn't in her blood. She didn't think that Jason understood, but he had backed down and no longer raised the issue. Just as well, she knew that she would not change her mind.

"Marcus, come here, won't you?" Heather called, intending to ask him to bring her a glass of water. Going up and down the stairs had become more and more of a chore lately. Marcus bounded up the steps two at a time, then stopped abruptly and slid halfway down the hallway before reaching their door. Heather didn't see it happen, but she'd watched it enough times to picture it clearly. Marcus was a ball of energy, and always looking for an opportunity to spend some of it.

"Whad'ya say?" Marcus asked, the words all one continuous string.

"Marcus, we've talked about this. In this house we speak properly, do you understand?" Marcus nodded. He had heard the speech many times over the last seven months.

"I'm sorry. What did you say?" he asked, this time more slowly.

"Would you please bring me a glass of water? I'm feeling pretty parched," Heather said, and Marcus sprang out of the room without hesitation. *If I only had his energy*, she thought.

Heather thanked him when he returned with the glass, and told him that he could go back to whatever he'd been doing. She could feel a headache coming on, and she was deciding whether or not to lie down to rest when she heard the door downstairs open and close.

A few moments later, Jason came up the stairs and entered the room. Heather was surprised, she hadn't expected him to be home for several hours.

"Why are you home?" Heather asked, realizing too late how that sounded.

"I'm happy to see you, too," Jason said, sarcastically. "I finished early. Well, actually, I didn't finish at all, but I decided to come home early anyway."

Heather raised her eyes in surprise. Jason was not in the habit of coming home early from work. "Oh, really? And why is that?" she asked.

"Just thought I'd spend some time with my lovely wife, that's all," he answered, smiling.

"That's sweet of you. You're just in time to join me," Heather said, returning the smile.

"Join you?"

"Yes, join me for a nap," Heather said, and laughed.

Chapter Forty-Five

Jason hadn't been able to sleep, nor had he wanted to. He'd laid beside Heather until she had started to breath heavily, and then had slipped out quietly. When he'd come home early from the studio, he'd hoped that he and Heather would be able to spend some quality time together. It felt to Jason as though they hadn't actually spent any time together in months.

Between Marcus, accommodations for their upcoming arrival, Heather's teaching, and his work at the studio, their time together had been stretched thin. Although he did his best to hide it, Jason was growing increasingly frustrated with their life at home. His love for Heather was as deep as ever, but he was quickly losing sight of what he had always expected married life would be.

He sighed audibly and sat down in the living room. He picked up the journal and a small notebook beside it. Jason had taken to making notations about the journal as he read and translated. Most were simple questions about what a word meant, but he also noted passages that seemed to contribute to the story of why Eustache had been arrested.

There were few such mentions, at least so far. Over the past few months, Jason had made minimal headway on the journal. Business at the studio had picked up significantly, and most nights he came home both late and tired. When he did find time to work on it, the struggles of translation caused progress to be slow.

Nonetheless, he was encouraged by the most recent passage, which described Eustache's actual arrest for the first time. He'd been in his own home when it had happened, the police barging in well after dark, waking his youngest son in the process. Eustache went into great detail about the event, describing it as perhaps the most terrifying moment he had ever experienced.

His wife, Josephine, had screamed and cried, begging the officers to tell her what they were doing. They had ignored her, refusing to say even a single word in explanation.

Eustache, for his part, had done his best to comfort her, telling her that it would be alright and that everything would be explained and sorted out. Jason read as Eustache lamented over the moment. It had been the last time that he would ever see his wife. The desperate cries of his son still troubled his dreams even so many years later.

"If I could go back and change things, for that I would give my life. I would give my future away in exchange for changing my past," Jason wrote. The translation was clunky and he knew it, but it was the best that he could do. The comment pulled at him. *What an unusual reaction*, Jason thought. The very idea of Eustache's life being unjustly taken made his blood boil.

He was angry, not just for Eustache, but for himself. He felt it rising and did nothing to quell it. He tried to go back to reading but found that he was no longer able to concentrate. He needed something more than a book to take his mind off of things; he needed a drink.

Book still in hand, he headed up the stairs, intending to tell Heather that he was leaving. When he got there, he set the journal on the bedside table and leaned over Heather. She was breathing even more deeply than before. Seeing no need to wake her, Jason quietly grabbed his jacket and went back downstairs.

He scribbled a note instead, leaving it on the table for her. Marcus had left the house a few minutes earlier, scampering outside to play with other children in the neighborhood. The weather outside was growing warmer, and all of the pent up wintertime energy was being exorcised.

Jason arrived at the saloon only a few minutes later, the walk being only a few blocks. He sat down at the bar and ordered an Old Fashioned, his drink of choice.

"Jason! Nice'ta see ya. Been a week or two," Garrison Henry shouted as he poured the drink. Over the last few months, Jason had become somewhat of a regular at the establishment. Not regular enough to have his own barstool, but regular enough to be on a first name basis with the proprietor.

"Ah, yeah, you too. Been working a lot, you know," Jason said. Glancing around, he noticed that the bar was surprisingly busy for a Saturday afternoon. It wasn't even dinner time and the saloon was almost completely full. "Looks like you have been too," he added.

"Oh, sure! Ever since the weather turned and they started that project along the river, things have been more than steady. Can't say I mind," Garrison said with a smile, always happy to have the extra business.

The barkeep slid a tumbler of amber liquid in front of him and told him to yell when he needed another one. *And a few more after that*, Jason thought as he took his first sip.

The bar's business did not diminish as the night wore on, more and more patrons flooding in the later it got. Within an hour, the place was nearly standing room only, and Jason thought that perhaps it might be time for him to get going.

Just after he'd made up his mind to go, a hand tapped his shoulder and a familiar voice sounded in his ear.

"Well, hey there stranger. Been a few years now, hasn't it?"

Jason turned, momentarily unable to place the voice. As he did, he noticed the blonde hair and impeccable dress of Faye Morris. Although it had been years since he had last seen her, very little about her had changed.

"Faye Morris, nice to see you. How have you been?" Jason asked, fumbling for a courteous greeting. He and Faye had never been close, and had he been the first to see her, it was likely that he would have left without making contact.

"Oh, you know, pretty good. And you? Still as tall and handsome as ever, I see," Faye replied, a coy smile adorning her otherwise ordinary face. She continued before Jason could say more, "I just moved back last week. When my parents moved to Wisconsin, I went with them. But my heart always belonged here, so when my engagement fell through, I knew this was where I needed to be."

"I'm sorry to hear about…," Jason started, but Faye cut him off once more.

"Oh hush, nothing for you to worry your pretty little face about. It was for the best, anyway. Tom was nothing but a drunk, spoiled rotten by his parent's money. Never earned a cent that didn't start out as theirs."

Jason just nodded.

"Well, come here, why don't you? I've been waiting for some friends to meet me. Sit with me until they get here, I've already got a table," Faye said, her smile returning. Jason wasn't sure what to say. He'd been planning to leave, but there was something about Faye's compliments that drew him in.

Jason glanced briefly at his left hand, realizing only then that he'd forgotten to put his wedding band back on. He always took it off when working with the developing chemicals, and his hand now felt naked without it.

"Just for a few minutes, alright?" Jason said, running his thumb over the place where the band should have been.

"Sure, of course. Now, let's sit down, shall we?" Faye said, and led him towards a table in the back corner of the saloon.

Chapter Forty-Six

Heather woke groggy and confused. It was dark in the room, no light entering from the windows. *Is it morning already?* she wondered before realizing that she'd only been taking a nap, not sleeping for the night. *What time is it?*

As if on cue, the grandfather clock downstairs began to chime. *Clang, clang, clang…*, the clock sounded one time after another, finally stopping after it had reverberated seven times.

"Oh, my goodness. It's seven o' clock!" Heather exclaimed to the empty room. She quickly scrambled from the bed, running her hands briefly through her hair before stepping out of the room and descending the stairs.

"Marcus! Jason! Is anyone here?" she called out, listening for a reply but not receiving one. After touring the rooms below, she concluded that no one was home. She cast her eyes once more along the empty space, only then noticing the scrap of paper on the table.

She read it aloud, "Went to the saloon. Be back for dinner."

She scrunched her nose and looked around again, as though one more look would magically reveal her family standing right before her. She was now both annoyed and concerned. She started towards the front door to look outside, only to hear it clatter open and then slam closed. Her nerves calmed at the sound.

"Hey! I wanted to know...," Marcus called out as he entered, stopping when he saw Heather. "I'm sorry, I didn't know you were up. I was just going to ask Mr. Baldwin if he minded if I went over to Johnny's for dinner."

"You haven't had dinner?" Heather asked, her concern flooding back. *Where was Jason? Why hadn't he returned yet?*

Marcus shook his head. "No, not yet. You were asleep and Mr. Baldwin left. So I've just been playing. I said I was hungry, and Johnny said I could come over for dinner. They always eat late. So, could I go?"

Heather didn't answer immediately. She was distracted by the note and the time, unable to process all of the variables at once.

"Sure, go. Just be sure that you're home by nine o' clock at the latest, okay?"

"Sure! No problem!" Marcus said, bounding out the door. As the door slammed shut, Heather thought she heard him yell, 'thank you!' It was an afterthought, but it was better than nothing.

Now that Marcus was taken care of, Heather's consternation returned. Jason had left sometime after she'd fallen asleep and was yet to return. Although he'd gone to the saloon with increasing frequency lately, it was still unlike him to be gone for three hours.

She vacillated between options for a minute, unsure of whether she should stay here or go out to find him. *He's probably just gone into the studio,* she thought. *After all, when he came home he did say that he had left work unfinished.* She knew that unfinished work stressed Jason out, but there was something else that nagged at her. She also knew that Jason did not drink when he worked. He always said that a sloppy photographer was no good for anything.

It was that thought that drove her out the door and towards the saloon. She dreaded the idea of walking all the way to there, but she felt compelled to go. Had her pregnant belly not prevented it, she would have taken her bicycle instead. As she walked, she alternated between concern and anger, both emotions posturing for the same internal space. By the time that she reached the saloon doors, it was concern that occupied her mind.

Heather had never been one to drink. Between her family history and the harsh taste, alcohol was something that she barely tolerated, much less enjoyed. She knew that Jason liked it, but she wished that he didn't. The only reason that she did not fight him on the topic was because he was always a happy drunk, and sometimes that wasn't all bad.

The saloon that Jason frequented was situated directly opposite the post office, on the far west side of the area considered to be downtown. It was a nondescript building. Just a building on a corner with chipped green paint and dirty windows. To the north were the railroad tracks, and Heather could hear one of those horns blaring in the distance. She shivered with the night's chill, and gripped her light jacket more tightly around herself.

Although the main swinging doors faced the east, Heather headed for the north side instead. It would not have been considered proper for a lady to enter through the front doors. Instead, she'd need to use the ladies' entrance, which was a smaller door set into the rear corner of the building.

Heather pulled at the door but only managed to move it a few inches. For an entrance made for women, the door was surprisingly heavy. She redoubled her efforts, and the door opened fully. She stepped inside, grateful to be out of the chilly night air. She glanced around the crowded room, first scanning the bar where Jason usually sat.

The saloon served food, and Heather felt her stomach growl at the smell of it. Pushing her hunger aside, she headed for the bar.

"Mr. Henry! Mr. Henry!" she called, trying to get his attention amidst the crowd. She saw his eyes glance over at her, and a sour expression cross his face. He did not acknowledge her, instead moving to the far end of the bar to help someone else. Heather was surprised, Garrison had always been pleasant to her.

She dismissed the thought and continued to survey the room. It was full of life, with men and women drinking, eating, and enjoying each other's company. Loud piano music drowned out all but the closest conversations, but it was clear that everyone was having a good time.

From where she stood, only some of the room was visible. Much of it was obstructed by the staircase that led up to Mr. Henry's living quarters. She walked towards the front door, attempting to get a better view of the entire room. After she'd reached it, she didn't see sign of Jason anywhere. He wasn't at the bar, nor at any of the tables. A group of men surrounded the piano, but Jason was not among them, either.

Her eyes scoured every corner. There were people everywhere, but nothing caught her eye until she saw a blonde woman in the far corner, kissing a man. Heather felt herself blush. *Such behavior, and in public!* she thought to herself. She turned her eyes away.

As her gaze shifted away from the woman, something caught her attention and made her refocus. Although the woman almost completely obstructed her companion, Heather couldn't help but notice that the man she was kissing had red hair.

She gasped out loud, although the room was much too loud for anyone to hear her. The world spun, her breath caught in her throat. The corners of her vision narrowed until there was nothing except those two people in the corner.

Chapter Forty-Seven

Jason felt his head swim. It wasn't the alcohol, it was the most intense shame that he'd ever felt. It bubbled and boiled within him, and he felt as though he may explode with it. His mortification was palpable, beads of sweat lining his forehead and his heart beating faster than he had ever felt it.

The instant that he'd looked up to see Heather's eyes on him, he had nearly fainted. Up until that moment, his only concern had been seeking out catharsis. He'd given no thought to anyone other than himself, and that knowledge filled him with a shame so deep he felt as though he may drown in it.

"Heather!" he'd shouted, practically shoving Faye off of him and completely unaware of her objection. Heather had not stopped, turning on her heel and leaving as quickly as she could. By the time that Jason pushed through the crowd, she'd disappeared. He ran through the swinging doors and surveyed the area outside. People milled about, but there was no sign of Heather.

Sure that he'd missed her, Jason returned to the crowded saloon and shouted for her once again. People were looking at him, but he didn't care. In that moment, she was all that existed in the world. *She should have been all along,* he thought. Gritting his teeth, he pushed through people until he reached the bar and saw Garrison.

"Did you see her? My wife, did you see her?" Garrison turned his eyes to him, and Jason was sure that he saw disgust written there. It was no more than he deserved, but that wasn't what he needed in that moment. "Did you or not?"

Garrison Henry pointed towards the back of the saloon, unwilling to say more. It was then that Jason remembered that the saloon had two entrances, and he raced for the door. He didn't push it open, he collided with it. The force of the impact nearly knocked his breath away, but he did not allow it to slow him down.

He fought the urge to run all the way back. He was simultaneously desperate to arrive and also more afraid than he had ever been. When he eventually made it home, he found the door locked. He tried the back door, but that was locked as well.

"Go away!" Heather shouted, apparently hearing his frantic attempts to get inside. "I don't want to see you here! Go!"

"Please, honey, let me…," Jason heard his voice crack and felt the hot streams of his tears as they fell down his face, "let me…," he trailed off. *Let him what? Let him explain? How could he possibly explain?* His thoughts raced, jumping from one cloud to another, each one disintegrating beneath him.

"I don't want to hear anything you have to say! Go away!" Heather shouted.

Jason watched through the window as Heather retreated up the stairs, attempting to get as far away from him as possible. He ran into the front yard and looked up at the bedroom window.

"Heather! Please!"

Hope flickered in his chest as he watched their window open. Before he had the chance to say more, he watched something escape through the window. Momentarily confused, he didn't even move, and the flying object hit him right in the face.

"No! I don't care. You aren't welcome here!" Heather shouted, slamming the window as an exclamation point.

Jason sat down in the grass and put his hand to his nose. It wasn't broken, but it throbbed anyway. He felt blood begin to drip down his face, but he didn't bother to try to stop it. His world began to spin once more, and he felt his hold on consciousness start to slip. He put his hand down to steady himself, and it landed on the object Heather had thrown.

He picked it up, realizing that it was the journal. It had probably just been the first thing that Heather had seen, but it felt more meaningful than that. He tucked the book into his jacket pocket and stood.

The sobs racked through him as he walked. He knew what he'd done, and he knew it was unforgivable. Even so, the worst part was the fear of what would come next. *Would she leave him? Would she move back to California? Would he ever see his child?* The thoughts were a thunderous cacophony inside his head.

Unable to quiet his panicked mind, Jason walked aimlessly. Although it had grown chilly, Jason was sweating. He felt the perspiration run down his back and soak his shirt, but he couldn't make himself care about any of that. All that existed in his world was regret.

Eventually, Jason ended up at his studio, the only place that he truly had to go. He walked inside and stared at the space. Somehow it seemed both cavernous and constricted. He was overwhelmed and wanted to hide. He left the front door open and walked directly into the office. He dropped his coat on the office floor and opened the closet door. Stepping inside, he closed the door behind him.

He sat there, in the corner of the cluttered closet, for what seemed like hours. The closet was dark, no light could penetrate the office from the windows outside, and Jason could hear nothing over the sounds of his own crying. He knew that had anyone walked in, they would have seen the most pathetic example of a man this side of the Mississippi, but it didn't matter.

At some point, the deep weariness that Jason felt overtook him, and he succumbed to sleep. As he laid in the cramped closet, his rest was fitful and troubled by nightmares, one after the other. He awoke at the sounds of footsteps outside the closet door, and noticed that he could make out the vague shapes of the boxes he stored in the closet. He'd apparently slept through the night and into the morning light.

When the door opened, Jason could do nothing but look up. It took him a moment to realize that it was Heather who stood above him. Surprise flooded through him. He had not expected to see Heather again, much less see her so soon. Unsure about what to say or do, Jason sat up in the corner and just looked at her.

"Get up," she commanded, and Jason did not argue. "We're going home. Let's go," she said, and once more, Jason simply did as he was told.

Chapter Forty-Eight

Heather wept. It was about all that she could do lately. Ever since she saw her husband kissing another woman, Heather felt as though her stable life had been ripped out from under her. Everything that she had worked so hard to build was crumbling beneath the weight of his indiscretion.

Jason had been repentant, there was no doubt about that. He had taken her yelling, her outrage, and her fury without offering excuse or justification. His remorse was evident, but it simply was not enough. *How could it ever be enough?* she wondered as she set down her bags and returned home for the day. She just didn't know how she could forgive what he'd done.

Her students offered her the best reprieve that she'd been able to find. While she was with them, she was able to silence the voice inside her that called out in anger. They provided the distraction that she needed to get from one day to the next, and for that she was grateful. Now that she was home, things were more difficult.

Heather stroked her enormous belly absentmindedly and reflected on the few weeks since that night, trying to sort out in her mind what had happened and why. As usual, she came up with few answers. Their life had been happy. It had been busy, sure, but it had been happy. They loved each other and looked out for one another. She could honestly say that Jason was her soulmate. *And yet…*, the voice inside her head nagged. She clenched her fists and tried to silence it. There could be no possible way forward for them if she let that voice win.

When she walked in, Jason was sitting on the couch, staring off into space. The journal sat beside him, open but ignored. She did not say anything. They did not speak much anymore, instead going about the chores of day to day life in silence. More roommates than partners. It wasn't what she wanted, but she didn't know how to make it change.

Jason looked up, as if just now realizing that she was there. "Hello, how was your day?" he asked, his tone perfunctory.

"It was fine. Marcus is staying over with Danny from down the street," Heather responded, her tone equally stiff.

This was their pattern. Each of them went off to work in the morning, made awkward, forced, conversation in the afternoon, ignored each other in the evening, and then went to bed. Wash, rinse, repeat. Heather was sick and tired of it.

"Did you do any work today?" Heather asked, harshly. It was a jab at Jason. Although he went to work each morning, most of the time he did very little, allowing client appointments to fall through and other obligations to drop. It was wildly out of character for him.

"I tried. Had a cancellation. Another one," Jason said, and Heather couldn't help but sigh. Word of what had happened had gotten around, and several of Jason's clients had dropped him. They couldn't be associated with behavior of that sort, they said.

"Great. Just great."

She watched as Jason put his head in his hands, idly rubbing at his temples with his thumbs. She guessed that he had a headache, and she caught herself hoping that he did. He'd hurt her, and now he was hurting. It seemed fair to Heather.

"Not going to say anything? Just going to sit there?" Heather said, voice rising. Jason turned towards her and shrugged.

"And what do you want me to say? That I'm sorry? That I'm horrified? That I loathe myself? I've said all that before and it didn't help then, why should it help now?"

Heather knew he was right, that there was little more that he could say. What she needed now was a miracle. She needed him to erase the past and make everything go back to the way that it had been. She laughed out loud at the thought.

Jason, unable to read her mind, clearly believed she was laughing at what he'd said. "You think that's funny? Because I sure don't. I want to be able to say that it was all just a dream, all just some sort of cruel nightmare that I can wake myself up from. But it's not, and I'm sorry!" Jason half-shouted, half-cried.

"I know you're sorry, but that's not good enough! You betrayed me, you embarrassed me, you acted as though I didn't even exist!" Heather hollered, returning his shout with one of her own.

"I know! And what do you want from me now?"

"I want you to be the man that I married! The man who loved me, and who would never betray me! Where is that man? Where did he go?"

"He's still me. I'm still me. I just lost my way, I…," Heather knew that she shouldn't, but she could not help herself. She cut him off before he could say more.

"You just lost your way? Lost your way right into another woman? How does a person, someone who calls himself a man, do that? You're worthless!" She continued on, accusation and curse flying from her mouth without regard. After she had finished, Jason left, practically running up the stairs. She did not stop him. She was immediately ashamed at her words, but the fire that burned within her had not yet settled. She felt justified.

A sob caught in her throat and she turned to the kitchen. She'd intended to prepare some soup for dinner, but now the very thought was exhausting. She plopped down at the table instead, letting the weight of the world fall out of her. She found herself doing the only thing that she could think of; she started praying.

God, You are so much stronger than I am. You are not shaken by the wind of the storm. But I am, God. I am not only shaken, but sinking. I have fallen out of the boat and cannot find my way to shore. God, if You are listening, could You please help me? Could You extend Your hand to me? I know that You brought the two of us together for a reason. You moved us from our homes, arranged for us to travel thousands of miles to meet each other. You moved Heaven and Earth to bring us to the place where we are now. Why did You do all of that if only to have us fall apart now? Where are You, God? Where are You now, when we need You the most?

Chapter Forty-Nine

Jason left the house the next morning before sunrise. He'd slept poorly, although that was nothing new. He rarely slept more than four or five hours and never had a night where nightmares didn't haunt him.

As he walked along the winding path by the river, he couldn't help but feel as though he was trapped. He'd behaved in a way that had brought him a deep shame, and he'd hurt the person that he cared about more than anyone else in the world. He had betrayed a trust and ruined the biggest blessing he'd ever been given.

For all of the wonderful things that Heather was, she was quick to anger, and her words echoed over and over again in his mind. *You are worthless.*

For his part, he had no fire within him to fight against those words. He'd made a vow that he would never allow himself to blame others for his mistakes, and that also meant taking the anger and hostility without retaliation. It was what he deserved, and he knew it.

The path was narrow and overgrown, hardly more than a game trail. He only knew about it because Bill had brought him along a few times when he came to take photographs. Although it had been his passion, Bill's outdoor work had never been of the same quality as his studio work. Nonetheless, he would often wake early in the morning to venture out and photograph whatever struck his interest.

One of those things was the high train bridge at the very far side of town. The bridge itself was not particularly impressive, but when paired with the river, it had a dynamic visual appeal. As Jason walked, he found himself reminiscing on those earlier days. Things had been so much simpler then, back before there were so many responsibilities and obligations. Back when he and Heather had simply been 'in love', with nothing more to do than enjoy each other's company.

Things were so different now. Not just because of what he'd allowed to happen, but because of how life had changed. They'd allowed themselves to fall into a pattern that minimalized the value of their marriage, prioritizing instead their individual choices. It was so obvious now, but it had happened so slowly as to be invisible back then.

He approached the crest of the hill, right before the path would wind down towards the river to the north. Towards the west, the hill sloped up towards the train tracks and the bridge. Jason turned left, off the path, and climbed the hill in large, sure, strides. It took him only a minute to ascend the slope, and after he did so he found his shoes soaked with the dew of the grass. He didn't mind, he would not need them for very much longer.

He looked out at the bridge. The west side of the river flowed over a large group of rocks, creating a beautiful cascade beneath the bridge. Or at least he'd once thought of it as beautiful. Now, it only seemed utilitarian. It was all just means to an end, nothing more.

He stood there, at the bridge's edge, and stared at the sunrise. It was the most generic of sunrises, an orange disc slowly piercing an ocean of pale blue sky. He broke his gaze and walked out to the middle of the tracks. Leaning over the edge, he looked down at the river below, the water moving lazily over the rocks. The distance between the bridge and the rocks was less than thirty feet. Not enough to do anything more than break a few bones. Or, knowing his luck, end up paralyzed. He grimaced at the thought.

No, the surest way to do it, the only way, was the train itself. It came faithfully every morning at 6AM, rocking back and forth as it rounded the bend and chugged over the bridge. By the time that anyone would see him sitting there on the tracks, it would be too late to do anything about it. He turned his back to the river, intending to sit down for the last time.

"Hey there, how ya doing?" a voice asked, startling Jason so thoroughly that he nearly fell. He spun and faced the direction he thought he'd heard the voice come from.

"Is someone there?" he called, realizing as he did so how ridiculous the question was. He'd clearly heard a voice, so either someone was there or he was out of his mind. Either way, the question didn't need to be asked.

"I sure am. So, how ya doing? If you're coming out to fish, you'll need to pick a different spot. Train comes round here in just a few minutes," a man's voice said. Still, it took Jason several more seconds to locate him. When he finally did, he gave a small wave, unsure of what to say in response. *That's the whole damn point,* he thought.

He took stock of the man as he pondered his predicament. The man was sitting on an outcrop of rock, fishing pole in hand. The line extended downward into the water, bobber drifting back and forth in the river. Although he was sitting, Jason could see that the man was tall, his long legs extended down and onto another rock beneath him. He was wearing an overcoat. Jason thought that it had been black at one point, but it was now gray.

Although his clothes and boots were clearly well worn, he seemed otherwise clean and well kept, no dirt or grime found home on him. His most notable feature was his head. It was shiny and completely bald, no sign of hair whatsoever. Even from a distance, Jason could see how smooth his head was, as if he'd been born that way. For some reason, Jason was afraid of this man, and he couldn't understand why.

"No fishing pole, eh?" the man said, and Jason realized that he had never answered the man's question.

"Oh, uh, yeah. Must have forgotten it. I was in a hurry this morning," Jason said, realizing how absurd it sounded but unable to think of anything else.

"Well, iff'n you don't mind some company, I've got a second pole. Always come prepared in case one breaks, ya see," the man said, and gestured to the rocks beside him.

Jason hesitated. He'd made up his mind, and if he didn't do this now he wasn't sure that he would ever get up the nerve again. His mind vacillated frantically, trying to find a solution. *When I hear the whistle, I'll just run up here. He won't be able to stop me,* he thought, and walked slowly down the bank until he stood on the rocks beside the man.

"Ira Gelb," the bald man said, extending his hand. Standing closer, Jason could now see the man fully. Although Jason had known he was tall, he hadn't realized quite how tall. The graying coat that he wore also hid the breadth of his shoulders, and the large, muscular frame beneath it. This was a man you wanted on your side of a fight.

"Jason Baldwin," Jason responded reflexively, taking the man's hand and shaking it. The man's handshake was a vice grip.

"So, no pole, dressed in a suit. Interesting start to a fishing trip," Ira commented, never taking his eyes off Jason. Breaking the handshake, Jason couldn't help but feel disconcerted. This strange man had derailed his plans and was now digging into things he had no business in. When Jason had left this morning, he'd dressed as he always did to go to work, not realizing that he would be quizzed about his attire.

"Wasn't really planning to fish. I was joking before. Just came out to see the sunrise," Jason said, attempting to craft a more believable scenario for the strange man.

"Mmhmm," Ira responded, clearly not buying the altered explanation. He continued, "well, that's good. For a minute there I thought you might mean to jump off those tracks. Or, even worse, stay standing on 'em."

Jason tried to hide his shock and discomfort. The man seemed to be reading his mind. Without thinking, he glanced at his watch. *The train should be here in five minutes*, he thought.

"Train's got a few minutes yet, if that's what yer wondering about," Ira said, and Jason's discomfort grew.

"Just wondering what time it was, that's all."

The man nodded, pausing for a few moments to look at Jason. "I see. Well, why don't you have a seat?" he asked. Jason thought about declining but decided better of it. He sat. "You know, I've known a few people where you are right now."

A quizzical look passed across Jason's face. *What did he mean?*

Ira continued, "Men who think they've got nothing to live for. Men who think they've done something that deserves an answer." Jason attempted to interject, but the man raised his hand and Jason fell silent, once again irrationally afraid. "My take has always been that there's always something to live for. No matter where you are or what ya done."

Jason sensed that it was now alright for him to speak, and he blurted out the first thing that came to mind, "I don't know about that."

"You don't think so? What's the worst thing that could happen to you, do you suppose?"

"I think the worst is hurting the people around you. I think that's the most shameful thing a person could do. What's a man good for if he betrays the person, the people, that love him the most?" Jason asked. Then another thought popped into his mind, "That'd be hard enough to live with, and rightly so. But even worse might be being punished for something you didn't even do at all."

His mind had flashed back to the journal, and now his thoughts raced. He was sitting here beside a stranger, contemplating how to end his life, while Eustache Dauger had bravely endured a lifetime in prison for a crime he didn't even commit. *You're such a coward,* Jason thought, completely disgusted with himself.

"An innocent man, huh? Can't say that I've met too many of those," Ira said, drawing his line back in and preparing for the next cast. "Seems to me that all of us are guilty of one thing or the other. We've all got something that we've got to live with. That's not always an easy thing to do, but what other choice do we have?"

Jason glanced up at the train tracks and then back down at his watch. Two minutes. Perhaps less.

"You know, what it comes down to is this: what kind of man are you? Every man has got to make his own choices, they can't be made for him. The only change that matters comes from people who want to change. Anyway, I think it's about time for me to find a new spot. You're welcome to stay here, I'll leave my extra pole and stop by on my way back to pick it up. It's right over there."

Ira smiled and nodded his head as he got up, carefully managing the rocky terrain. Jason watched him go. Just as he was walking out of sight, Jason heard a train whistle in the distance. It was still a ways away, but it was coming soon. Jason stood.

He took a couple of steps to the side, attempting to find an easier path up than he had taken down. As he did so, he saw Ira's fishing pole stuck in a crack between two rocks. Something else was sitting there beside the pole. It glittered in the sunlight and caught Jason's eye.

Taking a step sideways, he took a closer look at the object. He reached down and picked it up, his hands shaking slightly as he took it in hand.

The front of the book was worn and faded, but the lettering on the spine still shown.

Holy Bible.

Chapter Fifty

Heather had awoken late, sleeping until nearly noon. Sleep had come easily for the first time in weeks, although she could not explain why. It was the first night in nearly a month that she had slept through the night, much less slept in.

The house was silent. It was not surprising. By this time of the day, Marcus would be outside playing with his friends and Jason would be at the studio. Although the business was struggling, he still went in nearly every day.

She yawned as she descended the stairs, somehow still feeling tired even after so much sleep. Reaching the landing, she glanced over and into the living room. She was surprised to see Jason sitting there, the back of his head visible over the couch. She didn't say anything, heading instead to the kitchen.

Jason apparently heard her footsteps, standing up before she'd taken more than a few steps past the stairs. As he turned towards her, she nearly gasped in alarm. Had she not been half awake, she was certain that she would have.

For the first time since she had met him, Jason had shaved the small beard that adorned his chin. Clean-shaven, he looked a decade younger. She found herself thinking back to the last time that she had seen him like this and caught herself smiling. It felt refreshing, like cool rain in the middle of a heat wave.

"Heather, please sit down. I have a few things to say, and I'd like you to just listen."

Heather nodded. She wasn't sure what was coming, but she was afraid of it. She could not handle anything other than good news right now, nothing more than news that assured her that everything would be okay.

"I went down to the train bridge this morning. Left early. I've been really lost these last few weeks. And I know, I have no one but myself to blame for that. What I did was wrong. It doesn't matter what I was feeling; it doesn't matter what I was chasing or thinking. All that matters is what I was doing, and I know that."

"Jason, you've said all this, I…," Heather started to interject, far too tired to rehash where they had been. She wanted to start over, to put all of it behind her, behind them. Before she could say more, Jason started up again.

"I know that I've said this before, but it's important that I say this all again now. So please, just listen. Anyway, I was down at the bridge. Heather, I was at the train bridge because I planned to stand in front of it."

Heather felt the blood drain out of her face and her world begin to spin. She could not believe what she had just heard. She couldn't believe that he would do that! That he would abandon her that way, leave her alone and pregnant. It was unfathomable to her. No matter what he had done, she did not want him to die. She vacillated between sorrow and fury, unsure of which emotion would win. A sob escaped her before she could contain it.

"I felt as though I had ruined my life. I'd ruined my marriage. I'd hurt the only person that truly matters to me and violated a trust that seemed like it couldn't be repaired. I was lost, truly, and I felt as though the world would be better off without me. That you would be better off without me. That was all that I could think about, but I know that it sounds incredibly selfish.

"Anyway, when I was down there, I met a man. I've never seen him around here before. He called himself Ira. There was something about him that I can't put my finger on. It seemed like he knew me from the inside out. He said that everyone needs to make their own choices, and that change only happens when someone actually wants to change."

Heather exhaled. She hadn't realized it, but she'd been holding her breath.

"Heather, what I'm telling you is that change is a choice, and I have chosen. I've never felt anything like this in my life. It's as though everything inside of me is on fire, burning away what was and replacing it with something new. I know that it will take time to regain your trust, and that doesn't bother me. I will wait here for as long as it takes. I will wait until the end of the world for you. When the stars burn out and the world collapses in on itself, I will still be waiting, if that's what it takes."

Tears poured down Heather's face. All of the anger that had been inside of her went out, replaced by a peace that surpassed all understanding. Jason was crying, too, and she moved towards him.

His arms embraced her, enclosing her in the warmth and strength that she'd known for so many years.

She slumped into him, letting him take her weight. He held her close, as though he feared she may evaporate at any moment. She felt his heart thump in his chest, pounding hard but perfectly steady. *Boom, boom, boom,* one after the other.

"There's something else I found this morning, and you're not going to believe it," Jason said, and lifted up the journal.

Chapter Fifty-One

The whole story came slowly. As Jason told it, he found himself wrapped up in it. Something about the telling was a sort of vicarious catharsis, and Jason found himself savoring every moment.

"So, we already knew that Eustache Dauger was the attendant of a very powerful man. He had grown in position thanks, in large part, to his own father. After his father died, Eustache had worked under a man named Louvois, the son of his father's former employer. Louvois had not treated Eustache with the dignity that Le Tellier had shown his father, and he'd soon grown resentful of the lavish lifestyles of those he served. Once his wife, Josephine, had born him children, his discontent had only grown," Jason said, recapping information that he'd long ago gleaned from the journal.

"His daily employment consisted of keeping track of the day to day appointments of Louvois, along with tracking and organizing the manifests of shipments that were to be sent and received on his behalf. Because Louvois worked under the king directly, many of those parcels were simply being held temporarily, soon to be sent off elsewhere. It was a pretty boring job, based on what I've read," Jason said with a chuckle.

"Anyway, one day, Eustache had been going through the daily manifests when he came across a discrepancy. One of the crates that had been received was supposed to be sent directly to the king. However, it was instead being separated into two parcels. One would go to the king, the other to another location. The royal seal made it clear that whatever was inside was both important and valuable, so this deception was more than just a mistake; it was theft."

Jason felt himself shaking as he retold what the journal had revealed. It was still as shocking to him now as it had been the first time that he'd read it only a few hours earlier. After meeting the man at the bridge, Jason had felt like a man possessed. He'd returned to the journal the moment he'd arrived home, making more progress in a few hours than he'd managed to in months. Page after page of translation had flown by until he'd finally reached the climax. He calmed himself, and continued.

"After Eustache had discovered his master's plan to defraud the king, he'd been stricken with indecision. He knew that he should turn Louvois into the authorities and wash his hands clean of the situation. But the lure of the unknown riches had been too much for him, and he'd instead devised a plan of his own. Because he was in charge of the manifests, he simply altered the destination of the secondary crate and had it sent to a friend, using a false name, who would hold it until he was able to pick it up later. The original case was sent on to the king, albeit lacking its full contents.

"You see, if it arrived and was discovered to be in error, Eustache could claim ignorance. His employer had given the orders to siphon the valuables from the original shipment and had doctored the manifests. Eustache did nothing except switch an address. Eustache believed it to be a foolproof plan, and the contents of that crate would ensure that his family would never want for anything. They would be able to live out their lives without being in constant service to others."

Jason paused, his mouth dry. He took a sip of water from his cup before continuing, "Of course, the plan did not succeed."

"The failure started at the very beginning. Although the crates were both sent out as expected, the second crate had been stolen immediately after it had been delivered to his accomplice on the outskirts of Paris. He had been overtaken by thieves on the road, and everything had been taken. His friend barely survived the incident. After the thieves had beaten him mercilessly, they'd left him along the roadside to die.

"Once the delivery had reached the king, the missing contents immediately raised alarm. Louvois, who the king blamed initially, had been able to quickly shift the blame onto Eustache. Once he had been accused, Eustache was immediately taken before the king."

Jason sighed, "He was tortured mercilessly for several days, but he refused to give the name of his accomplice. Although he knew that the valuables had already been stolen, he also knew that his friend would face the same fate that he did if he mentioned his name."

"When the king had become convinced he would not speak, he sentenced Eustache to imprisonment. The king coveted whatever was in that crate, which is why his life was spared. Should he change his mind and name the accomplice, perhaps the king would show him mercy, at least that's what he was told.

"Eustache had been out of his mind with anguish, the seriousness of his crimes finally hitting him. He realized that he would never see his wife again and that his children would be without a father."

Jason felt tears beginning to well up in the corners of his eyes. Eustache had given up everything in exchange for something that did not truly matter. The idea of it was agony. He blinked back the tears and did his best to keep himself from choking up.

"He begged the king for one last visit with them, just to see them one more time, but the king denied him his request. Out of spite, the king also decreed that he was to be kept blind with a mask, and that his name would never again be uttered. No one would ever know who he was. He was sentenced to a lifetime of imprisonment without even the dignity of an identity.

"According to Eustache, it was that indignity which drove him to befriend the jailkeeper, Bénigne Dauvergne de Saint-Mars. As long as one person still knew who he was, he felt as though his life still had some value. Later on, he convinced Saint-Mars to inscribe his name someplace where it wouldn't be wiped away.

"Apparently, at some point, Saint-Mars told someone else that he had carved Eustache's name into the foundation stone of his home," Jason said, nearly breathless with excitement, "that's how Thomas and my father knew where to look, at least approximately. Whatever documents told that part of the story are now lost, but this journal verifies them anyway."

Heather listened intently throughout his story, her mouth opening and closing several times as she did so. When Jason reached the end, she had only one question left.

"So, Eustache wasn't innocent? He was guilty? After everything, all we went through, he was guilty?" she asked in a hushed whisper.

"Yes, that's right. Eustache Dauger was not innocent. He committed a crime and paid for it dearly. It cost him his freedom, his family, and his life."

Epilogue

The ship sailed gently on the water, the waves barely discernible as they lapped the bow. In front of them was a sight that Heather hadn't seen in nearly twenty years. Cannes rose from the sea, a beautiful cluster of buildings set into the hillside. The air smelled of salt, and seagulls screeched overhead. Jason stood beside her as they looked out over the railing.

"It's really something, isn't it?" Heather asked, still staring at the city in front of them.

"It really is. I remember when this was one of the worst sights in the world. I remember when this was just the place that had taken me away from my life," Jason paused, then continued, "and now I think of it as where my life truly began."

Heather smiled. She, too, couldn't help but think back on the when they had first met. It had been so long ago, but somehow it seemed like just minutes. Their childish flirting, those first moments of attraction. There had been something about that very first meeting that still seemed magical. Invisible hands leading the way towards the future.

They'd both known that they needed to return, somehow. There had been no debate when Heather had said it, and Heather knew that Jason had been thinking the same thing. They needed to come back to where it all began. It had taken them years to save up the money to make the voyage, but she knew that every dollar was worth it. There was something about being back here that made her feel brand new.

The ship docked and the they gathered their luggage. They'd only brought a few bags, just enough to get by. They walked slowly down the dock and then over the cobblestones. The streets were still lined with merchants and still smelled of bread and flowers, a combination that Heather breathed in deeply.

Not everything was the same, however. They saw the signs of new construction, buildings being torn down and rebuilt. Cannes was growing, and quickly.

"It's almost exactly the same. A few new buildings, but everything else is just the way that it was," Jason said, taking her hand in his.

"It's better than I remember it," Heather answered.

"Better? How so?"

"This time around, I get to enjoy it with you," Heather said, smiling. She could feel the blush on her cheeks, and something inside her smiled, too. Even this many years later, Jason still made her blush.

Heather thought of the boys, Marcus, Kenneth, and Elias. They had officially adopted Marcus about six years after they'd first taken him in. The last time that they had heard from his parents, they were somewhere out West, uninterested in having him back and unwilling to pay for it anyway. That had been years ago. Today, Marcus was an adult, already married and living in Ames. Their other two children were still young, three and eight years old, and they'd considered bringing them along. Dean had assured them that he would be happy to watch them for the duration, and they'd taken him up on the offer.

She thought about the years that they'd shared as a family, so many blissful years. There had been a few ups and downs, but she wouldn't have traded any of it for all the world. Even the worst moments of their life together had led to magnificent change. Sometimes it took being in the valley to appreciate the mountaintop.

Jason had been a stalwart for her in the years after their sons had been born. He'd always been loving, but in that time he had become her unwavering supporter. He was truly her best friend. More than that, it had been their faith that had bonded them together in a way that seemed as miraculous as their first meeting had been. The healing hands of a savior had invaded their lives, mending back together everything that had been damaged.

"We're almost there," Jason said, startling her out of her thoughts, "it's just up the hill."

Heather looked up to where Jason was pointing. At the top of the hill sat a narrow, two story building. The outside was almost exactly as she remembered it. The shutters had never been repainted, their green color now indiscernible, but everything else looked as though it hadn't aged a day. Heather looked nervously at Jason.

"Do you think she's still here?" she asked, her voice questioning. They had written to Adelia several times but had not received a response. Although they both knew they needed to return, both of them wondered whether it may be in vain. Adelia had been old when they'd first met her, and now she would be in her nineties.

"There's only one way to find out," Jason said, and walked up to the door. Knocking loudly, they both stood and waited for a response. For a long while, none came. When it finally did, the woman that answered was not Adelia.

"Mademosielle Dauger, est ce qu'elle est ici?" Jason asked, and the woman shook her head.

"Non, non, elle n'est pas ici." the woman replied.

Jason looked at Heather and shook his head. Adelia no longer lived there. Jason turned back to the woman.

"Savez-vous où elle est?"

"Oui, elle est par là bas," the woman said, pointing, "cherchez le signe qui montre 'apprendre'."

Jason thanked her and they turned away. Jason was smiling.

"Let's go, I know exactly where she is."

They walked the few blocks back towards the old shop where Thomas had once lived. Arriving, they saw that it looked nearly identical to how it once had, although clearly newer and cleaner. The building had been rebuilt after the fire, and Heather was sure that she knew who had been responsible.

They knocked on the door of the shop. When the door opened, they were greeted by a familiar face. When Adelia saw them, her face lit up.

The string of French that came next was too fast, even for Jason, but she soon slowed down and greeted them once more in English. They hugged and exchanged pleasantries before Adelia welcomed them inside.

The once crowded room was now clean and clear of clutter. Adelia had books on shelves, but they no longer dominated every square inch. Adelia looked frail and fragile, but she was as courteous as ever. When she offered her tea, Heather just about laughed out loud. In the years since her last visit, Heather had missed her tea on more than one occasion. She gladly accepted.

The three of them spoke for hours, discussing their lives and the changes they'd all experienced. To Heather, talking to Adelia felt like speaking with her grandmother, and it warmed her as thoroughly as the tea.

Eventually, the conversation returned to the reason they'd come in the first place, both then and now. Heather looked at Jason and nodded. She watched as he rummaged through his knapsack, eventually bringing out a delicate book, wrapped in string. He handed it to Adelia.

"Adelia, we think this belongs with you. It is the story of your ancestor, and we want you to have it," Jason said. They both watched her tug on the strings holding the old journal together.

"What is it?"

"That, Adelia, is the story of Eustache Dauger, written in his own hand. It is all of the answers that Thomas spent his life looking for," Jason explained.

Adelia looked awestruck, and tears fell down her cheeks. She hugged the journal to her chest and thanked them.

"Thank you, thank you. I cannot tell you how much this means to me. I feel as though you have given me my Thomas back."

Jason and Heather nodded to each other. They both knew that it was time for them to go. Adelia urged them to stay, but they insisted, knowing that she would begin reading the moment they left but not before.

"Where will you go?" she asked, standing up slowly.

Heather looked at Jason and smiled, unable to restrain herself.

"We're going to Paris, Adelia. Paris, at last."

Acknowledgements

To my friends who encouraged me, edited for me, and helped me along the way. I couldn't have done it without the ruthless editing pen of my friend Natalie, the translation aid of my sister Rachelle, the shared road experience of my longtime friend Tereca, the sage advice of my favorite neighbor Kathryn, and the general encouragement of many others.
Thank you all.

(Oh, and one last thing, I'll be on the lookout for that space odyssey you promised me, hun.)